BEAR
CLAW

Other novels by Alfred Dennis

Chiricahua
Lone Eagle
Elkhorn Divide
Brant's Fort
Catamount
The Mustangers
Rover
Sandigras Canyon
Yellowstone Brigade
Shawnee Trail
Fort Reno
Yuma
Ride the Rough String
Trail to Medicine Mound
Arapaho Lance: Crow Killer Series - Book 1
Lance Bearer: Crow Killer Series - Book 2
Track of the Grizzly: Crow Killer Series - Book 3

To see more books by Alfred Dennis
visit www.alfreddennis.com

BEAR CLAW

Crow Killer Series - Book 4

by

Alfred Dennis

Walnut Creek Publishing
Tuskahoma, Oklahoma

Bear Claw: Crow Killer Series - Book 4

ISBN: 978-1-942869-30-6
First Edition, Paperback
Published 2019 by Walnut Creek Publishing
Front cover painting: George Catlin/Weapons and Physiognomy of the Grizzly
Bear/Wikimedia Commons
Library of Congress Control Number: 2019905524

Books may be purchased in quantity and/or special sales by contacting
the publisher;
Walnut Creek Publishing
PO Box 820
Talihina, OK 74571
www.wc-books.com

This book is dedicated to my wife Jimmie and our beautiful children - Carl, Kim, Goldie, Kevin, and Michael.

Introduction

Jedidiah Bracket, the warrior the Arapaho called Crow Killer, sat before his cabin with his young wife, Bright Moon, enjoying the serene beauty of their valley. For the first time, he felt he could live his life completely happy in his valley with her. After fighting so many battles, he finally found the peace he sought for so long. Now, he hoped all his enemies were gone, where he no longer had to live by the code of the Arapaho Lance Bearer.

Four years had passed since Arapaho Chief Slow Wolf rescued Jed from the North Platte River where a sudden flash flood dumped him bloody and broken on its muddy banks. Jed's birthmark of a lance on his back plus the old medicine man's words foretold that he would become a great warrior. With guidance from the Arapaho warrior, Walking Horse, he had become a mighty Lance Bearer of the Arapaho Nation and a legend among the tribes.

Smiling over at his beautiful young bride, Jed did not foresee the problems riding to his valley at that time. He Dog, Walking Horse, and their warriors were crossing the mountains as Jed was finishing his coffee. The Cheyenne Chief, Yellow Dog, had been ambushed and killed by the hated Arickaree warriors of the north. Now, the new Chief of the Cheyenne, He Dog, and Jed's friend, Walking Horse, rode to ask for his help in avenging the death of Yellow Dog. Jed knew he would risk everything he wanted in life, if he rode with the warriors. If the raid on the Arickaree was successful and he was recognized, there would always be threats against his valley. His hopes of living in peace in the high valley with Bright Moon would be dashed forever.

As an Arapaho Lance Bearer, he had no choice, it was his duty to ride with his brothers against the enemy who had killed his friend and brother. Bright Moon was the sister of Yellow Dog, the dead Cheyenne, and she too wanted revenge for her brother's cowardly murder. There was no way he could say no and avoid this fight without losing face among the people.

Jed had no way of knowing another danger was seeking him out. The Blackfoot warrior, Bear Claw, wanted revenge against the Arapaho who had killed his father, Chief Lone Bull. Even now, Bear Claw was hunting down the demon bear killer, Crow Killer. The medicine man of the Blackfoot, Twisted Rope, had foretold that Bear Claw was invincible and could not be killed by mortal man. Jed thought Twisted Rope's vision was interesting since the medicine man of the Arapaho, White Swan, had foretold the same about him.

Jed only wanted peace, but before that could happen, he still had many trails to ride and many battles to undertake. His friends, Walking Horse and Red Hawk the Crow, would always be by his side in battle, but were they enough to combat the crazed Blackfoot called Bear Claw?

Follow Jedidiah Bracket, known as Crow Killer by the Arapaho, as he traverses the vast wilderness of the Rocky Mountains. Adventure, action, and romance come alive in this fourth book of the Crow Killer Series.

CHAPTER 1

From high on the north ridge, where Bright Moon had first looked down at the beautiful valley that was to be her new home, the cry of the great grey wolf sounded. The long moaning sound of the wolf's eerie howl carried across the endless meadows. Sitting at the log table outside their cabin, Jed and his new bride listened to the sad call. She shivered slightly, as the howl sent chill bumps running up and down her spine.

"The grey wolf sounds lonely tonight, my husband." Bright Moon frowned, then looked up at the darkening mountains.

Jed sipped on his coffee and smiled. "No, he cannot be sad. I spotted him today while I hunted. He has a new mate running with him now."

"The great grey one has a squaw?"

"He does." Jed nodded. "She's almost black. Her shiny hair glistens in the sunlight. She is a thing of beauty and almost as big as the grey."

"Soon we will have little ones running the valley."

"Do the howls scare you, my wife?"

"No, but sometimes they seem a little eerie."

Jed knew the Cheyenne culture well. Sometimes the cry of a nearby wolf pack racing through the night in pursuit of game was a bad omen to them. The wolves yipping and howling could be especially scary to women and children. Jed felt no danger or threat from the huge grey wolf. Many times, in the past three years, the grey had sent his moaning cry across the mountains, warning Jed of the close presence of grizzlies or other enemies. No, this valley was the wolf's home and he would be safe here where no one would harm him. Jed felt he owed the wolf his life many times over. He would protect the animal and see that no harm came to him.

"What are you thinking, my husband?" Bright Moon felt his attention drifting away from her. "Tell me."

"The wolf is my brother and he will never harm you." Her question brought his thoughts back to her. "Listen closely to his call. His voice will always warn you of danger."

"You speak as if he is human or thinks like a human." Bright Moon was curious. "Can this be?"

"I am alive today because of the grey wolf." Jed dumped out the dregs from his cup. He remembered the wolf calling to him, showing him the way home after the fight with the big sow grizzly. He was half frozen at the time so it could have been a mirage or his cold brain, but Jed felt the animal had really been there, calling for him to follow. "Listen for his call and he will always warn you of interlopers coming into our valley."

"When I was young, wolves were feared." Bright Moon shuddered. "They were huge, with long fangs, and they ran in packs. They killed children they found away from the village."

Taking her small hand, Jed reassured her. "He watches over us even now in the dark hours, my wife."

Bright Moon took one last look up at the mountain and wondered. Could the huge grey wolf be looking down, watching her even now? How could this be?

Waiting in the doorway, as Jed checked the corral gate and looked at the horses inside the enclosure, she moved back inside as he approached. Barring the heavy log door behind him, Jed checked his rifles and sat down in his elk-hide chair.

"Will my husband hunt tomorrow?" Bright Moon removed the coffeepot from the hearth, then banked the hot coals for the night.

Shaking his head, Jed pulled off his moccasins and leather hunting shirt. The muscles rippled across his chest and huge arms as he stretched. "No, the grass is long enough now. Tomorrow, we must start filling the barn for our winter feed."

When she had first arrived, Bright Moon had seen the small amount of grass hay left in the snug barn after the last winter. Jed said he meant to refill the barn to the rafters, but she couldn't believe he actually meant to fill the barn completely full of the wild growing grass. Never would a Cheyenne warrior work so hard to put up hay so his horses could be lazy and not dig for the grass over the cold times. She didn't understand why he was doing it.

"Why do you put the grass in the lodge? It grows all over the valley."

Jed laughed and drew her down on his lap. "Tell me, where will the grass be when the heavy snows cover the valley?"

"Under the snow." She answered, not knowing what he was really asking.

"Exactly, the grass will be beneath the deep snow where the horses cannot reach it."

"Cheyenne horses are smart. They paw through the snow to get down to the grass." Bright Moon still argued. "And the buffalo plow it up with their great horns."

Jed nodded. "Yes, they do, but they also lose much weight and strength working to get down to the frozen grass. Many even starve to death during the cold times."

"Yes, I have seen this." Bright Moon pretended to pout. "Still, it seems like much work to do when we could be swimming or riding the mountain trails."

"There will be plenty of time to swim and ride during the long summer months to come."

"If the horses die in the cold times, you could always steal more as the Cheyenne do."

"We are not horse thieves, Bright Moon." Jed laughed, he knew she still thought like a Cheyenne. "Besides, who would we steal them from? The Cheyenne and Arapaho are our people, and the Crow of Plenty Coups and Red Hawk are our friends."

"There is always the hated Arickaree or Blackfoot."

"Then we would have to watch for them to raid our valley." Jed shook his head. "No, it is a lot easier and safer to make sure our horses live through the hard times so we do not have to steal from others."

Bright Moon pretended to pout. "Perhaps safer, my husband, but I do not think it is easier."

Jed knew she would argue with the little black mule if given the chance. "Tomorrow, I cut hay."

True to his word, Jed had the scythe swinging as soon as the heavy dew of the morning had dried from the tall meadow grass. The steady ripping sound of the sharp blade laying down the green grass could be faintly heard across the valley. For three weeks, he dropped the heavy grass and after it cured, both he and Bright Moon brought the hay to the barn. The flat sled Jed had fashioned was carefully loaded and pulled into the shelter by one of the Pawnee horses. Jed had tried the little black mule, but she wasn't having anything to do with something following her. After kicking with both hind feet, then running off and wrecking the sled twice, he gave up and decided the horse would be much faster and safer.

"Mules are supposed to pull wagons." Jed muttered to himself. "What's the matter with you?"

The barn was filling fast with the dried grass as load after load was skidded from the valley floor to the building. Jed had fashioned roughly made pitchforks out of forked tree limbs for both himself and Bright Moon. They were prehistoric, but it sure beat bending and using their hands to load and unload the loose hay. Bright Moon still grumbled, but Jed loved the sweet smell of the fresh cut grass, spreading its aromatic fragrance around the cabin.

"Soon, the lodge will be full." Bright Moon looked in the barn. "Then what will we do?"

Jed shook his head. "It's a barn, Bright Moon, not a lodge."

"It is the lodge of several field people. I have seen them many times."

"You mean field mice." Jed knew there was no use arguing. "Okay, it's a lodge for the little varmints. It'll just take another few suns to finish the grass, then we will go swimming."

Bright Moon smiled. She knew he was trying to keep her happy. "I think my husband speaks with a forked tongue."

"Well, tell me, what do you think we're gonna do after we fill the lodge?"

"Then it will be time to bring in wood for our fires." Bright Moon frowned. "The water will dry up before we can swim."

"That's true, we have to cut wood for the cold times alright." Jed smiled. "But, I think we can find time to swim. I seriously doubt the creek will dry up."

Jed knew Bright Moon wasn't lazy, as he had watched her work for hours making him a new shirt or moccasins. The work didn't bother her, but she felt it was a waste of time to bring hay in for the winter. Like any other Cheyenne or Arapaho, she felt horses should fend for themselves.

Jed had laid down just enough grass to fill the barn and was busy forking loose hay inside as Bright Moon filled the last sled load of hay. Across the valley, the moaning call of the grey wolf made her straighten up and listen. The long, low cry called out again across the valley, but this time she heard something different in his call. The lonely howl sent chills up and down her back. Quickly clucking to the horse, she dragged the skid across the valley to the barn where Jed was standing atop the dry hay, stomping it down. Seeing the skid was only half loaded and the way Bright Moon hurried the horse, Jed jumped down from the tall pile of hay.

"What's wrong, woman?" Jed could see the worry in her face.

"The wolf, he calls out across the valley before the sun hides itself." Bright Moon pointed. "It is as you spoke of, his voice was different."

Walking to the edge of the small stream that separated the cabin and valley, Jed stood listening for several minutes. Once again, the moaning call sounded out, reverberating along the mountainside. Retrieving his rifle and shot pouch from where they lay across the outside table, he quickly unharnessed the horse.

"Stay here and see to your rifle." Jed swung up on the horse. "Stay close to the cabin."

"I fear there is trouble out there, my husband." Bright Moon stared out across the valley. "I can see or hear nothing, but I feel the wolf senses something is wrong."

Jed nodded as he looked out across the valley. "I will go see. Stay close to the cabin like I told you."

Crossing the small stream, Jed stopped the horse and waited, his eyes studying the ears of the little mule. She had her long ears pricked and he knew she too had sensed something off to the south. Quickly rounding up the small herd of horses, Jed drove them into the corral. Changing his rawhide bridle over to the piebald, Jed swung up on his horse. Waving at Bright Moon, he crossed the creek and rode out across the flat valley.

The piebald paint horse was in a hard run with his legs reaching out powerfully and his flying mane and tail waving in the passing wind. Despite his worry of an intruder, Jed felt elated with the wind blowing in his face, making his long black hair whip out behind him. It had been many months since he had let his horse run full out this way. The powerful stride of the great black and white horse was unbelievable, exhilarating. The horse seemed to run like the wind, never tiring.

Reining the horse in as he reached the edge of the valley floor, Jed sat several minutes studying the mountain trail leading up and out of the valley. Nothing showed on the trail, no sound, nothing. Jed waited, studying the horse's ears to see if the animal sensed anything. Suddenly, the black ears pointed up the mountain as the velvet nostrils of the muzzle flared. Turning the horse, Jed rode him into the heavy cedars that lined the slopes and waited. Higher up the trail, he could hear someone or something coming down the mountain trail. Suddenly, the piebald arched his neck and fidgeted as several war whoops came from up the trail and the sound of many running horses echoed along the mountain ridge.

Jed checked the priming of his Hawken and moved back onto the trail. From the haze of dust and flying debris, Walking Horse, He Dog, and several other warriors reined in their excited half-wild horses. Laughing and waving their weapons, they dismounted and pulled the surprised Jed from his horse. Rough housing and pounding him on the back, the warriors surrounded him. Walking Horse guessed Crow Killer would be waiting at the bottom of the trail so he told the warriors to race down the trail screaming.

"This time the great Crow Killer was scared." He Dog laughed and cleared his throat. "Well, maybe worried a little."

"We watched your face, my brother." Walking Horse pounded Jed's back. "He Dog is right."

Jed laughed as his best friends and brothers stood before him. "Tell me, with this ugly bunch coming at me yelling, who wouldn't be scared?"

"You got any good buffalo tongue steaks at your lodge?" Big Owl rubbed his stomach. "I'm hungry."

"How can Big Owl always be hungry?"

"My brothers have not fed me since the coming of the new sun." The big Arapaho complained good-naturedly. "Besides, I am a growing boy."

"Why are you here, my brothers?" Jed looked at the warriors surrounding him. "I did not expect you until the long days of the summer."

He Dog became solemn. "I have come to see my sister."

"Bright Moon will be happy to see you." Jed shook hands with He Dog and Walking Horse. "She has missed all of you."

"No, she will not be happy this time. We have bad news for our sister." He Dog nodded sadly. "Her brother has gone to be with his ancestors."

"What? How can this be? I am sorry." Jed was shocked as he knew the young warrior spoke of Yellow Dog. "Come, we will ride to my lodge."

Bright Moon stepped from the cabin as she recognized the Cheyenne and Arapaho warriors riding behind the loudly marked piebald as they crossed the valley. Still, too far to recognize their faces, the markings on the brightly marked horses with the Arapaho Lance markings and the tall headdresses of the Cheyenne Nation told what tribe they were from. Straining her eyes, she finally recognized He Dog and Crazy Cat and ran toward the small stream. It had been early spring since she had last seen them, when she left the Cheyenne village after her marriage to Crow Killer. She was elated as the warriors from her village could tell her of the people and news from the village. She knew warriors hated women's talk, but she would get it out of them.

Dismounting, He Dog smiled as he hugged her. "Marriage seems to brighten your smile, my sister."

"Yes, it does make her seem happier." Big Owl agreed with He Dog.

"I think she has gotten fatter." Crazy Cat teased. "Crow Killer does not make his woman work hard enough."

"And I guess Big Owl is hungry?" Bright Moon smiled.

"Always."

"I watched him eat a whole buffalo once." He Dog frowned.

Big Owl shook his head and laughed. "He Dog speaks falsely, I did not eat the hooves."

"Come, I will fix you some hot steaks."

"Buffalo?" Big Owl asked.

"No, our buffalo meat is gone now." Bright Moon shook her head. "You will have to survive on elk and deer meat."

Jed watched as the warriors took the plates of biscuits, wild greens, and elk steaks from Bright Moon, then sat down around the cabin and outside table. As the warriors ate, He Dog led Bright Moon down by the creek and spoke with her. Jed could see the small shoulders shake as he told her of Yellow Dog's death. He looked around at the gathered warriors and wondered, something was amiss. Only the older men, the cream of the Cheyenne Dog Soldiers and the Arapaho Lance Bearers were among these warriors. He could tell by the weapons they carried, the way their horses were painted for war, these men were here on a raid.

Jed knew it was bad manners to speak seriously before a meal was finished, but he ignored protocol and spoke to Crazy Cat. "Tell me, my friend, what has happened?"

Putting his plate down, Crazy Cat frowned. "A few sleeps ago as we hunted for wild horses, the Arickaree attacked us from ambush and killed our chief."

"They killed our chief like cowards from ambush." Lame Cougar repeated.

"Where did this happen?"

Crazy Cat frowned again and looked away. "We went to trade at Bridger's and were a sun's ride from the post, looking for the wild ones, when the Ree dogs attacked. They wanted to steal our trade goods and rifles."

Bridger did not allow fighting near the post, but the Rees were a warlike people and cared nothing about the old trader's laws. They had waited until the Cheyenne were a whole day's ride away from the post before attacking. They knew that far from the fort, Bridger would do nothing.

"So you have come here on a revenge raid?" Jed asked.

"We will have our revenge." Crazy Cat swore. "They killed our chief from hiding and without warning. Now, they will pay for their cowardice."

Most tribal warriors were honorable men who cared more about counting coup on an enemy instead of killing. Killings just brought more revenge killings. More honor was placed on touching a live enemy with your hand or coup stick, than killing one. Now, he knew these warriors minds, and they were here on a death raid. He could read it in their faces, as these warriors thirsted for revenge and blood, not honor. There would be no thoughts of counting coup on this trail, only death. He knew no tribe was more terrible on the blood path than the Cheyenne.

"You will raid the Arickaree?" Jed knew the answer before he asked.

"Not raid." Crazy Cat hissed. "We came to kill this enemy."

"None will live to speak of our chief's death." Lame Cougar chimed in.

"You plan to attack them from the west instead of taking the southern route?" Jed asked, but he knew what the consequences of such a raid from the west would be. The Arickaree people knew of Crow Killer, as they had heard the legend of the demon grizzly killer. They also knew the valley he claimed lay somewhere in the western mountains. If the Arapaho and Cheyenne mounted a raid on their village from the west, the Arickaree would blame him. He knew such a raid as this could forever prevent his chance to live in peace in his valley with Bright Moon. He knew the Arickaree were a dangerous and warlike tribe, with many warriors.

Returning to where the warriors waited, He Dog left Bright Moon down by the water where they could barely hear her sad song of mourning. Jed started to rise and go to her, but the young warrior stopped him.

"Let her have this time alone, my friend." The young warrior asked Crow Killer politely. "Has Crazy Cat told you of my brother's death?"

"Yes."

He Dog cleared his throat and looked around the sitting warriors. "We have come here to ask for your help."

"What does He Dog wish?" Jed already knew what the warriors wanted.

"That you accompany us and lead us to Arickaree Country." He Dog nodded. "We need the great Crow Killer with us. We are few and the Rees are many. We need the strong medicine of the bear to ride with us. We do not know this land very well. We must surprise and attack their village before they discover us in their hunting grounds."

Jed looked over at Walking Horse. "Does this raid have Slow Wolf's blessing?"

"Slow Wolf grows old before our eyes, my brother." The tall warrior nodded slowly. "He did not want this, but he has given his permission for this raid."

Jed had no choice, as it was his place as a Lance Bearer to defend his people, and now since his marriage to Bright Moon, the Cheyenne were his family too. Still, he did not want to bring this trouble to his valley. This raid, if successful, could bring the Arickaree here in force seeking revenge. With his new bride, he only wanted peace, but he had to honor his chief's wishes. Yellow Dog not only had been his brother-in-law but also his friend.

"I will lead you to the Arickaree lands." Jed looked over at the cabin. "But, I cannot leave Bright Moon here alone, unprotected."

"I know this, Crow Killer. We will leave two warriors here to watch over my sister." He Dog assured him. "She will be safe, I give you my word."

"When do you wish to leave?"

He Dog looked around at his warriors. "We will leave with the new sun."

"I will prepare my weapons." Jed watched as Bright Moon entered the cabin. "When the sun rises, we will depart."

"With the great Crow Killer with us, we will avenge Yellow Dog and kill the Arickaree." He Dog let out a mighty yell.

A shout went up from the gathered warriors as Jed disappeared inside the cabin. Every warrior present had great respect and faith in Crow Killer's ability as a Lance Bearer, fighter, and leader of men. Any of them would follow him to their death. All knew of his fights against the killer grizzlies, the Blackfoot, and the great Nez Perce warrior Black Robe, who Crow Killer had taken the great piebald horse from.

Entering the cabin, Jed found Bright Moon kneeling beside the fire preparing coffee. Looking up at him, she moved gracefully into his outstretched arms.

"I am sorry for your loss, my wife."

"My brother was a great chief. His life ended too soon." She seemed to wilt in his arms. "I should cut my hair and body in mourning."

Jed pushed her back and looked into her face. "You will not do that. You can mourn him in other ways."

"It is the custom of the Cheyenne."

"It is not my custom, and I forbid you to do it."

Leaning back into his chest, she nodded sadly. "I will do as you say."

"He Dog wishes me to ride with the warriors against the Arickaree." Jed looked into her tear-stained face. "Will that be enough to heal your mourning?"

"I wish the Ree dogs to pay for my brother's cowardly death." Bright Moon looked into his eyes. "Promise me, they will pay."

"I will ride with them, with the new sun." Jed moved to where his rifle stood against the wall. "Prepare as much food as you can spare for our journey."

"Bring me the hair of these cowards." Bright Moon picked up a knife. "Bring me many scalps."

"I will kill the Ree responsible for this cowardly deed." Jed shook his head. "But scalping, this I will not do. You know that!"

She understood and nodded. "I know the white part of you will not allow this, but they deserve to be scalped for the cowardly thing they have done. There was no reason for my brother's death."

"The Arickaree were wrong to kill him." Jed looked through the cabin door at the warriors. "I promise you, his death will be avenged."

"Ride against the Arickaree, then come back to me safely, my husband."

"I did not want any more fighting, Bright Moon. I wanted only to live here in peace with you." Jed laid out his war axe and bow. "But, I cannot refuse my brother's request that I ride with them in this."

"You are Crow Killer, the great Lance Bearer." Bright Moon smiled sadly. "It will always be your duty to protect the people. White Swan said there will never be peace for you."

Nodding, Jed rolled his sleeping blanket and laid everything on the log table. "He Dog will leave two warriors here with you. Do as they say, and stay close to the cabin while I am away."

Jed reined in the powerful built bay horse, as the column of warriors reached the high ridge overlooking the long valley and the cabin. Jed felt uncomfortable on any horse besides the piebald, but for this raid he would ride the bay horse he had taken from the dead Pawnee, Wet Otter. He stared down at the cabin and worried. He didn't want to leave Bright Moon.

"You do not ride your paint horse, my brother?" Walking Horse noticed Jed wasn't riding his favorite horse.

"No, he is far too easy to recognize." Jed looked down at the cabin. "I do not wish for him to be seen on this raid."

Walking Horse nodded his head as he watched Jed look at the cabin while the horses were blowing. "There is only one marked up as he is, and everyone knows Crow Killer rides him."

"I don't want to give the Ree a reason to come to this valley, if I can help it." Jed replied. "Now, I only want peace and to be left alone."

Walking Horse nodded. "I did not wish to involve you in this raid, my brother."

"It is no matter now, I am here." Jed looked once again down at the cabin before turning the bay. "He was my brother as you are."

"Do not worry for Bright Moon." Walking Horse followed the gaze of Jed's eyes. "The Wolverine and Spotted Feather will protect her until we return."

For two days, Jed kept the raiders in a fast trot until they reached the crossing on the Snake River. Black Horse Crossing was amply named for the horse head that stared down from his perch in a large oak tree. The horse head skull watched, staring with empty eye sockets, observing all who passed over the crossing. Jed sat knee deep in the cool river water, remembering the last time he had crossed here with Ellie. It seemed years ago, but actually had been less than two years before when he and Ellie passed this way. The Arapaho people called her Medicine Thunder, after her father Lige Hatcher, known to the Arapaho as Rolling Thunder.

Jed remembered the night clearly as they swam this same crossing on their way to his cabin, where Walking Horse lay near death. The same as now, there had been no time to enjoy the water or the ride back to the valley. Kicking the bay, Jed hit deep water, then slid off the side of the swimming horse, making sure to keep his rifle and powder above water.

The bay horse was a powerful swimmer, almost as strong as the piebald. Splashing ashore, Jed quickly donned his damp buckskins and watched the trees lining the riverbanks as the others came from the water. Patting the sleek neck of the bay, Jed smiled. The Pawnee had indeed given him a good horse.

"We will make camp down river, away from the crossing." Jed pointed to a clearing. "Post guards, all fires will be out before dark."

"Does Crow Killer think someone will be watching this place?" Crazy Cat questioned Jed.

Jed shrugged. "This I do not know, but we will keep a close watch on the crossing and our night camp."

"How much farther is it to the Arickaree village?" He Dog wanted to taste the blood of his brother's killers. He was restless, eager to ride against the Ree.

"If we ride hard, Bridger's Post is one day ahead." Jed looked up the east trail. "The Arickaree village may be one more sleep to the north. We will take another trail that will bring us to the valley where the Ree's normally make their summer camp."

He Dog looked across at Jed. "Then, we will be there soon?"

"No, little brother." Jed shook his head. "Our horses need rest and feed. We will stay here another sleep, and let them regain their strength."

Walking Horse spoke up. "My brother Crow Killer is right. We do not want to go into battle with fatigued horses under us."

"I know he speaks wisely, but I want to attack quickly." He Dog shook his head.

"One more day, more or less, will not matter, my chief." Crazy Cat spoke up as he dismounted. "Crow Killer is right. Let the horses rest in case we have to leave this land quick."

"No Cheyenne will run from this place." He Dog shook his fist. "We will kill these dogs or be killed."

Jed hadn't realized when he spoke to He Dog that the young warrior was now the hereditary Chief of the Cheyenne. He Dog was the only living son of the old chief, the successor to his position as leader of the Cheyenne Nation, now that Yellow Dog was dead. Yellow Dog's death seemed like an unreal dream. Now, he would never hear the good-natured ribbing of the young chief or enjoy the talks they had over the night fires. Now, He Dog was chief. His word was law and he would be obeyed on this raid.

He Dog finally agreed. "We will rest our horses and let them graze on the river grass for one more sun."

CHAPTER 2

A s Jed led the single column of warriors away from Black Horse Crossing, he rode far in advance on the west side of the trail, while Walking Horse took the east side. Now, they were close to Assiniboine hunting grounds, and if discovered, the Assiniboine would send runners to the Ree. For the raid to be successful, with only a few warriors, they must not be discovered until the moment of attack. Not a sound was spoken or heard from the mounted warriors. Every piece of equipment, that could make noise, was wrapped tightly in ermine skins to muffle the sound. The ground was sandy along that part of the trail, helping to silence the passing sounds of the horses. Several times, Jed had the warriors rest their horses by dismounting and leading them. Sometimes, he would have them hide in the tall foliage, lining the trail, as he and Walking Horse rode ahead to check out a threat. As was his valley, this was a beautiful land covered in every colored flower, but there was no time to enjoy such scenery. Today, Jed's thoughts were about keeping the ones following him safe from prying eyes, seeking to discover them in this far land.

Jed didn't know the size of the Arickaree village ahead. All he knew was what Crazy Cat had told him. One of the warriors who had shot Yellow Dog from ambush was a huge warrior with the sign of a lightning bolt, painted in yellow, on his horse. The totem custom among most tribes was to paint their lodges the same way they painted their horses. He Dog was enraged over Yellow Dog's death and adamant about wanting to scalp and eat the heart of this warrior. Jed knew if the young chief had his way, he would ride in search of the lightning bolt splashed across a lodge before attacking the village. However, Jed hoped cooler heads would prevail once they reached the enemy village.

Several smoke columns were spotted on the evening air as they neared the first village. Jed had the warriors conceal themselves in a heavy thicket as he and Walking Horse crept forward to investigate the smoke ahead. Most of the mud and thatch hogans were painted with one totem or another, but none carried the mark of the lightning bolt. Jed counted almost fifty mud lodges in this camp, which meant as many as a hundred able-bodied warriors could be present. Slipping back to where the warriors waited, Jed quickly reported his findings to He Dog.

"There are two more villages strung out down the small river for maybe three miles." Jed drew a quick sketch on the ground. "We could not see them closely."

"We will ride to these other villages and look for the yellow bolt of lightning, before we attack."

"My chief." Crazy Cat interceded. "We are too close to the villages. If we are to succeed, without being discovered, we must attack at first light."

"I want the huge warrior you spoke of." He Dog demanded. "He must be in one of these villages."

Walking Horse shook his head. "We cannot ride around here looking for this warrior. It would be foolish of us and dangerous."

"I want this one!" In a rage, He Dog slashed down with his hand. "I want his scalp to hang from my lodge pole. I want to eat his heart while it still beats."

"Listen to me, my chief. We will attack this village and the one you want will hear the battle and come to us." Crazy Cat pleaded. "He can do no less if he is a man."

He Dog paced back and forth as his mind was in turmoil between the safety for his warriors or death to his enemies. His need to avenge Yellow Dog impeded his good judgement. He wanted the huge Arick-aree, but he knew Crazy Cat spoke the truth. To stay in this place any longer than was needed, would place his warriors in danger. He knew the wise thing to do was attack at first light, before being discovered by a hunter or even a child who could sound the alarm. With only a few warriors, their only chance of a successful raid was to race into the village quickly, then retreat before the enemy had time to mount a counterattack.

Shaking his head, the young chief finally agreed. "Prepare yourselves. When the new sun spreads its light, we will attack."

"Who do we fight, He Dog?" Jed questioned the revenge minded warrior.

Staring at Jed, the youngster only smiled. "We kill anything that moves in that village; warriors, women, children, dogs, everything that moves will die."

"This will only bring more revenge killings, young one." Jed argued. "Let us kill only the warriors or women who come out to fight us."

"No!" He Dog shook his war axe. "You have told me of the need to attack with the morning sun, and I will do this, but my axe will taste the blood of anything that gets in front of me. I will kill all of these dogs who took the life of my chief and brother."

Jed looked straight at the young chief. "I will not kill children, they have done me no wrong."

"Crow Killer is an Arapaho Lance Bearer. He is free to choose who he makes war on." He Dog turned to his sleeping robe. "There will be no shame if you only kill warriors, but remember, one day these same children will be full-grown men."

Crazy Cat could only shake his head as He Dog walked away. "My chief mourns his brother. His mind thinks only of revenge and he needs much blood to erase his grief."

"I bet you a good horse, tomorrow, he gets the blood he wants." Big Owl laughed quietly.

"I will not take that bet." Crazy Cat looked to where He Dog had rolled up in his blanket to await the coming of day. "Now, his mind is full of hate and he thinks only of killing the Ree."

Jed leaned back against a small cottonwood tree, listening to the whippoorwill calls and the frogs croaking down along the river. The faint calling of a great northern owl sounded somewhere toward the village. Jed knew the Cheyenne and Arapaho were superstitious. They thought the calling of an owl from the dark was a bad omen from the spirit people.

Walking Horse tried to make out Jed's face in the dark. "You would say it is only a bird, my brother."

"That's all it is, nothing that can harm you."

"The night bird reaches out with his long talons and kills his prey." The warrior worried. "Some seers say whoever hears his call in the dark should leave the place where they are and flee."

"It's just superstitious beliefs, my brother. The owl is only a bird of the night." Jed tried to relieve Walking Horse's worries.

"Morning will show which one of us is right." Walking Horse rolled in his sleeping robe. "We will soon see."

The long strung-out column of warriors sat their horses in a straight line, facing the village, as the first rays of the morning sun started to lighten the land. The women of the village already had their cook fires lit, but no one noticed the waiting warriors, shrouded in the murky darkness of early morning. A low fog, heavy with mist vapors covered the banks of the small creek, making visibility at any distance poor. As He Dog motioned with his arm, the warriors started to inch forward slowly toward the village.

Jed nodded as he looked up and down the line at the feathered warriors. The Cheyenne had brought their magnificent headdresses and war paint of the dreaded Dog Soldier Clan. The Lance Bearers had their own paint and each warrior carried the lance that most tribes feared. Jed did not like the killing that was fixing to happen, but he was proud to ride in the same company with these warriors. Today, perhaps many of his friends would go to their happy hunting grounds, but he could think of no braver men to die with.

Slowly moving their horses forward, He Dog rode a few paces in front of the line, befitting his place as chief and leader of this raid. Less than fifty steps separated the oncoming line and the cooking fires. As they appeared out of the fog, an Arickaree squaw screamed and raced to her lodge. Screaming the war cry of the Northern Cheyenne, with bitter vengeance on his mind, He Dog slapped his war axe against the rump of his horse and rushed forward, splitting the head of the first warrior he raced past.

Complete bedlam and hysteria traveled the length and depth of the village as people raced screaming from their lodges, trying to flee the attacking warriors. As the column of savage raiders made their first pass through the village, many bodies were left bleeding, crushed under the horses and war axes of the attackers. Jed was curious, as he encountered only a few sleepy-eyed warriors on his first pass through the village, but not the hundred he was expecting to fight. He realized somehow they had gotten lucky. The main body of warriors was not present in the village.

Raising his war axe as the women and children huddled in a large group, Jed tried to block the onslaught of the crazed raiders and stop the carnage. Not one Arickaree warrior was anywhere to be seen, at least not alive. Pushing his horse in front of He Dog to stop another charge through the village, Jed tried his best to stop the needless killing.

"Enough have been killed, He Dog. Let us ride out."

Bloodied and torn, Crazy Cat nodded at the young chief. "Crow Killer is right, the missing warriors could come back at any time."

He Dog could only shake his head in rage. "There will never be enough dead Arickaree!"

"We go." Walking Horse turned his horse. "There are only women and children left to kill here."

"Then we will kill them!"

"No, we go now." Crazy Cat argued. "Listen to Crow Killer, my chief."

The killing fervor of He Dog finally relaxed, as his lust for blood cooled. "You are right, my friends. Let us leave this place."

As they rode from the village in a lope, Jed looked around at the warriors and they had many wounds, mostly superficial. Only two warriors, High Horn and One Bull, were seriously wounded and needed attention. After taking care of the two warriors, Jed mounted the bay and led the warriors south toward Bridger's Post. He could not understand why the warriors in the Arickaree village were absent. They had to be out there somewhere, probably hunting or on a raid. Also, there was danger from the other villages. The din of battle and the screams must have been heard, and more warriors could be racing to the village to help. By now, the other villages surely must have seen the smoke from the burning lodges, spiraling into the morning sky as well. Jed knew Ree warriors could spring on them at any minute. He Dog had his revenge, but now they must flee this place if they were to live.

The long trail from the valley, three charges through the village, and their flight for several miles toward Bridger's Post had fatigued the horses. Several miles from the village, Jed held up his hand and stopped the column of warriors. Looking around as Walking Horse, Crazy Cat, He Dog, and Big Owl surrounded him, Jed studied the trail ahead of them.

"Something is wrong." Jed could sense danger ahead. "No Arickaree follow us, this is not right."

"Perhaps, they wait ahead to ambush us." Walking Horse spoke up. "The ones following are pushing us into a trap."

"Why have no Rees from the other villages pursued us?" Crazy Cat questioned looking back down the trail. "Still, there is no other trail here. How could they have gotten ahead of us?"

"We do not know these mountains." Walking Horse warned. "There could be a hidden trail up higher. We could be riding into another ambush, as the one that killed our brother."

"What should we do, Crow Killer?" He Dog stared at Jed. "Tell us."

Looking back down their back trail, Jed turned his bay horse around. "I think we must go back the way we came to this place."

"But, surely there will be enemy warriors following us." Walking Horse intervened. "I have a bad feeling about this."

"Our medicine will protect us." Crazy Cat assured them. "Have no fear, my brothers, we are Cheyenne."

"I am Arapaho." Big Owl whispered to himself.

"Maybe it will." Jed nodded. "I think Walking Horse may be right. There may be warriors behind us, but there could be many others waiting in ambush ahead of us too."

"How does Crow Killer know this thing?" He Dog questioned him.

"For one thing, we spotted two more villages in that valley." Jed explained to the men. "Still, no warriors try to catch up with us. I think they just follow and push us into another ambush which the Rees are good at. I believe, like Walking Horse, the warriors from the village we raided are waiting ahead to attack us."

"How did they get ahead of us?"

"They might have been at Bridger's and a rider was sent to tell them of the raid." Jed was only guessing as he did not know where the enemy warriors were. "Brothers, we must decide, forward or back. We cannot be wrong in this decision."

"We go back." He Dog turned his horse.

The young chief quickly designated two warriors to look after the wounded if fighting broke out. He then kicked his horse back down the valley toward the stricken village they had just left. Watching He Dog, Jed felt proud of the young chief riding ahead, sitting his blood-stained horse so calmly with his shoulders square and proud.

"He is young, but he is a brave warrior." Crazy Cat laughed. "He Dog may get to kill more of the Rees before this day is finished."

Only the flashing black eyes of the young chief showed any emotion as he kicked his horse into a short lope. They had to reach and attack the Ree warriors ahead of them soon, before the ones at their rear could reinforce them. The raiders and their horses were tired from their long ride and earlier battle, but they may have to fight again soon. Now, with two warriors badly wounded, they were only eighteen strong against much greater odds.

Riding out from a grove of hackberry and locust trees lining the trail, He Dog reined his horse in hard. Before them, spread out across the valley floor, were at least forty Arickaree warriors. Sitting alone, at their front, was the one with the yellow lightning bolt painted on his palomino horse.

Jed quickly counted the Ree warriors and smiled. "My brothers, this is a good day; the enemy only outnumbers us two to one."

"That one in front likes the color yellow." He Dog pointed to the huge warrior with the painted horse. "He is mine. Soon his color will be red."

Ordering the others to wait, He Dog kicked his horse forward across the opening dividing the two groups. Reining in his horse, the young warrior pointed his war axe at the huge warrior and hurled insults, taunting the warrior. Several times, he raised his breechcloth and showed his nakedness to enrage the warrior.

"My chief, we do not have time for this." Crazy Cat called out a warning as he looked anxiously behind them down the trail to Bridger's.

"Go if you wish, Cheyenne." He Dog raised his war axe. "I will not retreat. My brother's blood calls out. I will kill this Ree dog or die here."

Crazy Cat scowled. "You know we would not leave you to fight alone."

Finally, complete silence settled across the field. The Ree warriors became still, waiting on their leader to respond to this insolent youngster. Seconds later, with a deafening scream of defiance, the huge warrior kicked his yellow horse forward, charging across the meadow, straight at the Cheyenne.

"Maybe, the young one bit off too much this time." Crazy Cat watched as the two warriors clashed together. "The ugly one is a ferocious fighter and our chief is still very young."

"He is only a Ree dog." Hide Walker raised his war axe and screamed. "He Dog is Cheyenne."

"Maybe so." Big Owl agreed. "But he is an awful big Ree dog."

Jed watched as the two screaming warriors pushed into each other. He remembered well, the day on the Blue River when his good friend Bow Legs had lost his life the same way. Bow Legs had taken up the challenge from a huge Pawnee warrior, knowing his chances of defeating the warrior were slim. The little Arapaho Lance Bearer was much smaller and had little hope of winning the duel. However, he had a huge heart, and with one last desperate attempt, his knife somehow managed to find the Pawnee's heart and kill him. That day, Bow Legs had given his life to save the honor of the Lance Bearers and the life of Walking Horse. By killing the huge warrior, Bow Legs had won a truce with the Pawnee so Walking Horse would be taken to Jed's valley where his life could be saved.

Jed watched the raging fight as he watched that day when he was helpless to go to Bow Legs' aid. Today was the same, and now he had to hold back from charging forward to help He Dog. The young one wanted this fight and challenged the older, bigger Arickaree to avenge Yellow Dog. Jed knew if He Dog was killed, then he would have died bravely and would always be honored by his people. He could not ride forward to help, if he did, He Dog would be humiliated. All he could do was watch and hope the young Cheyenne would somehow survive this fight.

Repeatedly, the war axes clashed as the two horses pushed together, then broke apart for another charge. He Dog fought with passion, screaming like a madman every time his axe bit into the Ree's war shield.

"This must end soon or we will be caught between two enemies at the same time." A warrior looked worriedly back down the trail.

"We cannot interfere in this fight." Crazy Cat glared at the warrior. "Have courage, it will be over soon, one way or another."

He Dog seemed to fall sideways as the Ree pushed his horse into the other horse making him stagger. Quick as a cat, the young chief raised back up, swinging his heavy war axe, catching the Ree deep in the stomach, unhorsing him. Slipping from his horse, He Dog stood over the gasping man. Placing his foot on the warrior's heaving chest, the young Cheyenne pinned him to the ground.

"This is for my brother, Yellow Dog, who you killed like a coward with no honor." Pulling his skinning knife, He Dog slashed deep into the helpless Ree's chest, removing his still beating heart. Screaming, he raised the bloody heart to the watching warriors, then bit into it. That was enough for the Ree warriors who panicked and quickly fled, as Jed and the others charged forward.

Scalping the dead Ree, He Dog swung on his horse and waved the bloody hair to the cheers of his warriors. Taking the palomino from the dead warrior, he tied the grizzly trophy to the horse's mane, and followed Jed at a lope behind the fleeing enemy. Jed knew the fighting for today was finished. The Ree were in flight, they had seen their bravest warrior killed and his heart eaten by a mere youngster. Their lust for battle was broken. Maybe, if there were warriors coming from Bridger's Post they might take up the pursuit of the raiders, but Jed did not think so, not today anyway.

Jed had been right, as the warriors crossed the Snake at Black Horse Crossing, no pursuit had been detected by Walking Horse or Crazy Cat as they trailed the column of Cheyenne and Arapaho warriors. He noticed as the warriors rode past him, all were covered in dried blood, mostly Ree blood. As they swam the Snake, the red blotches were cleansed from their bodies. They had gone into the battle naked, except for their breechcloths and headdresses, so no blood showed on their leather hunting shirts or leggings as they donned them after the crossing.

"We were lucky today." Jed looked at the warriors as Walking Horse and Crazy Cat caught up where he sat waiting for them. "We lost no warriors and very few were badly wounded."

"I think Yellow Dog's spirit looked over us this day." Crazy Cat spoke up.

"Our medicine was strong." Walking Horse agreed. "The ugly one should have killed He Dog this day."

"If he had, we would have been in for a long fight." Jed knew the Ree warriors had been shaken and discouraged by losing their leader to such a young warrior. Their resolve to fight had left them as they watched the young Cheyenne eat the heart of their best warrior. Yes, He Dog had been lucky to win over the larger and older warrior. If he had not won, the Rees would have rushed forward to attack in a frenzy.

"It was the rage in his heart that helped He Dog win." Crazy Cat nodded solemnly.

"Has He Dog had enough revenge now?" Jed asked.

Shaking his head, Walking Horse looked over at Jed. "This great victory today will only make his lust to kill stronger. Never will He Dog forget his hatred for the Arickaree dogs."

"Today he was lucky. We were lucky and we all still live." Jed responded.

As Jed approached the crossing, he could see the others waiting beside their horses on the far shore. Wading into the river, he quickly washed the dried blood from his body and shook his head. For once, after a battle, he didn't have a single scratch on him. Walking Horse ducked his body under the cool river water and scrubbed himself with sand from the bottom. Leading their horses into deeper water, they started the animals swimming.

Wading from the river, Jed handed his horse to Big Owl, then walked to where the two wounded warriors lay on their sleeping robes.

Both warriors were badly wounded, but neither uttered a sound. After examining each man's wounds, Jed walked to where He Dog and Crazy Cat were waiting.

"Both have bad wounds." Jed shook his head. "Very bad."

"And we are far from your lodge." Crazy Cat added.

"We must make a travois for One Bull." Jed sat down on his sleeping robe. "High Horn will be weak, but for now, he can still sit a horse."

"One Bull is that bad?" He Dog looked over at the wounded warriors.

"The arrow went deep and causes him much pain."

Crazy Cat spoke up. "Will a travois be able to cross the high passes?"

"Where it can't go, One Bull will have to be put on a horse or carried." Jed accepted some jerky from Big Owl. "Hopefully, he won't have to leave the travois."

He Dog called two warriors to him, then pointed across the river. With a nod both men mounted and re-crossed the Snake. "They will stand guard and make sure we are not attacked during the night."

"The Ree have been whipped this day." Crazy Cat proclaimed. "I do not think they will come to this place."

"I would come if it were my people who had been slaughtered." He Dog declared.

"You have already proved that, my chief." A Cheyenne warrior called Hide Walker spoke up.

Jed noticed since the fight with the Ree warrior, the Cheyenne and Arapaho warriors treated He Dog with more respect, or perhaps, admiration. He knew the tribes respected and admired a warrior with a fighting spirit. There was no doubt the young Cheyenne Chief had proved his mettle and leadership qualities this day.

Daylight found the raiders already mounted, heading away from Black Horse Crossing. Jed wanted to return to his valley as quickly as possible. He knew the trails following the Snake River and there was no way an enemy could get ahead of them on these narrow passes. The trail from the crossing was just too steep and mountainous, and only one trail followed the river. Still, he wanted to return to Bright Moon to see about her safety. The memory of Sally Ann's tragic death would always haunt him and make him worry for Bright Moon's safety.

Both wounded warriors were in agony, but neither would let the others know of their pain. High Horn had an arrow pass through the fleshy part of his thigh. The pain made it difficult for him to sit a horse, but Jed did not see the wound as being dangerous or life threatening. One Bull's wound was different, as the warrior had taken an arrow to his chest and it was very serious. A travois had been made to carry the warrior back to the valley. Still, Jed knew the travois would be a bumpy ride, very hard and painful on the wounded warrior.

"Why do we not make a sling for him as you did for me?" Walking Horse had been watching the pain-racked face of the warrior. "The trail is rough. The travois is hard on him."

"A sling would be good." Jed nodded. "But, we do not have the rawhide or an old gentle horse to put it on."

Walking Horse agreed. "Crow Killer is right. Our war horses are all young and would not allow such a thing on their back for very long."

Big Owl frowned in thought. "One Bull is in pain and needs no more hurt to come to him."

The slow progress up and down the mountain trail was torturous, but it had to be endured. He Dog kept two warriors far behind the slow moving column, just in case they were being followed.

The trail back to his valley had been hard on the wounded. As Jed reined in at the high ledge and looked down on his cabin and long valley, the two men tried to be cheerful and smile.

"Be brave, Cheyenne, we are almost to Crow Killer's lodge." He Dog knelt beside the travois. "It is only a short distance now."

"I am okay, my chief." One Bull tried his best to smile.

Wolverine and Spotted Feather, the two warriors He Dog had left behind to stay with Bright Moon, noticed the ears of the black mule suddenly focused on the north trail out of the valley. Something had her attention, somebody was coming down the mountain pass. Calling to Bright Moon, both warriors took up their rifles and slipped out of sight behind the tall oaks. The little mule let out a long bray just as Wolverine pointed at riders coming into sight as they made their way slowly down the mountain.

"It is them, they have returned." Bright Moon started for the creek.

"Wait!" Spotted Feather warned. "We will wait until they ride closer so we can see their faces."

"I know my own husband, warrior." Bright Moon started forward again.

"I told you to wait, woman." The warrior grabbed her arm. "Stay back until I tell you different. This could be a trap."

"Listen to him, Bright Moon." Wolverine cautioned her. "Wait until we can see their faces plainly."

Bright Moon glared at the warrior, but stayed where she was ordered. Spotted Feather was right, at this distance she could not tell who it was for sure.

"I am sorry, Spotted Feather." She apologized. "I was excited to see my husband Crow Killer."

The warrior nodded seriously. "We understand, but I do not think Crow Killer would be happy with us if you lost your pretty long hair."

Smiling, she nodded quietly. "I will do as you ask."

Both warriors cursed as Bright Moon laughed and bolted for the creek. They could not believe the speed with which she could run. Running at full speed, they barely caught her as she stopped at the water's edge. A few minutes later, as they held her arms and waited, the riders crossed the valley floor and rode up to the stream. Smiling, Bright Moon waded into the shallow water, laughing as Jed pulled her up on the horse in his lap.

"You have returned sooner than we thought." Bright Moon hugged him.

"Your woman is hard to control, Crow Killer." Spotted Feather glared at Bright Moon. "She needs a stick taken to her."

"I know my husband." Bright Moon laughed again. "But, you can hit me if you want."

"Women!" Spotted Feather swore, shaking his head. "That mule is easier to control."

"We have a few wounded ones and two are very bad." Jed reined in the bay horse at the corral. "We must get them inside and treat their wounds quickly."

This bad news sobered Bright Moon's happiness at reuniting with

Jed. Sliding from the horse, she knelt beside the travois and felt One Bull's head. "Bring him to the lodge. He has many evil ones in him."

Standing beside her, Jed nodded. He knew she meant both warriors had high fevers caused by their wounds. Quickly, several warriors helped One Bull and High Horn into the cabin. Jed wished Ellie or Little Antelope was there to help. He knew Bright Moon would care for the men the best she could, but she was young and he wasn't sure how much she knew about healing the injured.

Water was quickly heated, and with the help of the older warrior Crow Wing, Bright Moon cleansed the wound of One Bull. The arrow had penetrated the warrior's right shoulder, and the wound was inflamed with redness and swelling. Jed was right, neither Bright Moon nor Crow Wing knew the healing ways of Ellie or a medicine man. All they could do was clean the wound and put on the healing salve Ellie had left there for Walking Horse when he was sick. Moving to where High Horn sat weakly in Jed's chair, Bright Moon examined his wound. The warrior had been lucky as the arrow had passed clean through the fleshy part of his thigh. After cleaning the wound, she applied the salve and covered it with clean cloths, then tied them off.

"It is all I can do." Bright Moon apologized. "I will look at the others, then fix food."

Taking her by the arm, Jed smiled down at her. "You did a good job with them. You make me proud."

"I wish I knew the healing medicine, as my sisters do." The slender woman shook her head. "High Horn's wound will be very sore for many days. Lone Bull I do not know, his wound is much worse."

"You did fine, Bright Moon." Wolverine spoke up.

After a good night's rest and a hot meal, most of the warriors had recovered from the long ride and were bantering one another. Each one had to brag and tell of his part in the raid as was the custom of the tribes. Jed knew when they returned to their village a great celebration lasting far into the night would be given in their honor. The drums would beat steadily as the younger women of the village danced in their finery, trying to catch the eyes of the heroic returning warriors.

He Dog called Jed and Walking Horse outside to the corral. "I worry for my people. I will take my warriors home today."

"I understand." Jed nodded and looked over at Walking Horse. "And you, my brother?"

"I cannot leave my wounded."

"We will take care of High Horn and One Bull, then we will bring them home when they are strong enough to sit a horse." Jed argued. "Your people may need you also."

"Perhaps you are right, my brother." Walking Horse agreed. "Our great Chief Slow Wolf grows feeble. He cannot protect his people now."

"Go with He Dog, my brother." Jed smiled.

The young Cheyenne Chief looked away, ashamed. "I was wrong to get you and Bright Moon involved in this trouble with the Arickaree. Now, I ride away and leave you here alone in this place."

"I did not have to go, my chief."

"A warrior with pride and honor always has to go." He Dog shook his head. "To do less would be a dishonor."

"We will be fine." Jed tried to change the subject. "Besides, I was getting fat just sitting in my lodge."

Looking at the full barn of dried grass, He Dog smiled and questioned Jed. "Why would a warrior do all this work? I do not understand. One day, my brother, you must tell me why you work this way when you could be hunting or swimming."

"Your sister wants to know the very same thing." Jed laughed.

Shaking hands with Jed, He Dog smiled. "Keep safe, my brother, watch like the hawk."

"I will take care of her." Jed knew the young chief worried about his sister.

"And yourself, Crow Killer." He Dog called to his warriors. "We go!"

Walking Horse gripped Jed's arm, then pulled him into a bear hug before stepping back. "I will do as you say, then I will see you when you bring our warriors home."

"Have a safe journey, my brother."

"Look to your watch fires. The Rees might have followed us here." Walking Horse frowned and looked up at the high mountains. "I know the grey wolf watches for you. We heard him call out as we rode down the mountain."

"Do not worry, my brother. I have two lookouts posted at all times." Jed smiled.

"Two lookouts?" The warrior was curious. "What is the other one?"

"The great grey wolf watches over this valley." Jed pointed to the valley. "And don't forget the little mule."

"Oh." Walking Horse laughed, he had forgotten about the mule. "Yes, I remember her."

"She is a good watcher." Jed smiled.

"Before I leave, I tell you this, my brother." Walking Horse nodded. "Chief Slow Wolf asks that you come to see him soon."

"Is something wrong?"

"Slow Wolf grows feeble, but I think it is something he wishes from you." The warrior swung up on his horse. "He would not tell me what he needed, only that he wishes for you to hurry."

"Tell my chief I will come as soon as One Bull and High Horn can ride."

"Thank you, my brother." Walking Horse looked down from his horse. "I will tell him."

Big Owl led his horse up to a large rock to stand on while he mounted the animal. Watching, Bright Moon grinned at him, as he made a face and flopped himself over the horse. The horse seemed to sag as the huge warrior straightened himself comfortably on his back.

"Perhaps, Big Owl should get a shorter horse." She giggled.

"Maybe Bright Moon should respect her elders more." The warrior kicked the horse after the others.

"I pity the poor thing having to tote Big Owl over the mountains."

"Yes, Big Owl is a big man." Jed laughed. "But, he is also a great Lance Bearer."

Walking to the creek, Jed and Bright Moon stood watching as the warriors disappeared across the long valley. The tall waving grass, abounding with brightly colored and sweet smelling flowers, quickly closed in and hid the men and their horses as they passed. Sunflowers grew everywhere in the valley, growing taller than the valley grass. The pretty yellow and black colors along with smaller blue and red flowers appeared to blanket the valley.

Bright Moon watched as they rode out of sight. "My brother offered me the hair of the Ree."

Jed nodded quietly. He had noticed the bloody trophy still hanging stiffly from the mane of the yellow horse, before the warriors departed. "I am glad you didn't take it."

"It would not bring my brother back to me." Bright Moon bit her lip to hold back the tears. "I will see to One Bull and High Horn."

"One Bull looks bad."

"Without White Swan or Medicine Thunder's medicine, I fear he will be with his ancestors soon."

"And High Horn?"

"The arrow tore his flesh, but I think his leg will heal with time."

Catching the piebald, Jed took his rifle and crossed the small stream below the cabin. He wanted to check the high pass for any evidence of enemy tracks along the trail. He didn't figure the Arickaree would come to the valley so soon after the raid, but he needed to put his mind at rest. He also needed to be alone with his own thoughts for a while. He knew the Arickaree way was to wait and lull an enemy into thinking they were safe, then launch an attack. Jed knew alone, he could evade any enemy coming into his valley, but he had Bright Moon and the two wounded warriors to think about.

Nothing showed on the rocky trail, only the older tracks of their horses and the travois' drag marks were visible. He wished he could wipe out all the tracks, but he knew that would be impossible.

Carefully, the piebald paint picked his way across the rock strewn trail climbing first, then dipping back down as the trail meandered along the steep mountains. Even on the sunny passes, the wild flowers grew along the trail, giving off their sweet fragrances as he passed. Nothing sounded along the trail. Only the moaning wind called out as it caused the limbs of the trees to sway. Jed smiled as he breathed in the clean mountain air. Nowhere, could a man find the tranquility and beauty that lay on the face of these mountains, his mountains.

As the morning passed without incident, Jed looked up and gauged it was past noon as the sun was already high and on its downward spiral. He had found nothing disturbing along the trail so there was no need to ride any further. Reining the piebald around, he turned back to his valley. Passing the high ridge, he looked down at the cabin and nodded. This was his home and his valley, and he would fight to protect it from any enemy riding against him.

As he passed the high ridge and started down the trail, the sun broke out over the ridge where the bright light, as in the past, suddenly flashed brightly from the sheer wall. Reining in, Jed studied the light that almost blinded him. Slipping from the piebald, he made his way to the rock ledge only to have the light distinguish itself as before. Walking back a few paces, Jed watched as the light flashed on again. Several times, he moved forward only to have the light flee from his view. Looking up at the sun, Jed nodded. He knew it was the rays of the sun hitting some object that projected the shining light.

"So you are not supernatural at all. You just need the sun to reveal yourself to me." Jed laughed. Mounting the piebald, Jed raised his hand. "I will return soon supernatural one to find out your secret."

Early the next morning, after returning to the cabin, Jed sat outside at the log table sipping on his final cup of coffee. Looking at the tin cup, he smiled. He had come to enjoy his coffee in the early predawn morning, watching as the valley and its wildlife came fully awake. The distant call of a bull elk trumpeting his challenge could be heard across the valley as the sun showed its glowing face above the eastern rim.

"What will you do today, my husband?" Bright Moon touched his shoulder as she sat down.

Jed looked at the double-bladed axe he had stood against the cabin. "It's time to start bringing in firewood for the winter."

"The cold times are still a long way off."

"You are right, but it will be here sooner than you think." Jed replied.

"Are the cold times bad, up this high, when the sun hides its face?" Bright Moon looked up at the high mountains.

"Sometimes it can get rough." Jed admitted. "But, we will be warm and cozy before our fire, or under our warm robes."

"Everything will be white, all covered in snow?"

"Everything." Jed looked back at the cabin door. "How are the sick ones?"

"High Horn is still in pain, but he gets better."

"One Bull?"

"He weakens. This morning, he refused to eat." Bright Moon frowned. "I think the spirit rider will come for him soon."

"I'm sorry. He was a great warrior and he will be missed." Jed frowned.

"I do not think even our medicine people could have saved him." She shrugged. "I think the Arickaree dogs put evil spirits on their arrows."

Jed knew she was just talking. If the Rees had put some poison on their arrows, High Horn would be getting sicker too. He knew the enemy sometimes dipped their arrowheads in dung or in the poison from the ivy or oak, but he did not think that's what was killing One Bull.

"One Bull's wound is bad and no one could save him. I do not think he wants to live." Jed stated sadly.

Bright Moon shuddered. "I have seen the old ones of our tribe will themselves to die and then they went to be with their ancestors."

Picking up the axe, Jed kissed her softly. "I will start gathering wood. Call out if you need me."

CHAPTER 3

urther down the valley, above the cabin, there was a good stand of oak and cottonwood trees. High winds, from a bad storm, had knocked down several trees causing them to die and dry out, perfect firewood to warm the cabin. Jed started trimming the smaller limbs, then used the Pawnee horse to skid the logs to the cabin. By nightfall, he had several small trees lined up alongside the wooden saddle he had made to hold the logs while he sawed them.

Last trapping season, as he traded his furs, he had bought a one-man bow saw to cut the logs into lengths. Looking at the gleaming new blade, he smiled, knowing it would make the task a whole lot faster and easier than chopping each log with the axe, as he had done the previous winter. Dragging one of the limbs onto the saddle, Jed went to work with his new saw. The sharp teeth bit through the dead wood easily as the ripping of the blade cutting could be heard across the valley. Bright Moon would come out occasionally to help stack the cut wood against the cabin.

The day was warming up, causing Jed to shed the deer hide hunting shirt and work bare-chested. Bright Moon smiled uncontrollably as she took in the rock hard muscles as he pushed and pulled on the saw. The heavy back muscles bulged powerfully as he wielded the blade. She beamed with pride. No woman in the whole Cheyenne Nation had a warrior like Crow Killer.

Stopping, from time to time, to check on the wounded men, Jed had already stacked a cord of wood against the cabin wall by nightfall. Lige

Hatcher had warned him of this practice of putting cut wood against the cabin walls, saying it would cause the wall timbers to rot faster. Still, Jed persisted, as the high country snows and winds were very fierce at times. Trying to go outside to bring in firewood from a woodpile was hard and could be dangerous. Finally, near nightfall, after bringing in the horses, Jed sat down before the small cook fire. He was tired, but it was a good feeling, something a man felt good about after a long hard day's work.

Sitting beside High Horn, Jed could tell the warrior was deep in thought. "How is my brother's leg today?"

Flexing the injured leg gently, the warrior nodded. "It is still sore to the touch, but it mends."

"And One Bull?"

"He suffers much. The evil ones will not leave his body." High Horn looked over at the bed. "I fear he will not be with us much longer."

Jed watched as Bright Moon swathed the man's sweaty head with cool cloths trying to comfort him. He could tell One Bull had weakened and could plainly see what High Horn had said was true. Pouring himself a hot cup of coffee, Jed sat back against the hearth.

"I must return to our people soon." High Horn sipped on his coffee.

Jed shook his head. "Your leg will not allow this."

The warrior persisted. "I will wait for One Bull to go, then I must return."

"You are still too weak, my friend. Alone, you would not reach the big river." Jed argued. High Horn couldn't walk by himself yet, much less mount a horse. "You must wait a few suns yet."

Morning found Jed back at his work, dragging and cutting firewood. Today, he started felling green trees to mix in with the dry wood. Dried wood burned hotter and easier, but green wood, when finally burning, held a fire longer throughout the night. The winters were long and cold, and from early fall until late spring a fire was needed almost all the time to warm the cabin. Jed intended to have at least ten cords of firewood stacked in rows along the cabin wall before he was finished cutting.

Dragging the last two logs in for the day, he watched as Bright Moon walked toward him. Something was wrong, he could tell by the stoop of her shoulders.

"Is it One Bull? Is he dead?"

"Yes, my husband, he has gone to sleep with his ancestors." Her eyes filled with tears. "I could do nothing."

"You tried your best." Jed held her. "Death comes to all of us, some sooner than others."

"I know, but he was so young."

"Come, I will prepare a scaffold for him to sleep beside Silent One." Jed led the horse to the cabin.

"I do not think he would like to sleep forever beside an Assiniboine." Bright Moon clucked her teeth the way Cheyenne women did when they disagreed about something.

"You are wrong. One Bull has met the Silent One and he liked him." Jed nodded. "It is an honor to rest beside a warrior like the Assiniboine."

"I did not know this, my husband."

"Prepare him for his journey. We will take him to the place where he will sleep."

Bright Moon looked up at Jed. "Will you let his horse journey with him?"

The question surprised him. He knew the Cheyenne practiced the custom of killing a deceased warrior's favorite war pony and laying it under the scaffold so the warrior could ride into the hereafter well-mounted. Whites did not practice this ritual, but most of the horseback tribes did.

"I will speak with High Horn."

"High Horn is sad." Bright Moon looked back at the cabin. "He and One Bull grew up together."

Jed understood the sadness very well. "It is always sad to lose one so close."

High Horn sat at the outside table as Jed removed the harness, releasing the horse across the stream with the other horses. The warrior sat watching as he trimmed and cut poles for the scaffold.

"I should be helping you, Crow Killer. One Bull was my friend."

"Your leg will not permit this." Jed cautioned him. "You would, if you could."

"Will you bring me a horse so I can ride to the place where he will rest?"

"I will do this." Jed looked at the warrior. "Should we leave a horse for him to ride to hunt the shaggies?"

"No, you have few horses." High Horn replied. "One Bull will understand."

Jed sat looking at the uncut logs, knowing he should start with the blade again. One Bull had been placed on the high scaffold to rest beside Silent One, where he could look out over the valley. For High Horn, the short way to the knoll had been a painful ride, but he was grateful to Jed for helping him out there.

As the blade started to cut into the green limbs, Jed noticed as High Horn limped out to the table and sat watching him. Putting the saw down, he walked over to where the warrior sat.

"In two sleeps, I must return to our village."

"You are still weak, my brother. You could hardly make it to the burial place yesterday." Jed explained.

High Horn shook his head. "I will go. I must return to my people."

Jed couldn't understand. "Why must you travel so soon?"

"When we rode on this trail my woman was heavy with child." The warrior looked out across the valley. "By now, I may have a new son."

"The baby will need a father." Jed argued. "Wait a few sleeps, my friend, and let your leg become stronger."

"No, two sleeps, then I must return."

Jed went back to his work knowing the warrior had made up his mind and would not be talked out of leaving. He also knew the chances of High Horn making it across the great mountains and rivers in his condition was very slim. Two more cords of wood had been stacked in neat rows as Jed hung the saw up, out of the night dew. Walking inside, he took the plate of food from Bright Moon and sat down.

"Does High Horn still insist on leaving?" He looked over at the warrior.

"I must, unless you need me here, Crow Killer." The warrior nodded between bites.

Jed looked over at Bright Moon. "My woman wants to see her sister, so we will ride with you."

High Horn protested. "You have much work to do here at your lodge."

"There is plenty of time during the summer months to finish." Jed finished his supper and stood up. "We will prepare for our journey."

"Thank you, Crow Killer."

Two days later, everything was ready for their departure. Anything of value had been cached in the secret cave Jed had found on his hunts for the killer bears. The heavy steel traps were left hanging on their pegs in the horse barn. Jed knew no Indian would have use for these iron things. The extra horses were turned out on the valley floor to fend for themselves. Jed had left them before and they hadn't roamed away. He hoped they would be here when he returned. Counting the little mule, he now had nine horses to feed during the cold times. He didn't need near that many, but he had become like the Arapaho warriors. They counted their wealth in horses, so he kept them all.

Jed helped High Horn and Bright Moon mount their horses, then he swung on the piebald. Taking one last look around, Jed turned his horse away from the cabin, toward the south. The black mule, loaded down with their sleeping robes, cooking utensils, and two extra rifles, followed Jed as he led her across the stream. Bright Moon led the horse of One Bull behind her. Jed had wanted to give the horse to High Horn, but he had refused the gift, asking Jed to return the animal to the dead one's family.

The climb up and over the torturous steep trail was very telling on the wounded one. His face was absent of all color as he clung painfully to the back of his horse. Only by gripping the animal with his knees and hanging onto the heavy mane kept him from sliding from the animal's back. Reining the piebald in as they topped over the first mountain pass, Jed slid from his horse and helped High Horn slowly to the ground.

"We will rest here for a while."

"These sore bones thank you, my friend." High Horn sat down softly on a flat rock. "I think you were right. I should have waited a few more suns."

"We are not far. We could return to my lodge." Jed offered.

"No." High Horn shook his head. "We will not waste this day. I only need a little rest."

By sundown, they had made only half the distance Jed normally made the first day on the trail. He knew High Horn was in severe pain from his leg wound and could not understand how he thought he could return to his village alone. The warrior could not even mount his horse without a helping hand. All day, Bright Moon kept a close watch on the wound to make sure it did not break open again.

Finally, after passing another painful day for the wounded man, they reached the bank of the big river. The current was slow and lazy, but there was still plenty of deep swimming water to cross.

"What do you look for, my husband?" Bright Moon reined her two horses in next to Jed. "Your eyes keep searching the far bank."

Jed had been watching the mule's ears. She sensed something across the water. Her eyes and ears were pointing to the same clump of bushes. Jed helped High Horn from his horse and onto a dead log lying on the sandy riverbank.

"We will camp here tonight." Jed spoke loud enough for his voice to carry across the river.

"I thought we were going to cross tonight so we could dry out before morning?" Bright Moon asked him curiously. "You have changed your mind, why?"

"There's something over there watching us." Jed stopped her as she began to turn. "Do not look across the river, just act normal and see to High Horn."

"Is it the Rees?" Bright Moon whispered. "They have come here?"

"I don't know. In this land, it could be anyone, friend or foe." Jed led the piebald and black mule down to water.

"Would they not show themselves if they were friends?" High Horn spoke up.

"We will give them time." Jed ignored the far bank as he helped the wounded warrior to his sleeping robe. "How is your leg?"

"Stiff, in pain, and useless for walking."

Whispering quietly, Jed handed the reins of his animals to Bright Moon. "Make camp, laugh, and walk around. Whoever they are, keep their attention."

"Where do you go, my husband?"

Laughing and speaking loudly again, Jed sauntered off down the river. "I will bring firewood so you can cook, woman."

"Yes, cook!" She answered him loudly.

Bright Moon and High Horn watched as Jed picked up a few pieces of driftwood, then disappeared into the heavy foliage lining the river.

Bright Moon shook her head and looked over at High Horn. "I will unload the mule, then hobble the horses on the grass."

"Be ready with your rifle, woman." High Horn lay studying the riverbank.

"Why?" Bright Moon looked at the warrior. "Do you feel an enemy is across the river?"

"I think Crow Killer goes hunting, but not for wood."

"What are you saying, warrior?" She questioned him.

High Horn looked across the broad river. "I believe your husband crosses the river. He suspects something is over there watching us."

"He will cross the river alone and without his rifle?" Bright Moon looked to where Jed had left his rifle before walking away. "We should go across and help him."

"Listen to me, woman. We will wait here." The warrior frowned over at her. "Our rifles will reach him if they are needed."

Removing his clothes, Jed slipped silently through the bordering shrubs and underbrush of the river. Crawling quietly down to the river, he submerged himself in the cool water. Without making a sound or disturbing the water, Jed slowly dog-paddled across the wide river. Pulling himself out of the water, he waited concealed under the heavy brush, listening for any sound from the far timber. For several minutes, his sharp ears listened, trying to detect the slightest of sounds. Nothing was heard, not the bark of a squirrel nor the call of a jay or crow, nothing.

Crawling forward through the heavy cane and brush on his belly, occasionally Jed would stop and listen. Minutes later, still no sound came as he continued to inch forward silently. As he crawled, the sand from the riverbank had completely covered his wet body, causing him to blend in with the ground.

Suddenly, Jed froze in place as he found himself looking into the eyes of a coiled water moccasin. Only the flicking tongue of the snake moved as his beady eyes watched where Jed lay motionless. The moccasin had been lying under a dead log, hidden from Jed's view until he crawled up to the viper. Both pairs of eyes, man and snake's did not blink or move in the slightest as they studied each other. Jed knew he was within striking range of the snake. However, from the bulge in the reptile's body, he must have just eaten making him sluggish and too full to strike. Retreating slowly, back out of the snake's reach, Jed searched the thickets for any more snakes before moving forward again.

Jed knew he had just missed by inches, one of the worst deaths a man could suffer. If the moccasin had struck, he would have hit him in the face or neck. The moccasin's venom was deadly and a terrible, agonizing way to die. Next to the rattlesnake, the water moccasin was the most venomous snake there was and probably meaner.

Shaking the cold chill that ran down his back, he slowly pushed his way along the underbrush. This time, he moved even slower, taking in every ounce of ground before he crawled forward. He knew he had been lucky. White Swan had said no man would ever kill him, but he didn't mention anything about a water moccasin.

Jed lay almost across from where Bright Moon moved about the small fire, singing as she made camp. Suddenly, he heard a noise close ahead, then again, a faint sound carried to his ears. Finally, he figured the sound was from a horse swishing its tail, trying to rid itself of the swarms of pesky red-headed flies that were so abundant along the river. Slipping forward, then parting the foliage enough to peer out, he spotted two horses tied to a tree, less than twenty paces away from him. There was no wind moving to bring his scent, so the horses hadn't detected his presence yet. Slowly pivoting his head toward the river, he found what he was looking for. Two warriors were concealed behind a dead log, watching the camp across the water.

Crawling a few feet forward, Jed raised to a kneeling position, remaining hidden behind a large elm tree. Both horses finally noticed him and pricked their ears, but their owners were so engulfed in watching Bright Moon, they did not look behind them. Jed recalled Walking Horse's warning; in enemy territory, always watch your horse's ears. These warriors apparently hadn't learned that one good lesson.

"The woman has much beauty." The larger of the two nodded. "And I have never seen a horse such as this black and white one."

The other warrior shook his head. "Have you not noticed there were two warriors guarding the woman?"

"One is hurt. I watched when the other one helped him to the ground."

"It does not matter, his arms are not injured. They have rifles against our bows."

"The Bat is scared, maybe?" The bigger warrior grinned. "When the new sun comes, they will cross the river. When they are swimming and helpless, our bows will strike."

"We should go, Prairie Runner, leave this place." The one called Bat pleaded. "We have already lost our friends on this stupid raid."

"That is why we must kill these warriors." Prairie Runner argued. "We must have something to show for this trail. I will not return to our people with nothing."

"You would have your life."

"No, I would only have shame." The bigger warrior shook his head. "I want the woman and the horse."

"I have a bad feeling about this thing. We should go from this place." Bat requested a second time.

"Do as you wish, but I will have the woman for my own."

Bat peeked over the log and looked up and down the riverbank. "Where has the other warrior gone to?"

"He goes for wood like a squaw."

Jed slipped silently to within ten paces of the hidden warriors. He had never seen warriors like these. Except for a small scalp lock protruding from the side of their head, they were completely hairless. They were a lighter skinned people, and their muscles were smooth, not bunched in mass as the Arapaho. Jed had never known or heard of warriors such as these, and wondered where they had come from.

"He has been gone a long time. He should have returned." Bat looked around. "Where is he?"

Jed shook his head in disgust at the foolish ones. "I am right here."

Whirling, both warriors grabbed for their war axes as they stared in disbelief at the naked warrior covered in sand standing before them. In their entire life, they had never seen one so heavily muscled and scarred as this warrior was. Bat stood frozen, trembling as he stared at the wild caricature standing before him. Prairie Runner advanced a step toward Jed with his axe raised.

Jed was armed only with his skinning knife as he stood before the two warriors. "Put your weapons down or die here."

Prairie Runner laughed. "You are only one man against two."

"I do not see two men. I see two dogs, cowards, waiting to ambush a defenseless man and woman."

"We will see who is a coward." The bigger warrior charged forward right into Jed's flying foot that caught him across his face, breaking his nose as it knocked him senseless. "Now, it is your turn."

Dropping his war axe, Bat shook his head in fear. In disbelief, he watched as the older, stronger Prairie Runner had been disabled so easily. Bat knew to fight was useless. He would stand no chance against this warrior.

"Do not kill me." The warrior trembled so hard, his teeth chattered. "I did not wish to ambush you or take your woman. I said nothing."

"What tribe are you?"

"Paiute."

"Where is your village?"

"Far south of here." Bat watched fearfully as Jed moved around him.

"What are you doing this far north?"

Bat expelled a long breath and nodded at Prairie Runner. "That foolish one led us here to raid."

"Just the two of you?"

"No, there were many of us until we ran into many warriors east of this place." Bat shrugged. "These warriors attacked us from ambush, killing many of my people."

"East of here?"

"Yes."

"How long ago was this?" Jed was curious, wondering if the warriors were the Rees looking for the ones that attacked their village.

"Maybe four sleeps."

"Why are you still in these mountains?"

"They pursued and killed more of us until only me and that one remained." Bat nodded at the unconscious warrior. "They were ferocious warriors, blood crazed."

"Yet, he still wanted to attack us as we crossed the river?"

Bat nodded. "Prairie Runner is a foolish leader. Now, he has gotten us both killed."

"You are not dead yet, Paiute. Have heart, I may spare you." Jed replied.

Motioning the smaller warrior ahead of him, Jed drug the unconscious Prairie Runner until they reached a grove of small elm trees growing along the bank. In plain sight, across from Bright Moon's camp, Jed deposited the unconscious warrior and started rolling out a roll of rawhide he had found on one of their horses. Ordering the other Paiute to lay down, Jed quickly bound their wrists and legs with strong coils of rawhide. Standing back as the unconscious one came awake, struggling against his bonds, Jed smiled at the feeble attempts and curses the warrior made. Spread-eagled tightly, both their arms and legs had been tied to the near trees so they could hardly move. Both men lay on their backs looking up at Jed, wondering what was going to be their fate.

"What happened?" Prairie Runner shook his head trying to remove the blood from his eyes and nose. "Why am I bound like this?"

"You are bound because you acted foolishly, Prairie Runner." Bat relaxed, not trying to fight the cruel cutting rawhide. "As I was foolish to follow you."

"If I was free, you would not speak like this."

"No, Prairie Runner, I know your heart now. You are a coward. If we were free, I would kill you." Bat criticized and threatened him.

Jed shook his head as he listened to the two warriors argue. "Maybe I should free you both and let you fight."

Disgusted with the aimless bickering, Jed walked back down the riverbank and out of their sight. Both of the men sickened him as neither showed pride nor honor as a warrior should. Moments later, returning to where the two men lay bound, Jed walked to where they could see him. Both men inhaled deeply as their eyes widened, focusing on what he held.

"I have brought someone to watch over you during the dark time." Jed held the snake close to their faces, then stretched the maddened water moccasin out on the ground. Holding the snake's wiggling body on the ground between the two terrified men, Jed pushed his hunting knife through the snake's tail, pinning it to the ground. Quickly stepping back as he released the snake's head, Jed wiped his hands with sand. Several times, the viper struck at the cringing bodies. Both bound men screamed in fear, trying their best to pull away when the moccasin drew its head back for another strike. Jed could still see the bulge in the snake's midsection, probably a rabbit or squirrel he had recently eaten. The meal made the moccasin lazy and passive until Jed disturbed him. The misfortunate animal that had been eaten probably had saved his life back on the riverbank.

Jed smiled, the two Paiute didn't know it, but he had pinned the snake so he could not reach either of the frightened men. Looking across the river, Jed could see Bright Moon and High Horn watching curiously at what he was doing.

"If you lie real still, the snake may go to sleep and not strike you." Jed turned toward the river. "Be still now."

"Do not leave us here tied like this." Prairie Runner pleaded. "We will leave this place."

"What, you do not desire my wife or horse any longer?"

Bat shook his head. "Do not beg him."

Turning his back on the two terrified warriors, Jed waded into the river and swam back downstream to where he had left his clothes. He knew the snake could not break away and strike the tied men. He only wanted to frighten them into leaving this country and never return. He smiled as he exited the water. After tonight, he doubted these two warriors would ever want to raid here or anywhere else again.

Dropping an armful of wood at the fire, Jed looked over at Bright Moon and High Horn, and shrugged. He knew, from this distance, they could not see what had transpired across the river, but they could see he had captured two warriors.

"Tell me, my brother." Jed looked across at High Horn. "Have you ever heard about a tribe that call themselves Paiute?"

"I have heard of these people that live far to the south." The warrior commented. "But, I know nothing of them nor have I ever seen one."

"Across the river there are two who say they are Paiute." Jed nodded. "With the new sun, you will see them."

High Horn could see the two bodies lying on the ground from where he sat. "Are they dead?"

"No, but after the night they will spend, they probably will wish they were." Jed felt no guilt as he had heard what the two warriors had intended for them. "They meant to attack us as we crossed the river with the new sun."

"You did not kill them?" Bright Moon asked.

Jed smiled. "I believe what they are suffering, as we speak, may be worse than death."

"What have you done, my husband?"

"You will see in the morning, woman. Now, I am hungry."

Splashing out of the river, Bright Moon could not believe her eyes. Two warriors staked out between the trees with a venomous snake pinned between them, made chill bumps on her arms. Death would have been far better than the agonizing ordeal these warriors had suffered throughout the long night. She could see both men's eyes were transfixed on the snake. They were almost crazed with fear.

"They have suffered much, my husband." She couldn't believe Crow Killer would do such a thing.

High Horn could only lean against his horse and grin at the helpless men and the maddened snake. "I think they are lucky to be alive."

"That they are." Jed shrugged. "Did you know, wife, they wanted to kill me and High Horn, then take you and my horse as their captives? They just couldn't decide which they wanted the most, you or the horse."

Only the snapping coal black eyes of the woman spoke as she flashed them at the Paiute. "Perhaps, you should release the snake first."

"Take the horses and ride up the trail a ways. I will let our friends go." Jed nodded at High Horn, then helped him up on his horse.

"You should kill them, Crow Killer, or tie the snake to them." High Horn glanced back at the warrior as they left.

Walking to where the two Paiute lay, Jed quickly cut their rawhide thongs and waited as they stiffly regained their feet. Grabbing the water moccasin by its head, he pulled his skinning knife from the tail and flung the viper into the river.

"We are even now, snake. You let me live and now I have given you back your life." Jed watched as the snake swam away downstream.

"What will you do with us?" Bat asked in a subdued voice.

Looking at the two men, Jed shook his head turning to where the horses waited. "Nothing, I think I have done enough to you already."

Swinging up on the piebald, Jed took one final look at the two shamefaced warriors who hadn't moved from where they stood. They were beaten, humbled men, and Jed knew they would not try to follow. Scared as they were now, he doubted they would make it safely back to their village. These two against the many enemy warriors between here and the south, weren't good odds. He could not believe the one called Prairie Runner had led raiders so far north into hostile country. The Paiute had made a foolish decision, one he would regret as long as he lived, if indeed he survived the trail ahead.

Walking Horse walked to Slow Wolf's lodge and stepped inside. The old chief greeted him weakly as the warrior found himself a place across the fire from him. He could see that Slow Wolf was getting weaker as the days passed.

"You have sent for me, my chief?"

Nodding his head, Slow Wolf's eyes were still bright as they looked across the fire. "Thank you for coming, my son."

"When my chief summons, I will always come."

"Have you heard if Crow Killer is on his way to our village?"

"No, my chief, we have heard nothing since leaving his valley." Walking Horse explained. "I fear he will not return here until the wounded ones can ride."

"I grow weak, my son." Slow Wolf stared into the fire. "Crow Killer may come here too late."

"You have many suns yet, my chief." The warrior knew his words were false as he said them.

"Send Big Owl to the river to look for him."

"I will go."

"No, Walking Horse, you will remain in the village." Slow Wolf stared into the fire. "Soon, I will go to meet my ancestors, then you will become chief."

Walking Horse knew he was in line as the next hereditary Chief of the Arapaho after Slow Wolf. Still, the thought of losing a leader like Slow Wolf, one he had followed and learned from since he was a child, saddened him. He remembered the great Lance Bearer in his prime, one of the most feared of the Arapaho. He dropped his eyes. Where had the days gone? Only yesterday it seemed like Slow Wolf was leading them into battle or on the buffalo hunts. Walking Horse knew that whatever sickness was inside the old warrior, it was killing him quickly. The leadership of the old one would be sadly missed.

"I will send Big Owl."

"Thank you, my son."

Walking Horse looked across at the frail old warrior. "If my chief would tell me what he wants from Crow Killer, maybe I could do this for you."

"No, as I said, I cannot let you leave the village." Slow Wolf shook his head. "What I will ask of Crow Killer will be very dangerous."

"Crow Killer is my brother." The warrior stared at Slow Wolf. "If there is danger, I should go."

"No, my son, soon you will be chief of our tribe. I cannot allow you to do this for me." The old head shook. "When you are chief, then perhaps you will understand my words."

"What is it, my chief?"

"I can only tell Crow Killer." The old head nodded slowly. "He must do this."

"As you wish, my chief."

Little Antelope stood outside the lodge as Walking Horse returned from his talk with Slow Wolf. "What did our chief want, my husband?"

"He would not tell me. He asks for Crow Killer." Walking Horse looked down at the little woman. "He wishes me to stay close to the village."

"Why?"

"Our chief is tired. He feels he may die soon."

"What could he want of Crow Killer?"

Walking Horse shrugged. "He would only say the trail will be dangerous."

"Dangerous?" The small woman's head snapped up as she looked at Walking Horse.

"I must send Big Owl to the river to look for Crow Killer."

"Go then, I will prepare a meal for you, my husband." Little Antelope watched as Walking Horse walked away. "Dangerous." The word slipped from her mouth.

Two days later, the Yellowstone with all its majestic beauty came into view as they pushed their horses down the rocky trail, past the outcropping where the Crow scouts always waited. None of the Crow were in sight as Jed led Bright Moon and High Horn down to the crossing of the mighty river. It puzzled him that there was no one to challenge them as they neared the water.

Slipping from the piebald, Jed moved beside High Horn and took his reins. "Only one more river to cross and you will see your wife and new son."

"If the young one has been born yet." High Horn was in pain, but eager to cross the Yellowstone and get home to his lodge. "I have much to thank you for, my friend."

"Your friendship is all I ever ask."

High Horn nodded. "The lance unites and bonds us as brothers, Crow Killer. You will always be a friend."

"Are you ready to go see your sister?" Crow Killer looked over at Bright Moon.

Laughing, Bright Moon slapped her horse, and with One Bull's horse in tow, she hit the current of the slow moving river. Jed smiled as she slid her body from the horse, hanging onto his mane as she paddled beside the swimming animal. He was proud of her. Not only was she pretty, but she had much courage and was always game to do anything. Holding both his and High Horn's rifles above the water, Jed watched as the injured man eased his hurt leg into the water.

Splashing ashore, Jed glanced back across the water as he helped the wounded warrior mount his horse. Several Crow warriors waved at him from the opposite bank. Jed had never seen the scouts as he rode down to the river crossing. Normally, they would have challenged him before letting him pass.

Raising his hand, Jed turned his small band toward the Arapaho village. Walking Horse had said the village would be camped along the small stream, just a half day's ride ahead. Looking up at the high sun, Jed knew that would put them at the village almost at sundown.

"Soon we will be home, Bright Moon."

"It is good, my husband. It will be good to see Little Antelope again."

"And maybe the small High Horn." The warrior laughed despite the pain in his leg.

A young boy, out hunting for rabbits, watched as they passed down the trail leading into the village, then raced ahead, giving a warning that strangers were coming. Mounted warriors raced from the village, surrounding them yelling and screaming in shrill voices that aroused the whole village. Drums started beating, calling the villagers from their lodges. There was complete hysteria in the village as the great Crow Killer had come home and he had brought the wounded High Horn back safely.

Walking Horse walked from his lodge and greeted Jed as he dismounted and helped High Horn to the ground. Throngs of villagers tried to push close, wanting to touch the two warriors. Laughing and yelling the whole village was jubilant. The safe return of their warriors was cause for celebration.

Jed watched as High Horn greeted his wife and new baby, then nodded as he was helped to his lodge. Walking Horse smiled as Bright Moon was pulled into the arms of the smiling Little Antelope. The villagers, after greeting the newcomers, slowly started to dwindle away.

"It is good, my brother has returned." Walking Horse looked about the horses. "I do not see One Bull."

"We could do nothing. One Bull has gone to be with his ancestors." Jed dropped his eyes. "Nothing."

"His wound was bad." The warrior nodded solemnly. "I was afraid he would not make another sun."

Jed looked around the village. "He died with much honor, fighting for his people. I must tell his family. "

"He was young yet and had no squaw, only his aged mother." The warrior looked over at Little Antelope. "I will have Little Antelope tell her."

"Come, we will release your animals and unload the mule." Walking Horse looked at the black mule and shook his head in disgust. "Why do you use such an animal as this one?"

"It's simple, my brother." Jed smiled as the little mule dropped her droopy ears and waited patiently where she stood. "She is the best watchdog I've ever owned. She has warned me of danger many times."

"But, the fat one at the post would give you five good horses for the contrary little beast."

"That was his offer alright." Jed would never part with the little mule. He knew it was partly because she was such a good watchdog, but mainly because as long as she was with him, he still had part of Silent One too.

Stripping the mule of her load and halter, he turned her loose with the other horses. Hundreds of horses were grazing along the small stream and spread out throughout the village. Jed never could figure out how the warriors in the village remembered which horses was theirs. Turning back to the village, the two warriors sat down outside the lodge and relaxed against the backrests. Jed smiled as he looked about the busy village. It was good to be back among his people once again. His valley was beautiful and peaceful, but sometimes, even though he wouldn't admit, it could get lonesome. He missed talking with Walking Horse and riding on their hunts together.

Little Antelope walked outside and smiled down at the two warriors. Jed noticed the beauty of the little woman hadn't changed, as he smiled up at her.

Quickly regaining his feet, he greeted her. "It is good to see my sister again."

"And it is good to see Crow Killer once again." Little Antelope smiled as Bright Moon pushed through the entrance. "And thank you for bringing my sister."

"She wouldn't take no for an answer." Jed laughed. "You know your sister."

After a brief visit, the two women walked away toward the small creek below the village. Jed watched the two sisters who were almost identical in looks.

"They are almost twins." Walking Horse nodded.

"Almost."

"You should go now and meet with Slow Wolf." Walking Horse changed the subject. "The old one has asked many times for you."

"What does he want?"

"This I do not know, but do not be surprised by his looks." Walking Horse suggested. "He has aged much, my brother, since you spoke with him last."

"I will go now and speak with him." Jed turned and walked back to the village and the large lodge that belonged to Slow Wolf. His curiosity was aroused as he wondered what the old chief wanted of him.

CHAPTER 4

Stopping before the large lodge, Jed cleared his throat before stooping to enter. The lodge was dim inside with only the glow of the small fire, casting enough light to show the old one's figure sitting against his backrest. Greeting Slow Wolf with a raised hand, Jed took the seat across from him.

"Crow Killer, my son, it is good you have returned to your people." The voice was low, not as strong as Jed remembered.

"It is good to be home, my chief."

"Did you have a safe journey?"

"We did… we met no enemies on the trail."

"That is good, my son." The old head nodded. "My woman says One Bull did not return with you."

Jed couldn't help notice the wrinkled, shriveled-up hands that were once the strong, vibrant hands of the great warrior. "No, my chief, One Bull went to live with his ancestors several sleeps ago."

"And High Horn?"

"He is with his woman and new son." Jed smiled. "He will recover from his wound."

"Daughter… High Horn had a daughter." Slow Wolf laughed quietly. "Perhaps, one day he will live to have a son."

Jed neglected to mention the Paiute warriors they had encountered at the great river. The fight with the pale warriors wasn't worth bringing up. Studying the old one, Jed remembered the strong Arapaho Chief that had pulled him from the Platte River and made him a Lance Bearer. When his mother still lived, she spoke of neighbors who had been suffering from the onslaught of crippling arthritis. He feared this disease was what Slow Wolf suffered with. It had only been four years since he was first brought to the Arapaho, and back then this warrior had been strong and powerful. Whatever the sickness was, it was killing Slow Wolf quickly.

"You have asked to see me, my chief?"

"Yes, my son." The old head nodded slowly. "I would ask a very great and dangerous thing of you."

"Ask… I owe you my life." Jed remembered Slow Wolf had saved him from the war axe of Walking Horse when he was found on the muddy bank of the Platte. "Ask of me what you wish."

"I did not want to send Walking Horse and the others to fight against the Arickaree, but the Arapaho and Cheyenne are allies. I had no choice."

"This is so, but still it was a great raid, my chief." Jed smiled. "Our warriors made us proud."

"Yes, Walking Horse and Big Owl spoke of it." Slow Wolf looked into the fire. "But, we lost a brave Lance Bearer."

"He died with honor."

"I need to ask a dangerous thing of you, my son. If you do not wish to do what I ask, I will understand." Slow Wolf looked into Jed's eyes. "As I said, it will be very dangerous."

"I am listening."

"Many years ago when I was young, the Arapaho raided north into Shoshone hunting grounds. Our great chief Iron Breast led the raid. Our medicine went bad when the fierce Shoshone warriors discovered us in their territory and a great battle was fought. We were trapped in a place called the Serpent Canyon, a large rock formation that looks like a coiled snake. Our chief took an arrow to his heart, killing him instantly. Several others were killed at this place and many were injured. We were hard pressed in this fight and could not bring our chief's body back to the Arapaho."

"So you left him somewhere in Shoshone territory?"

"As I said, we had no choice. To survive, we had to retreat quickly to our lands." Slow Wolf nodded. "The enemy was gaining more warriors and fighting hard against us."

"What do you wish of me?"

"I swore when I became chief, I would bring Iron Breast's remains home and bury him with his ancestors." Slow Wolf explained sadly. "I have never been able to keep my promise, in this I have failed. The spirit of Iron Breast has roamed Shoshone lands alone all this time."

"This is what you wish me to do?"

"Our great Medicine Man White Swan watched a great warrior appear in his smoke. He watched this warrior bring the bones of a dead warrior home to be with his father. He said he watched again in his smoke. The same warrior with the Arapaho Lance on his back would do this for Iron Breast and me. That warrior, he saw in his smoke, was you, Crow Killer."

"Has it been many years since this happened?" Jed asked.

"Yes, I was a young man then."

Jed watched the old one as his hands shook. "To ask this of me, you must have left your chief where you could find him."

"We buried our great chief in a shallow grave, then retreated quickly from Shoshone lands." Slow Wolf dropped his head, his voice barely audible. "We ran like cowards to save ourselves."

"No one would dare say the great Slow Wolf was ever a coward."

"We left behind a great warrior."

"Where would I find the place you left this warrior?"

Slow Wolf bent forward slowly, looking across the fire, straight at Jed. "You must understand, since it will be a very dangerous trail, I cannot let Walking Horse share this journey with you. Soon, he may be needed here to take my place. You will be alone in this."

"I understand. Tell me, my chief, where to find this place." Jed repeated.

"Many years ago, the place the whites call Baxter Springs, used to be Shoshone hunting grounds. The white village was not settled yet. Two sleeps north of this place, you will find the place called Serpent Canyon, and beneath the head of the snake is a cave. The place is easy to find, but it is evil. We buried our chief in that cave so his body would not be desecrated. I have been ashamed for deserting his body all these years."

"You had no choice, my chief."

Slowly the old head nodded. "We should have all died at that place."

"You would have if you had stayed and fought." Jed argued. "Your bravery has always been beyond question. Your people love and respect the great Slow Wolf."

"Before I ride my spirit horse, I must bring Iron Breast home and bury him with his ancestors."

"I will ride with the morning sun."

"Hurry, my son. I fear my days are numbered. Go, before I too go to meet my ancestors."

Jed smiled. "You will live to see this happen, my chief. I promise."

"That is all an old man can ask for." Slow Wolf nodded. "Ride with care, my son. The lands you enter are covered with Arapaho blood."

Jed was met by Walking Horse as he walked back to the lodge. He knew the warrior was curious about what Slow Wolf wanted.

"Ride with me to the river with the new sun."

Walking Horse looked over at Jed and nodded. "The women have food prepared."

Sitting outside the lodge after their meal, Jed looked across at Walking Horse. "You have not asked what our chief wants of me."

Shaking his head, the warrior puffed slowly on his pipe. "It is not my place to ask. I will wait for Crow Killer to speak if he wishes."

Jed slowly told of Slow Wolf's request.

Walking Horse listened intently. "I was too young to remember Iron Breast, but I have heard many tales from the old ones of his bravery in battle."

"I will leave Bright Moon here in your protection." Jed looked at the smoking pipe. Many times since watching Lem Roden smoke, he had wanted to buy one at the trading post. The aroma of the tobacco smoke was pleasing to him. "She is not to know where I will go."

"Bright Moon will not like this." Walking Horse responded.

"This trail will be dangerous, and my mind must stay free of worry." Jed shook his head. "She must remain here, safe with Little Antelope and you."

"Who will tell her, that she is to remain behind?"

"I will tell her tonight." Jed stood up. "In the morning, we will ride to the river."

"Slow Wolf refuses to let me ride with you?"

Jed nodded. "You are needed here, my brother. If Slow Wolf should get worse, you will be the new Chief of the Arapaho People, and they will need you to protect them."

"I know this is true, but it is my wish to ride with you."

"Not this time, old friend."

Jed shook hands with Walking Horse on the bank of the Yellowstone, then with a wave, he kicked the piebald into the river. He had said his goodbyes to Bright Moon and Little Antelope long before the sun had come up. Swimming alongside his horse, Jed wondered how this trail was going to turn out. He had ridden so many dangerous trails since becoming a Lance Bearer. Riding into the Shoshone hunting grounds would be another, and perhaps, the most dangerous trail of all. Slow Wolf and Jed's white stepfather both had said they were some of the most warlike people of the north. Only the Blackfoot were as ferocious. The old ones said the Shoshone fought like fanatics when attacked or when their lands were invaded.

Swinging on the piebald, Jed waved once more across the river, then rode up to the high ridge where the Crow scouts would be watching. Chief Plenty Coups had been true to his word and always kept warriors guarding the crossing against any enemy. It was because of the Crow warriors watching over the Yellowstone that the truce between the Pawnee and Arapaho had held so long. None had reported any horse stealing or raids between the two tribes along the great river for two years.

Further to the northeast, there was no peace, where the Sioux were always raiding their neighbors. The Crow people were notable horse thieves and they raided further south into Comanche hunting grounds as well. Jed laughed as the Comanche were great horsemen and pretty good horse thieves themselves. After losing horses to the Arapaho or Crow, their warriors just rode north and stole their horses back. It was a game for warriors to amuse themselves and seldom ended in death.

Four young Crow warriors sat their horses on the high pass as the piebald pulled the last sharp rise in the trail. Today, Jed's mind was on the thing he had promised Slow Wolf, not on the beautiful flowers lining the great river. His thoughts remained only on the long, dangerous trail he knew awaited him.

Reining up in front of the warriors, Jed held his hand up.

"What do you want here, Crow Killer?"

"I must ride to Plenty Coups' village."

All four of the young Crows could plainly see the medallion hanging from Jed's neck. They knew this Arapaho had a free pass through their hunting grounds. They also knew the last warrior to challenge the demon had died at his hands.

"We will ride with you."

"Is Red Hawk in your village?"

The oldest of the young men shrugged. "Who knows where Red Hawk might be, but I believe he has just returned from a raid."

"Against who?" Jed was curious.

All four warriors laughed. "Our young chief steals from anyone who has good horses worth taking."

The village buzzed with chatter and excitement as the villagers noticed who rode with their young men. All knew the great Crow Killer, the good friend of Plenty Coups and Red Hawk. Reining in at the lodge where the spotted stallion was picketed, the warriors left Jed and turned back toward the river. Sliding from the piebald, Jed smiled as the huge form of Plenty Coups came from his lodge.

"My son, Crow Killer, it is good to see you." The great bear paw of the chief wrapped around Jed's shoulder. "It has been many suns since you have come here to visit."

"It is good to see the great Plenty Coups." Jed smiled looking at the chief. He was thankful he never had to meet this warrior in battle when he was in his prime.

"Come, we will eat, or you will eat. Medicine Thunder warned me about eating too much." The chief laughed and shook his head.

Following Plenty Coups inside his huge lodge, Jed took a seat on a pile of buffalo robes. Looking about the chief's lodge, Jed looked up at the hanging bows and lances, and remembered the time he had slipped in and stole the headdress. He was lucky as the spirit people had been with him that night. Taking the hot stew, one of the women handed him, Jed thanked her and started eating hungrily.

Plenty Coups smiled over at his guest, one that he thought of as a son. He remembered the first time he had met Jed, when the Arapaho had crossed the Yellowstone into Crow hunting grounds looking for buffalo. No fear had shown in the young Arapaho Lance Bearer's face even when confronted by the mighty Plenty Coups and his warriors. The bond between them had been sealed that day. No other warrior, maybe not even Red Hawk, had the powerful medicine of this young warrior. Many had tried, but no warrior could match him in battle.

The entrance to the lodge darkened as Red Hawk ducked inside and yelled loudly, deafening all inside. Grabbing Jed, as he stood up, the warrior held onto him with a mighty grasp. Anyone watching would know the closeness these two warriors shared with each other. Red Hawk and Crow Killer were the cream of the Arapaho and Crow Nations. Plenty Coups, frowning at his son, did not stop the jubilation of the reunion.

"So the mighty Arapaho Lance Bearer comes to see us lowly Crows." Red Hawk joked. "It is good to see you, my brother."

Jed looked over at the handsome warrior and smiled. "And it is good to be back with my friends and brothers."

"Is the great Crow Killer lost or have you come to hunt the shaggies with me?"

"Neither, I'm afraid." Jed shook his head. "I have come to ask for your help, with the great Chief Plenty Coups blessings of course."

Red Hawk looked over at his father. He knew whatever brought Crow Killer here asking for help must be important. "Is Walking Horse sick again?"

"No, it is not Walking Horse this time, but something much more dangerous."

For once the young Crow grew quiet. "For you to ask, it must be serious. Why did Walking Horse not come with you?"

"Chief Slow Wolf is very weak." Jed shook his head. "He needs Walking Horse to remain with his people. Soon, I fear he will be chief."

"I remember Slow Wolf. He was a mighty and very dangerous

enemy." Plenty Coups spoke up. "We fought many battles, stole many horses from each other, and he had much honor. He will be missed even by his enemies."

"How dangerous is this trail you take us on?"

"We may not return from this one." Jed shook his head seriously. "I wouldn't blame you if you said no this time."

Red Hawk smiled. "You know I like danger as much as Crow Killer does."

"We ride against the Shoshone to the north." Jed smiled. "I do not do this because of the joy of danger."

"It will be just the two of us against the whole Shoshone nation?"

"Just the two of us." Jed nodded. "Against hundreds, maybe."

Red Hawk looked closely at Jed. "Are you serious, my friend?"

"Very serious."

"Well, at least they cannot say we had them outnumbered." Red Hawk laughed. "That is always my enemy's excuse when we raid their horse herds."

Frowning over at his son, Plenty Coups questioned Jed. "Tell us why you ride against the Shoshone. Their lands are far from here."

Jed quickly told Plenty Coups and Red Hawk what Slow Wolf had asked of him. Explaining where they were headed and how dangerous it could be. He looked over at the face of Plenty Coups studying him closely.

"If you would rather your son not accompany me on this trail, I will understand." Jed shrugged. "I know how much you think of this one. This is a dangerous trail and we may not survive. I know you will worry until his return."

Plenty Coups looked at Red Hawk. "My son is a grown man and a Crow warrior. Even though at times he does things and acts like a child, it is his place to choose what he will do."

Laughing, Red Hawk looked with affection at his aging father. "In your day, my chief, you would already have your horse and weapons ready to leave."

"Probably, but in my day, I too sometimes acted like a child when danger presented itself." Plenty Coups chuckled making his huge stomach bounce. "This is a dangerous thing you undertake. Both of you must think wisely before you ride against the Shoshone."

"It is at least six sleeps to Shoshone Country if we ride hard." Jed looked at Plenty Coups. "We will have plenty of time to plan what we will do."

Reaching above his head, Plenty Coups brought down his beaded pipe pouch. "Let us smoke and ask the medicine people for their blessings on this trail."

"My father thinks it is folly. I think it is just another great adventure. I will get to see new country." Red Hawk laughed.

Jed smiled. "Like the time you went into Nez Perce lands to steal the spotted stallion."

"It makes a warrior's blood come alive." Red Hawk nodded clenching his fist. "This trail will bring us much glory."

"Yes, my son. The last time your blood boiled, you came home wounded. You almost got killed and probably would have if Crow Killer had not helped you."

Red Hawk faked sadness, shrugging his shoulders. "But, my chief, a warrior only lives once."

Plenty Coups frowned. "Yes, and in your few years you have already lived three lifetimes."

Tamping the ceremonial pipe full, the old chief picked a hot ember from the fire and started the tobacco burning. The aroma was pleasant as the smoke filled the lodge. Jed had sent Plenty Coups a whole pouch of the white man's tobacco that he had traded for at Bridger last season. Passing the pipe around, the three of them took several puffs each before the bowl burned out.

"We will speak no more of this." Plenty Coups tapped the ashes from the pipe. "It would do no good to try to talk some people out of drowning."

Red Hawk pouted playfully. "The only sad thing is if I am killed, the pretty maidens might mourn themselves to death."

"Tell me, my son, have you spoken with the medicine woman since she came here?"

"No, my chief." Jed shook his head. "She lives in the white village, Baxter Springs."

"Crow Killer has a new wife now, and I have heard she is very beautiful." Red Hawk knew Plenty Coups thought Jed would take Ellie for his woman.

Jed did not know how the Crow had heard of his marrying Bright Moon or how pretty she was.

"Hopefully both of you will return safely and with honor." Plenty Coups dismissed the two men he thought most of in this world. "We would not want one homely maiden to mourn for you, Red Hawk."

"Bah, I would not want that either."

Smiling and shaking his head with pride, Plenty Coups watched as Jed and Red Hawk passed straight shouldered and proud, through the doorway of the lodge. He could not help but worry, as the trail they were planning to go forth on was a dangerous one. He had made war against the Shoshone many years ago. They were a mighty enemy to fight.

Outside the lodge, in the dimming evening sun, Red Hawk and Jed led the piebald down to water, then turned him loose on the lush grass of the valley floor. Jed was amazed as he looked over the hundreds of beautiful horses grazing about the village and out on the valley floor. The Crow were the greatest horse raisers and owned the fastest buffalo runners of any tribe.

"How many horses do you own, Crow Killer?"

"Eight and one mule."

The Crow laughed. "You still have the little black mule?"

"Yes, she is as we speak at the Arapaho village with my woman Bright Moon."

"I own maybe a hundred head of fine racers." Red Hawk boasted. "I wish there were more. Never have I owned a mule. I have ate some mule meat, but never owned one."

"What do you need that many horses for, my brother?" Jed shook his head as he looked over the great horse herd. "How do you tell which horse is yours and which isn't?"

"You never know when you may have to buy a wife." Red Hawk laughed. "And all of my horses have the red mark on them."

"Red mark?"

"There." The warrior pointed to red paint on a horse's forehead.

"I see." Now, Jed understood and remembered how White Swan knew of his killing the young Crow many years ago. Walking Horse had painted a red lance in blood on the horse.

"Come, we will go to my lodge and eat, then you will rest until it is time to leave." Red Hawk with Jed following walked back to the village.

"I was serious, my friend." Jed stopped outside the lodge. "This is a dangerous trail, if you rather not go…"

"Why does Crow Killer go?"

Jed sat down beside the lodge. "When I first came here, Slow Wolf saved my life, then made me a Lance Bearer and gave me great honors. I owe him much more than my life. I would walk through fire for my chief."

"As I would for my father, Plenty Coups."

"Tell me, besides the adventure, why do you go?"

"I owe you my life." Red Hawk smiled at a pretty maiden as she passed by the lodge. "Besides, somebody has got to get you out of this mess you have gotten yourself into."

Long before the rising of the new sun, Red Hawk had one of the young horse guards catch the piebald and his spotted stallion. Several young Crow warriors watching the crossing waved as they passed by their campfire. Red Hawk was making good time as he kept the horses in a steady trot through the night since departing the village. Mile after mile passed beneath their horse's feet as they continued at a steady pace toward the north. The two warriors from different tribes were many miles away from the Crow village as the sun rose over the land.

"This trail will bring us to your valley."

"Traveling at this pace, we'll reach there in two more suns." Jed acknowledged. "We will stop at the cabin for more supplies."

"The horses will need rest soon."

"They can rest during the dark time." Jed agreed. "We will make camp at the great river."

Riding up to the cabin, they found it undisturbed. Jed had been worried the Rees might follow the raiders back to his valley and burn the cabin and barn. He wondered, if the Rees had mistaken the Paiute raiders for the ones that had destroyed their village. Shaking his head, he knew this was practically impossible, as surely they had been recognized as Cheyenne and Arapaho warriors. Still, in all the confusion and with no living Ree warriors left alive, the terrified women might have made

68

ALFRED DENNIS

that mistake. Unbarring the door, Jed laid his rifle and other weapons inside the door, then walked back outside to where Red Hawk was holding the horses.

Smelling the newly arrived animals, the loose Pawnee horses crossed the creek to greet the newcomers. Jed was glad to see them. He was relieved the horses hadn't strayed away with the wild ones.

"Your horses are puny, but the Pawnee never have been good judges of horseflesh." Red Hawk laughed as he looked the horses over, gauging whether they were worth stealing or not.

"Not worth stealing are they?" Jed knew Red Hawk was just kidding him about the horses.

The handsome head shook, then looked again at the horses. "I have never raided the Pawnee for their horses."

Jed could only shake his head as he fastened two of the horses in the corral and released the piebald and spotted stallion out on the valley floor. Turning, he walked back inside and started a fire for their supper. Red Hawk stayed outside skinning three rabbits he had managed to bring down with his bow as they rode into the valley. An hour later as the sun cast its shadows, both men sat at the log table outside, eating rabbit and hot biscuits.

"Your new wife, tell me, is she a good cook?" Red Hawk bit into the hot back strap of one rabbit. "I know she must be beautiful."

Looking over at the Crow, Jed smiled. "How do you know she is beautiful? You have never seen her."

"The sister of the sharp-tongued one would have to be beautiful." The warrior laughed. "I hope she is not as sharp tongued as Little Antelope."

It was Jed's turn to smile. "They are sisters."

"And Cheyenne."

"That they are." Jed nodded, thinking wistfully of Bright Moon. "Yes, my wife is very beautiful and yes, she is a good cook."

Red Hawk smiled, as he hadn't met Crow Killer's new wife, but he could tell Jed was happy with her. He never understood how a man could be happy with just one wife, even if she was pretty, when he could have many. It had to be the bad influence of Jed's white blood that held him to only one wife. Red Hawk was glad he was Crow, one of the most adulterous of all the tribes. The Crow were all handsome people as Red Hawk was. However, they were also habitual horse thieves, women stealers, and willing to take anything that caught their eye.

"We will leave at first light." Jed laughed as Red Hawk shook his head, trying to figure him out. "You best get some sleep."

The crossing of the Snake went easy. No tracks, other than the fur bearers, showed on the trails from the cabin. With the river behind them, it was only a half day ride to Baxter Springs. Looking up at the sun, Jed reined in beside the immigrant road leading to the small settlement. He knew Carter's farmhouse was only a few miles down the sandy trail and then Baxter Springs would be next.

Sliding from the piebald, Jed looked up at Red Hawk. "We will wait here until full dark."

The warrior nodded, he knew the white village was close ahead. "You do not want anyone to see us pass through your village?"

Jed nodded his head. "The ones ahead all know me and I do not wish anyone to know we are here."

Red Hawk looked down the road. "Do we fight the Shoshone or these whites?"

"I want to keep our presence here unknown, at least until we have done what we came to do." Jed looked down the dusty road. "In this country, I do not know who to trust and who not to. Yes, if possible, I would like to pass without being seen."

"It will not be so easy to keep the Shoshone from knowing when we ride onto their lands." Red Hawk quipped. "If they are like most tribes, they have eyes everywhere."

"We will ride to my white father's house first." Jed thought of Ed Wilson and his dead sons. "He may know more about the Shoshone than we do."

"Did he not kill a white man to keep him from riding to the Shoshone?" Red Hawk looked over at Jed. "Medicine Thunder told me of the killing."

Jed thought of Willie Beck and nodded. "He did kill, to help me."

"The whites take the killing of another white very serious, do they not?"

"Not if the dead one is guilty of a crime against his neighbors."

Red Hawk was curious. "And this one was guilty?"

"Guilty as sin."

"Does not Rolling Thunder's daughter Medicine Thunder live here in this village?" Red Hawk remembered the beautiful young medicine woman who had saved Plenty Coups life. "That is what Walking Horse spoke of."

"She does." Jed nodded. "Why?"

"You do not want to see her?"

"No, I do not want to see anyone."

"She is very beautiful." Red Hawk smiled wistfully. "With one such as her you would only want one wife."

"You plan on stealing her, my brother?" Jed laughed.

"How many horses would Rolling Thunder ask for her?"

"My friend, she is not Indian." Jed shook his head. "You can't buy a white woman like that."

"Perhaps, I can buy the Indian half of her." Red Hawk shrugged innocently. "How many would he take for her Indian half?"

"Enough of this talk, let's ride."

Bright Moon had been awake and watched as Walking Horse and Jed rode away during the night. Now, her and her sister Little Antelope sat before the lodge preparing deer hides for hunting shirts. Tanning hides was hard work. Despite their slender appearance, both women were strong.

"Does Crow Killer make you happy?" Little Antelope looked over at her sister. "Do you miss your village?"

The Cheyenne were a close-knit family and they lived all their lives together in close proximity. The family clans had strong bonds that were very hard to break.

"Yes, I miss my people, but my husband comes first." Bright Moon did not look up. "He is my life now."

"As Walking Horse is mine."

"Yet, you have had no children."

Little Antelope's face blushed a little. "No, we have not been blessed by the spirit people."

"Does this not disappoint Walking Horse?" Bright Moon looked over at her sister. She knew all men wanted sons.

"We have not spoken of it." Little Antelope pulled hard on the scraping tool. "Only time will tell."

"I am not judging, nor being nosy." Bright Moon averted her eyes. "I just worry if I will give Crow Killer a son."

Little Antelope laughed. "It is too soon, maybe you rush things. You have not been married very long."

"Our mother had four children, but both of her sisters had none." She looked again at Little Antelope. "Were they cursed or something?"

"Do not worry, little sister. You will give Crow Killer many sons."

"Let's finish this hide, then go for a swim." Bright Moon smiled. "As we did when we were children in our village."

"I have not been swimming in a long while, except to bathe." Little Antelope nodded. "I will tell Walking Horse where we go."

Walking Horse walked outside just in time to hear the last of the conversation. Looking over at the two women, he shook his head. Jed had left Bright Moon in his care. She was his responsibility as was Little Antelope. He wanted them to remain near the village for their safety and his piece of mind.

"You may go, but stay in view of the village." The warrior looked down at the women. "The skins will make soft hunting shirts."

"We wanted to go to the deep pools near the big rocks."

"No, it is too far from the village." His voice was harsh. "I forbid it."

"You could go with us, my husband." Little Antelope smiled. Walking Horse hardly ever spoke in such a hard tone. She knew he was worried about something. "You would protect us."

"I have to speak with Slow Wolf, perhaps then we will see."

"Would Walking Horse tell me where my husband went so suddenly during the night?"

Shaking his head, the warrior looked at the woman. "I cannot do this."

"Why?"

"Because Crow Killer asked me not to speak of it."

"Is he in danger?"

"Perhaps, we will all go to the falls when I return. Have the horse herders catch us three horses." Walking Horse had ignored the question and walked away toward Slow Wolf's lodge without looking back.

"My husband worries about something."

Bright Moon frowned. "Walking Horse and my husband keep something from me, as if I was a child."

Little Antelope knew Jed rode into danger, but would not speak of it and worry Bright Moon. "You are almost a child, little sister."

"No, I am a married woman."

Minutes later entering the lodge, Walking Horse sat down across from the old chief. "My father, we may have trouble."

"Tell me, what it is?"

"The night herders spotted a strange rider watching the village last night." Walking Horse looked across at Slow Wolf. "His horse was black and his face and body was painted black. They said he left this hanging on a limb and seemed to float away when they approached."

Slow Wolf took the piece of leather with the bear tooth hanging from it. "What does it mean, my son?"

"I do not know this." The warrior shook his head. "I have sent Big Owl with warriors to track whoever it was."

"He did no harm to anyone or steal horses?"

"No, I do not think he was here to steal. He just showed himself to be sure the night herders found this amulet."

"Have Big Owl keep warriors out riding at night until we find out what this one wants." Slow Wolf explained. "One does not ride in the dark time, painted in black, for no reason."

"I agree. He came here for something, but for what?" Walking Horse shrugged.

"The night herders knew nothing more?"

"They were frightened, my chief." Walking Horse replied. "They say he was like a ghost rider who disappeared when they rode close to him."

"They just spoke of what they saw." The old one nodded. "Remember, they are young, untried boys."

"Maybe they are young, but they are still Arapaho."

Big Owl was waiting as Walking Horse exited the lodge. "We found nothing, no tracks, nothing. It was as if he just disappeared into the night, like the young men said. He was a ghost maybe."

"There is no such thing as ghosts, Big Owl." Walking Horse frowned as they walked back to his lodge. "Keep guards riding day and night until we find this ghost, or figure out what he has come here for."

"Finding a ghost may be hard, Walking Horse." Big Owl stopped and waited while Walking Horse spoke to the women.

"There is no such thing, my fat friend."

Seeing the horses and the women waiting beside the lodge, Walking Horse took one of the horses from Little Antelope and turned the others loose. "There will be no swimming today. Neither of you are to leave sight of this lodge." Mounting, he rode away with Big Owl.

"Something is very wrong, my sister."

"You are right, Little Antelope." Bright Moon watched the disappearing backs of the two warriors. "I have never seen Walking Horse this way before. He worries about something."

"I have seen him this way before and it always involves trouble of some kind." Little Antelope went back to scraping the hide.

CHAPTER 5

Swinging up onto the piebald, Jed started west on the immigrant trail as the dark of night fell across the road. He wanted to be well past the Carter farm before the moon showed its face throughout the land. He also wanted to pass through Baxter Springs without being seen by the townspeople. From past experiences, Jed did not trust the people of the settlement. He only wanted to check on his stepfather, then ride on to Shoshone lands. Hopefully, he could locate the canyon Slow Wolf spoke of quickly, then find the cave containing Iron Breast's bones without the Shoshone discovering them in their land.

The light showing in the Carter house was just a small speck in the dark when several loud barking hounds started coming toward them.

"I think we have been discovered." Red Hawk's voice spoke through the dark.

Jed didn't know the dogs. There weren't any dogs at the Carter farm when he passed there with Bright Moon only months before. The horses were used to the continuous barking of the village dogs so these dogs did not spook them. Still, it was annoying as the dogs followed at their heels, causing a steady racket as they rode past the Carter farm.

"Who's out there?" Jed recognized Carter's voice. "Call out or I'll fire."

Riding away from the road, Jed bypassed the yelling voice in the dark. Several blows from Red Hawk's bow sent the barking hounds running home. They could still hear Carter yelling out in his booming voice a mile away from the farm.

"Whites are not very quiet." Red Hawk looked over at Jed's dark silhouette. "They are louder than a buffalo stampede."

"It is just their way. They are alone out here." Jed kicked the piebald into a lope. "Some fear the night time or what's out in it."

Jed kept to the shadows as they passed through Baxter Springs, avoiding the few coal oil lamps that lit the stores and lone saloon. Boisterous talking and the banging of piano music sounded from the saloon doors as they passed along the street without notice. Jed watched the shadowy face of Red Hawk as he tried to look inside the building to see what was making all the noise. Smiling, he knew the Crow had never seen or heard anything like this before. Passing the doctor's office, Jed could see Ellie's silhouette inside the lamp lit home. He remembered the good times they shared, but they were never meant to be together. Their worlds were so far apart and so different. Now, he had Bright Moon, and he was happy and content.

Red Hawk noticed Jed's gaze. "Was that Medicine Thunder inside that lodge?"

"Yes, it was her silhouette behind a curtain." Jed knew Red Hawk had no idea of what he was talking about, silhouettes and curtains.

"We should have stopped. Perhaps, I could have bought her." The warrior joked with Jed.

"I'm afraid, my friend, you are lucky you did not stop."

"And why is that?" Red Hawk didn't understand.

"I don't think you would want Medicine Thunder for a wife." Jed smiled. "She would not let you have any other women or steal horses anymore."

"She would be so cruel?"

"Yes, my friend, she would."

Crossing the Pennybrook, Jed heard the sound of Ed Wilson's old bluetick hound sounding the alarm, then wagging his tail as they rode into the yard. Slipping from his horse as the door opened and his stepfather appeared in the doorway, Jed hollered a hello. Not wanting

Wilson to become alarmed at the late night visitors, he spoke again. "It's me, Pa. Don't shoot."

"Jed?"

"We're coming in." Jed motioned at Red Hawk. "Call off your hound and don't shoot Red Hawk."

Wilson stepped through the doorway holding a lantern. "Who did you say was with you?"

"Red Hawk."

Wilson hollered at the dog and motioned them in. "You two, bring yourselves on in here."

"Let us put the horses in the corral, then we'll be in."

"Very well, I'll start you some supper." Wilson nodded. "You know where I keep the feed."

Red Hawk had never seen inside a white man's house before. Sitting at the table drinking coffee, Wilson had poured, the warrior looked curiously at the metal stove that put off so much heat. No fire showed, but somehow, the fire was kept penned up inside the iron thing. Adding to his curiosity, there was a huge mirror sitting atop a dresser that made him step back as it reflected his image.

"I think it holds evil spirits. It sees me. It looks at me." The warrior was spooked.

Jed laughed. "No evil spirits, my brother. The mirror is the same as looking into a clear stream, it just reflects your image clearer.

"No, it is like you are alive in two places." Red Hawk was truly startled by his image looking back at him. "It is not the same as looking in water."

Jed watched the warrior as his step-dad placed ham, eggs, and fried potatoes with biscuits before him on the table. He knew the tribes sometimes found nests of eggs from the turkey or prairie chicken, but Red Hawk probably had never eaten a fried egg before.

"It is the same as a turkey egg." Jed picked up his fork and cut into the egg.

Also, Red Hawk had never seen the iron fork or spoon of the white man before. For some tribes, eating with anything metal was taboo, bad medicine. He had never seen the Arapaho people eat with anything but carved-out wooden eating utensils. He remembered Bright Moon at first refused to feed him from the metal spoons he had at the cabin. To the Cheyenne, metal spoons or forks were bad medicine.

"Pa has some wooden spoons if you want one."

Smiling, Red Hawk picked up the fork. "If I am to ride against the Shoshone, one small metal thing should not scare me."

Wilson's head jerked as he heard Red Hawk's words. "What did he say? I heard him say Shoshone. Are you riding into Shoshone Country?"

"That's why we're here, hoping you might be able to tell us something about the Shoshone lands to the north."

"I will tell you this, they're a warlike people." Wilson bit into his supper and shook his head. "They stay up north. They are plain mean. We leave them alone and you should do the same."

"Is that why you killed Willie Beck?" Jed already knew the answer as he looked across the table at Wilson. "Ellie said he was about to give them rifles so they could kill me."

"Ellie told you the truth. He was gonna do just that."

"So you killed him?"

"He wouldn't listen when I told him to go back to town." Wilson shook his head. "He was a fool. He forced me to kill him."

"And the Shoshone? Tell us about them."

"All I know is what Lige Hatcher told me about them." Wilson shrugged. "And believe me, that wasn't good."

"Did Lige ever speak of a place called Serpent Canyon?"

"No, not that I recall."

Finishing their meal, the three men sat out on the porch listening to the calling of the night creatures. Jed knew the way Red Hawk looked at the pipe in Wilson's mouth, that the warrior did not understand why he wasn't asked to smoke the pipe as in the villages.

Smiling, Jed tried to explain to Red Hawk. "In the white world, my brother, the pipe is his own personal property and no one else may smoke it."

Nodding, the warrior smiled. "This is bad manners. Everyone should share the ceremonial pipe."

Wilson lit his pipe as the old bluetick hound opened up with a long, loud bawl down on the Pennybrook. The villages of the Crow had many camp dogs running loose, but Red Hawk had never heard one running with such a loud mouth.

"He will catch what he chases?"

"He won't catch the coon, but he will put it up a tree."

Red Hawk shrugged. "Then what will he do? A dog cannot climb as a cat can."

"Well, if Pa doesn't go down and shoot him out for supper, the dog will come home when he gets tired sitting under the tree."

"When will you be leaving?" Wilson wanted to hear more about their quest into Shoshone Country.

"When the new sun rises." Jed looked over at Wilson. "How many days is it to the beginning of Shoshone lands?"

"Maybe two days." Wilson thought back to his meeting with Willie Beck. "Jed, I wish you and Red Hawk would forget this foolishness."

Jed nodded. "I wish I could, but what you ask is impossible. I have given my word."

"Word to who? I have already lost two sons. I can't lose you, Jed." Wilson argued.

"Don't worry, Pa. With Red Hawk helping me, we will be fine."

"I wish I could believe that." Wilson shook his head. "You are only two against many. I have heard terrible things about the Shoshone."

"Red Hawk is a great warrior, the greatest in the Crow Nation." Jed tried to assure the older man. "He will protect me."

"Well, I see your minds are made up." Wilson tapped out his pipe. "Goodnight then. I'll see you two in the morning.

"Goodnight, Pa. I'll ride back by on our way from Shoshone lands."

"I'll have some breakfast ready." Wilson nodded at Red Hawk. "After we eat, I will ride with you and show you the back trail to Shoshone lands."

Jed took the trail Wilson showed him, a shortcut leading to Shoshone Country. It was the same trail Wilson had killed Willie Beck on last summer. Soon, they would be entering lands the Shoshone claimed as their hunting grounds, and from then on, they had to ride with caution. They would have to travel slowly, avoiding detection as the wily coyote or bobcat would do. Being discovered in the lands of the

Shoshone would end their quest for the remains of Iron Breast before they could reach the cave they sought. Jed knew the Shoshone believed any foreign tribe found encroaching into their lands was an enemy. In the land of the Shoshone, they would not be welcome, and worse still, they would be killed on sight.

"I think from here on, maybe we should travel at night." Red Hawk spoke up.

"In the dark, we would never find the canyon." Jed shook his head. "We must look for the serpent's head that Slow Wolf spoke of, in the daylight."

"You are right. Then we must ride like ghosts, very quiet and unseen."

As they passed deeper into Shoshone land, Jed only had the long ago landmarks, from the old chief's dimming memory, to go on. Already, several small hunting parties of warriors had been sighted, but so far they hadn't been discovered. Finally, on the third day after leaving Wilson's farm, riding in the lead, Red Hawk spotted what they searched for.

"There." The brown finger pointed across a small valley where the stone image of a snake's head stood high in the air.

Jed knew this must be the entrance to what Slow Wolf had called Serpent's Head Canyon. "It is the rock Slow Wolf spoke of."

"We must be careful, my friend." Red Hawk sat the spotted stallion, next to the piebald, looking out across the flat land. "There is no place to hide as we cross. It is all open meadow to the canyon."

"We will wait until dark to cross." Jed slid from his horse.

Waiting out the daylight hours, the two warriors took turns watching over the horses as the other slept. Jed studied the meadow thoroughly before the sun set, memorizing in his mind the serpent's head location.

After the setting of the sun, the horses plodded slowly across the grass covered meadow in the shadowy darkness of the moonlight. Only the slight sound of their muffled feet plodding through the deep grass could be heard. Jed wanted to locate the cave and retrieve the bones of Iron Breast, then make a hasty retreat from Shoshone lands before the rising of the new sun. He knew every minute they lingered in this place, they were in danger of being discovered.

"Slow Wolf said the cave was right under the serpent's head." Jed slid to the ground and led the piebald forward, feeling for the rock wall.

"I do not like disturbing the bones of our ancestors." Red Hawk hung back as the opening to the cave was located. "The spirit people look over our dead ones and protect them."

"The medicine of White Swan has brought us here." Jed looked into the black entrance. "The spirit people are with us in this. Iron Breast wishes to go home."

"We will need a light." Red Hawk did not want to enter the cave in total darkness. "Evil ones could be inside the dark place."

"In the dark of night, a light would be dangerous." Jed shook his head at the idea. "A light could be seen by any who are camped out here."

"In the dark, the cave will be dangerous." Red Hawk repeated. "Who knows what awaits us in the dark."

Jed smiled, as he knew old superstitions were hard to break, even for the great Red Hawk. Most tribes believed anything to do with the dead required a medicine man must be present to perform the death rituals and ceremonies. Common warriors were not welcome or in touch with the spirit people. All burial plots were sacred, never entered or disturbed in any way except to bury a deceased one. Much ceremonial chanting and smoke offerings had to be performed by a holy man before entering such a place. Red Hawk worried that by not following these protocols would turn the spirits against them.

"We can wait until it is light, or we can light a torch."

"This is your trail, my brother." Red Hawk answered. "I will do as you think wise."

Jed moved closer to the dark entrance. He knew Red Hawk could be right, any kind of danger could await them in the cave. He remembered the snake back on the river. Moving back to where the warrior waited, he decided to wait until light.

"You take the horses back to the trees and hide them, I will wait here. When the new light comes, I will find the remains of Iron Breast and bring them out."

"I will watch for your signal." Red Hawk sounded relieved that he would not have to enter the cave. "Our horses are the strongest runners in the nations. If we are discovered, the Shoshone will not be able to run us down."

"Maybe so, providing we can escape this canyon before being hemmed in." Jed remembered Slow Wolf saying it was a box canyon. That was how the Shoshone had trapped them long ago and forced them to fight their way out.

"We made it this far unseen." Red Hawk shrugged. "You get your chief, and I will be ready with the horses."

Jed sat by the mouth of the cave waiting on the early sun to light up the valley. He didn't know what was worse, the annoying mosquitoes steadily buzzing about his head or waiting in the dark. So far, their luck had been phenomenal. Coming this far into enemy territory without being discovered by a roving party of warriors was almost itself a miracle. Maybe, they were kept safe by the intervention of White Swan's medicine. Jed knew the old medicine man was with his ancestors, but his medicine still protected them.

As the dimness of the early morning brought a degree of light into the cave, Jed looked into the interior as far as the light would allow. He wondered if he was beginning to think like Red Hawk, fearing the unknown spirits. Perhaps, he had lived with the Arapaho too long. This was different from retrieving the bones of Billy Wilson, scattered by the grizzly. Today, he must go in the cave and dig up the dead remains of Iron Breast, a human being.

He forced himself to move forward as he could not go back without the remains he had promised Slow Wolf. Entering the cave, Jed pulled his skinning knife and started probing the soft floor for the remains. The old chief had said the grave was shallow and near the center of the cave. Finally, the knife struck something solid just beneath the soil. Digging quickly, Jed excavated the first bone, he had found the grave of Iron Breast. Faintly, he heard the warning call of a blue jay coming from the timber below the cave. Peering out of the entrance cautiously, Jed spotted two warriors sitting their horses only yards from the cave's entrance.

Something alerted the Shoshone, and somehow they knew he was there. Jed suddenly realized what they were looking at. In the dark of night, they had completely overlooked the horse prints they left outside the cave. Their luck had finally run out, but he already knew before starting this trail, their chances of remaining unseen were slim to none. Retrieving his skinning knife, Jed waited concealed beside the entrance of the cave as the two Shoshone warriors gestured at each other. Finally, one of them slid from his horse and started slowly forward. As the lone warrior approached the cave, Jed watched as the second warrior slipped sideways from his horse. Jed could see the feathered shaft of Red Hawk's arrow protruding from the man's back. Springing from the cave, Jed drove his knife into the vitals of the oncoming warrior, killing him instantly. Quickly filling the leather bag with all the remaining bones he could dig up, Jed raced to where Red Hawk was dragging the dead bodies to the cave.

"Perhaps, the spirit people will not be mad. We have left two bodies for the one we have taken."

"Hurry, let us leave this place." Jed quickly followed Red Hawk back to the horses. "Where are the Shoshone horses?"

"I could not catch them. They ran when my arrow found the warrior." Red Hawk shrugged. "I think it could be bad luck for us if they return to their village."

"It doesn't matter, we're leaving this place quick." Jed replied.

"The horses ran back the way they came, and one was covered with blood."

"Then we must hurry." Jed nodded. "The Shoshone village could be near this place."

Jed had to balance the contents of the bag in front of him. His quiver, bow, and lance lay strung across his back. Carrying his rifle, he had to control the piebald mostly with his knees. They had to ride fast as they retraced their steps away from the canyon. Now, there was no time for caution. They knew the enemy would be on their trail as soon as the dead warrior's horses returned to the village.

Stopping their horses in a tall stand of oak and spruce trees, Jed studied the terrain as he looked around. "We might turn back to the north. They might not look for us there."

Red Hawk shook his head. "No, if they are following, they will have to track us. By then, with luck, we will be far out of their reach."

"You're thinking our horses can outrun theirs if they spot us?"

"My great spotted one can outrun their horses, but I do not know about the one you are riding." Even in this time of great danger, Red Hawk still had to joke.

"Okay, we'll head straight home." Jed shook his head. "I'll take the lead, you watch behind us. Holler if you spot anything following us."

Jed knew it had taken them three days to reach the cave, but coming north they had been riding slow, making sure they didn't run into the enemy. Going back, they would be riding hard, throwing caution to the wind. Ignoring what lay ahead, the ride may take two days to clear Shoshone hunting grounds. He also knew when the enemy warriors found the cave and the two dead bodies, the Shoshone would be madder than a stirred up hornet's nest. The killing could not be helped, and if they ran into more trouble, they would take care of that problem if and when it came.

All day they rode, riding fast across the open land from one belt of timber to the next. Entering the heavier trees and brush, they would slow their horses to a walk until they reached another open space. After checking for any signs of the enemy, they would race to the next tree line. Some of the meadows were wider and much longer than others. In the open, they could be seen, but they had little choice as they had to cross and take the chance of being discovered. Jed knew the horses were tiring at the pace he was setting. The next bunch of trees they entered had a small stream flowing along the base of a plateau. Riding into the water, he let the horses drink, and then rode them straight down the waterway for as far as they could go. Several times, they had to step over downed trees, chest high on the horses, just to move forward. Gradually, the waterway was becoming a tangled mess of brush the deeper they rode into it. Finally, Jed had to give up and work his way through the thick underbrush moving back toward the open meadow.

"Wait, Crow Killer, riders approach. I heard something." Red Hawk whispered.

"Should we make a run for it or hide here?"

Slipping from the spotted horse, Red Hawk trotted to where he could see the oncoming Shoshone, then returned to where the horses stood. "I was right, they come. Some follow behind us in the water and some are coming through the trees."

"How many?"

"Maybe thirty warriors, maybe more." Red Hawk hastily swung up on the appaloosa. "They have warriors out in front tracking us."

"Let's go." Jed nodded. "We can't let them get ahead of us."

Bursting out of the trees, Jed only nudged the piebald into a short lope, wanting to conserve his strength. Holding onto the cumbersome bag, rifle, and sleeping robe, plus trying to rein his horse was just too much. Relenting, he let the robe slip from his hand.

Red Hawk kicked the spotted horse up next to the piebald and reached out his hand. "Let me carry the bag for a while."

Thankfully, Jed nodded and handed the bag over to the Crow. "Thank you, my friend, it was getting quite heavy."

"We must let the horses water at the next crossing we come to." Red Hawk advised. "They will need it when the real chase starts."

"You're the expert on horse stealing, my friend." Jed nodded.

"But, this is not horse stealing." Red Hawk laughed. "Before this trail is over, it is going to be a horse race. Whoever rides the strongest horses, will win out."

Jed turned to look at their back trail. So far, nothing showed as they raced into another stand of trees. Pulling to a halt at the small stream, the warriors slid from their horses. Jed took the heavy rawhide bag from Red Hawk as he dismounted.

"It is almost sundown. We'll ride until full dark, then under the cover of darkness, we'll rest and graze the horses a few hours." Jed pulled the piebald back from the water. "Then, my friend, with the coming day, I believe we will be riding for our lives."

"Have no fear, Crow Killer." Red Hawk grinned in his good-natured way. "I have seen their horses. They are mountain horses and cannot match these two racers."

"While the horses rest and while our enemy sleeps…" Jed hesitated a moment not liking what he was fixing to say. "Remember when the redheaded Billy Wilson took Little Antelope and your horse?"

"Yes, I remember." Red Hawk nodded. "Seems like many suns ago."

"We could do as you were going to do that night, to the Nez Perce."

"Yes, we could even the odds. Maybe even make them give up their pursuit." Red Hawk agreed.

"It wouldn't be honorable." Jed didn't like what he was suggesting. Killing a warrior while he slept was despicable to him, but to survive here, far from their lands, they didn't have a choice.

"Would you rather have your honor, my friend, or your life?" Red Hawk shrugged. "Think about your woman who waits for you. Remember, these warriors chasing after us want to make a fight and take our hair."

"I know what you speak is true." Jed nodded. "I know what you say to even the odds would be a good thing."

"If we do not get caught sneaking into their camp, it would be a good joke on the Shoshone." Red Hawk laughed.

Jed had been raised white, supposedly a civilized human being. He did not yet completely think like an Indian. For the tribes, killing their enemies seemed natural, a way of life to gain fame, glory, and the adoring looks of the young maidens. He did not like what he was proposing, but he knew to survive against so many, he and Red Hawk would have to try to cut down their numbers a little. Jed knew most warriors were superstitious and believed their spirits would wander forever in the dark if they were killed at night.

Total darkness fell across the meadows and tree lines, making it very difficult to see as they rode slowly, feeling their way through the heavy timber. Their horses were tired, as they had been ridden many miles since leaving the Crow village several days ago. Trying to stay ahead of the ones pursuing them, Jed and Red Hawk had been riding at a fast pace all day. The horses needed a few hours of rest and some good grass to help revive their strength and energy. Neither man wanted to kill this way, but the hostile Shoshone were pressing them hard, and they were not giving them any alternatives. Both men knew a face-to-face battle with thirty of the warlike Shoshone would be suicide. Also, this was a new land to both Jed and Red Hawk, so neither man knew the landscape. They did not know how much longer they would have to run from the enemy before they would be out of Shoshone hunting grounds.

"It is a good plan, Crow Killer." Red Hawk hobbled the spotted horse and placed his weapons on the ground. "I will go back and see where our friends make camp for the night."

Jed nodded, knowing it would not do any good to argue with the Crow to get him to wait so they could go together. Hobbling the piebald, he moved all their weapons to where the horses grazed. He hadn't eaten since the night before at the cave while they waited on daylight. With the Shoshone picking up their trail and following on their heels, he hadn't felt hungry.

Now, his stomach growled, causing him to reach for the bag of jerky on his side. Unwrapping some of the jerked elk meat, he had taken from the cabin, Jed took a few swigs of water, then found a comfortable spot against an oak, chewing hungrily on the tough jerky. Hardly finishing one piece, he stiffened as the dark shape of Red Hawk trotted through the gloom to where he waited. Watching as the warrior caught his breath from the hard run, Jed waited for him to speak.

"We must catch the horses and leave this place quick."

Jed did not hesitate or question the warrior. Leaping to his feet, he took the hobbles from both horses and replaced their rawhide bridles. Placing his bow and quiver of arrows across his back, he handed the reins of the spotted one to Red Hawk.

The warrior nodded as he knelt and took a few sips of water, then swung up on the appaloosa. "They have four warriors with torches following our tracks." Red Hawk handed Jed the leather bundle. "It will be slow tracking, but I think they will come to this place very soon."

"It's not really fair disturbing a man's supper." Jed handed Red Hawk some jerky, and then nudged the piebald in a slow trot to the south.

"Yes, my friend, but it would have been more disturbing if they had caught us for their supper."

"I'll bet one thing, we would have been much easier to chew than this dried meat." Jed whispered as they cleared the timber and once again crossed the meadow lands in a trot.

"My stomach does not care how tough the meat is, it's hungry."

Riding at a slow ground-eating trot, Jed kept the horses moving with just a few stops for water throughout the night. Following the stars, Jed kept them straight on a course south toward Baxter Springs. Finally, with the break of day, Jed reined in and slid from the piebald.

"We will let them graze for one hour." Jed looked at Red Hawk. "If you think we have that much of a lead on them."

The warrior looked over their back trail for any signs of the Shoshone. "I believe we have stretched our lead now."

"How do you think the horses are holding up?"

The Crow only nodded as his eyes checked over the grazing animals. "They are a little tired, but they have great hearts and will run away from our enemy if asked."

An hour later, after checking their back trail again, Jed had them in a hard trot to the south. This time, Red Hawk carried the leather pouch, letting Jed rest his arms. Still, no sight of Shoshone warriors showed behind them.

At midday, Red Hawk reined in and pointed at a large rock promontory, less than a mile ahead. "I remember that high place as we rode through here."

"I do too, my friend. We are still at least a full day away from the small river that Pa said was the boundary line of the Shoshone hunting grounds."

"I hope Crow Killer does not think a little water will stop these warriors from following us." Red Hawk laughed. "We have killed two of their warriors and they wish our hair."

"I was hoping maybe they wouldn't find out about that."

"Look, Crow Killer." Red Hawk pointed at a lone figure waving a blanket from the tall ridge.

Jed's dark eyes followed the warrior's finger as he pointed up the mountain. "It appears, my friend, that we have been found."

"Let's ride." Urging the horses into a hard run, the powerful animals threw up dirt clods as they pounded south. Red Hawk could hear the distant war cries of warriors coming in from their right side.

Jed knew more riders were following from behind as well. He also knew safety still lay almost a full day ahead and the Shoshone were riding fresher horses. Reaching out, Jed took the leather pouch from Red Hawk.

Trying to skirt around the ridge, to get away from the warriors that might be there, Jed and Red Hawk let the horses run. They only slowed the horses down to a short lope when they became labored in their stride. Crossing the long valley, Red Hawk looked behind to see the small figures of the following warriors just breaking from the timberline at least two miles back. Slowing the horses to a walk, Red Hawk watched the pursuing warriors trying to gauge their speed.

"Red Hawk, look!" Jed reined the piebald to a sliding stop.

Five Shoshone warriors broke out of the timberline, almost on top of them. "The odds are getting much better now, Crow Killer." Red Hawk laughed. "Only five against us now."

Checking the priming of his rifle, Jed looked over at the Crow. "Check your rifle, my friend."

"What will we do?" Red Hawk watched as the five warriors came toward them at a hard lope. "Our enemy is in front and in back of us now."

"We will take their horses." Jed watched the oncoming warriors as he slipped from the piebald and set the bag on the ground. "They are a gift, my brother. Now, the ones behind will never catch up."

Red Hawk nodded as he slipped from the spotted one and aimed his rifle across his horse's withers. The five Shoshone came on without hesitation, right into the waiting barrels of the rifles. Jed took a sharp bead on the lead rider and squeezed the trigger. His shoulder felt the recoil of the large caliber rifle as the bullet knocked the screaming man backward from his horse. Another warrior fell as Red Hawk fired. Quickly, Jed reloaded and brought down a third warrior. The last two tried to rein away, but even the fastest horses had no chance of outrunning the far-shooting Hawken rifles. Both rifles roared again, dropping the two fleeing warriors from their horses. Jed walked out to check on the downed warriors as Red Hawk quickly rounded up the loose horses.

Jed knew this time, they had no choice. They had to kill these warriors or they would be delayed long enough for the other warriors coming up fast behind them to catch up.

Turning the bodies over, he found two of the warriors were still breathing. "They are all just youngsters."

Red Hawk shook his head as he scalped the dead warriors and broke their weapons. "No, they were foolish young men to ride against our rifles armed only with the bow."

The two wounded warriors had watched as the Crow scalped their friends. Both were still young warriors, not blooded in war, but they tried to conceal their fear from the hated enemy.

Jed stood over the wounded men. "I will permit you to live this day, Shoshone. Tell the ones that follow to go back or they will die as your friends did."

The young men could not help cringing as the bloody Crow holding the scalps of their friends approached where they lay on the ground. "Do not let him take our hair, tall one."

"Why, Shoshone? Your foolishness got your friends killed." Red Hawk held the scalps up for them to see. "Are you any different from them?"

"We were doing as our chief told us." One spit at Red Hawk, but if you want my hair, kill me first, Crow dog."

The warrior screamed his faint war yell as he flung his skinning knife at Red Hawk, then spit at him again. Red Hawk laughed as he smeared both men's faces with the bloody scalps, then looked to where Jed waited. "You are lucky today, Shoshone. I would scalp you alive if he was not here."

"He is brave, Red Hawk." Jed spoke up. "Let him live and tell of the great Crow Warrior Red Hawk."

"Yes, he is that." The warrior turned away from the wounded youngsters. "You live, Shoshone, because of him. I would have cut your throats."

Riding the Shoshone horses, Jed and Red Hawk led their own horses to let them rest. Red Hawk had picked out the two strongest animals. After hanging the bloody trophies in the other horse's manes, he turned them loose, and with a loud yell, he headed them back to the north. He knew when the horses with the bloody scalps of their young warriors were found, it would infuriate the Shoshone into madness, wanting revenge. Maybe in their rage, the Shoshone would run their horses into the ground trying to catch up.

Today, Red Hawk tasted victory and his fighting blood was up, wanting more of the enemy to challenge him. Jed didn't like the practice of taking scalps, but it was a ritual that most tribes followed. It was the means for many warriors to prove their valor in battle. Two of the young warriors were Red Hawk's kills so he could do as he wanted with them.

Jed knew Red Hawk well, and most of the time, he was laughing and carefree, but not now. His fighting blood still ran hot and he wanted more warriors to fight. He had never known a warrior like the Crow, fun loving at times, but at other times he could turn deadlier than any warrior. He also knew they had been lucky this day. The young warriors trying to slow their retreat had been killed very quickly, not giving the ones following time to catch up. With at least thirty warriors closing in on them, he knew trying to fight against such great odds was suicidal.

CHAPTER 6

Red Hawk led the appaloosa and piebald horses since Jed had his hands full with the rawhide pouch. Several times, they spotted the oncoming Shoshone far behind, as they crossed a long meadow. They covered several miles as the day wore on toward nightfall, holding the horses to a slow lope as they neared a small creek.

"They will not catch us now, my friend." Red Hawk guessed the warriors following were at least two or three miles back.

"It's still probably two days until we reach Baxter Springs."

"You do not return to your white father's lodge?"

"Can't, wouldn't want to bring these unwanted guests to meet him would we?"

Red Hawk laughed. "That would be a good joke on him alright."

"I don't think he would appreciate the joke."

Reining in at a small stream, Jed and Red Hawk watered the horses and let them blow for a few minutes.

"They are catching up." Red Hawk motioned with his jaw.

"Their ponies must be near give out by now." Jed turned the bay gelding he was riding. "Surely they cannot pursue us much longer."

"Hate makes a man do things he should not be able to do." Red Hawk watched as the riders came closer. "And I believe these warriors hate us."

"Their horses do not hate us."

"Let's stay here a few moments longer, Crow Killer." Red Hawk raised his rifle. "I would like to tickle them a little more."

"Let's go." Jed shook his head at his friend.

"You take away all the fun in life." Red Hawk complained. He was indeed a strange one. The warrior could be happy and friendly like a child one minute, and then the next minute, deadly as a rattlesnake.

Dark shrouded them as a heavy fog moved in blanketing the countryside as it closed in around them, hiding the stars. The night before had been crystal clear, but this night was different. Both men stood beside their horses in the murky gloom of the fog.

"We cannot travel in this mess." Jed could hardly see anything, barely even Red Hawk who stood beside him.

"Neither can the Shoshone." Red Hawk shrugged. "The horses will be able to rest while we wait for the new sun to show us the way."

The long night was eerie as the two men stood waiting, listening for any sound to betray an enemy coming closer. The fog thickened, becoming so heavy one could almost cut it with a knife. Jed missed his warm sleeping robe as the night air, heavy with fog, chilled him to the bone. Leaning against the piebald for warmth, he chewed absently on another piece of jerky.

Not a word was spoken by either warrior as the night passed. Both men knew in the quietness of the fog their voices would carry far. Suddenly, almost as quick as it had come in, the fog lifted, showing Jed and Red Hawk the stars. Both men mounted and pointed their horses to the south.

"I am glad the fog has lifted." Red Hawk swung his legs absently against the smooth hair of the Shoshone horse. "Now, I can see my enemy."

Shaking his head, Jed smiled. "I just hope we don't see them anymore."

"We will, my friend, if the spirit people are good to us."

"That could get you killed."

Red Hawk laughed quietly. "What a way to go, with beautiful maidens weeping under my scaffold."

"You'd be happy to die just so women would mourn you?"

Red Hawk laughed. "Of course, my friend, wouldn't you?"

Jed was baffled. "You really want to die?"

"Of course not, but it is an interesting thought to see beautiful women crying over me."

With the new sun peeking slowly over the horizon, Jed kicked the Shoshone horse into a slow ground-eating lope. He could only shake his head, listening to Red Hawk. If he lived to ride a hundred trails with the warrior, he would never understand him.

"They still follow us." Red Hawk looked behind them and grinned. "The spirit ones above smile on us this day."

"How are their horses still able to keep up?" Jed couldn't believe his eyes. "I thought you said they were a bunch of culls."

Red Hawk shrugged. "I guess nobody told their horses they should have quit many miles back."

Finally, passing through lands they recognized, Jed and Red Hawk figured out their exact location from the many landmarks they remembered. Just before sundown, Jed figured they would cross the small creek, the boundary Ed Wilson called the beginning of the Shoshone hunting grounds. Neither, Red Hawk nor Jed was foolish enough to think the creek would slow the Shoshone in the least. They had lost seven warriors to the men they were chasing, probably some were sons, and these warriors wanted blood. A mere stream would not stop them as long as their horses could continue the chase.

Stretched out in a hard lope, the horse Red Hawk rode almost dumped the warrior as it stumbled and went to its knees. Quickly sliding from the limping horse, Red Hawk leapt on the spotted stallion. Not a stride was missed as he kicked the appaloosa and followed Jed. Trying to save their horses, Jed had let the oncoming warriors close the gap. Now, less than a mile separated the two parties as the Shoshone forged forward in a last chance to overtake the fleeing men.

Finally, the chase was over. The Shoshone horses started to fall back, they were finished. Pulling their tired horses to a stop, the warriors screamed out their frustration. The pursuers knew they were beaten and would not catch their prey this day. Reining their horses to a walk as the Shoshones fell back and the long chase ended, Red Hawk raised his arm in triumph and yelled out a loud Crow war cry. Jed shook his head in dismay as the warrior stood up on the appaloosa and raised his loincloth, insulting the warriors even more.

Several of the Shoshone rode their horses forward, daring Jed and Red Hawk to stand and fight. Laughing, Red Hawk waved and followed Jed to the south. The long race had been hard on the following Shoshone horses. However, the spotted stallion and piebald, with the help of the horses taken from the dead Shoshone, were still strong and able to run.

Kicking the horses into a slow trot, Jed smiled over at Red Hawk. "We are close to the creek."

"That is good, my friend." Red Hawk shook his head as he pointed behind them. "Because, I believe our friends found fresh horses from somewhere."

Jed could not believe his eyes as he looked back, there were horses running loose everywhere. He figured fresh horses must have been brought to the Shoshone by horse herders from a nearby village herd. Jed shook his head as he stared in disbelief at the oncoming horsemen mounted on fresh horses, racing toward them. Switching to the piebald, he kicked the horse and raced toward the creek a mile ahead. Somehow, he hoped, but didn't believe, the invisible boundary would stop the Shoshone warriors.

"It will be dark in an hour." Jed yelled over at Red Hawk. "We are almost at the creek."

"And they still do not catch up with us." Red Hawk laughed.

"You are right, Red Hawk. Our horses are too strong."

Reining in hard at the small creek, Jed blinked in surprise. Sitting horseback across the water with rifles resting across their pommels was Lige Hatcher, Ed Wilson, and several farmers and people from Baxter Springs. Splashing across the shallow creek, Jed laughed, shaking hands with several of the men he knew.

"What are you doing here, Pa?"

"We heard you two might have gotten yourselves in a little trouble over there." Wilson laughed.

"Kinda." Jed smiled again. "It was nip and tuck back there for a while."

"Yeah, we watched from up there." Hatcher pointed at a high knoll. "I'd say it was a pretty darn good horse race." Translating his words in Crow to Red Hawk, Hatcher waited for the response he knew would be forthcoming from the warrior.

Grinning, Red Hawk shrugged and spoke to the old scout. "Tell us, Rolling Thunder, which is the best horse; my spotted one or Crow Killer's paint?"

Rolling his shoulders, Hatcher laughed. "I'd say it's a toss-up. They're both great animals. I wouldn't mind having either horse to ride myself."

Patting the appaloosa horse on the neck, Red Hawk became serious. "Tell me, Rolling Thunder, would this fine stallion be enough bride payment for your daughter Medicine Thunder?"

"What?" Hatcher was shocked at the question, watching Red Hawk as he grinned. "Let me think on it, Red Hawk."

"Peers to me, y'all have been in a close up fight." Bate Baker looked nervously at the blood-splattered Red Hawk, then across the creek at the oncoming Shoshone.

Jed knew Red Hawk's English was limited, so he probably understood a little of what Baker had said, but not all. He shook his head as he knew the warrior was only joking with Hatcher about his daughter, or was he, one never knew with Red Hawk.

"We had a small fight, it was nothing."

"Here they are boys, get ready." Hatcher turned his attention across the creek as the Shoshone pulled their heaving horses to a stop at least fifty yards back from the water.

"I believe they are a little mad." Red Hawk looked over at Jed, then taunted the Shoshone by raising his rifle.

"Tell me, my friend, were you serious about the bride price?"

"Certainly, I was serious." Red Hawk pretended to be deeply hurt that Jed doubted his sincerity and his proposition had not been taken seriously. "I would not hurt Rolling Thunder's feelings by offering less."

"Stop that dang fool before he gets us in a fight." Baker warned Jed.

"They're not crossing, Bate. Quit whining." Hatcher frowned over at the trader, then grinned over at Red Hawk. "You men see to your weapons, and be ready if they charge."

"I ain't whining, Lige." Baker frowned. "I just don't want to see a blood bath right here."

"Worried about your fur trade business, Bate?" Wilson shook his head. "I didn't know the Shoshone traded their furs with you."

Baker cursed. "They don't. They trade with the Frenchies in Canada."

"Smart Injuns, they probably get fair prices up there." Wilson quipped.

Again, Red Hawk raised his rifle and screamed across the water at the watching Shoshone. Two warriors from the Shoshone rode forward, pointing at Jed and Red Hawk, then drove their lances deep into the ground along the creek bank. He knew they were too smart to charge across the creek in mass, straight into the deadly rifles of the whites.

"Magnificent looking fellas ain't they?" Jake Carter spoke up.

Jed smiled over at the tall skinny farmer. With all the confusion and his attention across the creek on the Shoshone, he never noticed the farmer in the group of men. "Good to see you, Mister Carter."

"And you, Jedidiah."

"You got yourself some hounds since last time I was here."

"So, that was you that passed a few nights ago right after dark?" Carter nodded. "Yep, bought 'em from old Morgan Lehigh. Been running coyotes away from my place with them."

"It was us, alright." Jed nodded, remembering his conversation with Lem Roden about Lehigh's bear dogs. "I thought about buying me some of those dogs at one time."

Jed looked across the creek at the Shoshone, he already knew what was going through the warrior's mind. The buried lances, the pointing and raised fists, and the stoic looks as the two Shoshone sat their horses calmly across the creek, meant only one thing. Jed knew they had been challenged. He also knew Red Hawk would never turn his back and leave this place without answering the challenge. To leave would label him a coward, and this could never be. Jed knew once again, he was trapped and could not ride away, leaving Red Hawk to take up this fight alone.

Dismounting, Jed and Red Hawk both stripped to their breech-cloths and placed their weapons atop their leather hunting shirts.

Walking to where Hatcher sat his horse, Jed pointed to the rawhide pouch beside the pile. "If things go wrong over there, Lige, take this bag to Slow Wolf as quick as you can."

Red Hawk laughed, then swung on the spotted stallion and looked over at Hatcher. "You take my horse to ride if like Crow Killer says, if things go wrong."

"He's learning a fair amount of English."

Jed shook his head as he looked over at Red Hawk. "Too much sometimes."

Hatcher knew a challenge had been made and what was fixing to take place. He knew Jed and Red Hawk could not turn their backs on this fight, and to do so would label both of them cowards throughout the tribes. Jed probably did not care what he was called, but the hotheaded Red Hawk would die first. Never would he ride away from this place with the challenge unanswered. The Crow's pride was just too strong. To lose face here and have to face his people in shame was not happening.

"What's in it?" Hatcher looked down at the bag.

"Inside are the remains of one who died in Shoshone lands long ago." Jed sprung upon the piebald. "Slow Wolf asks that this one be brought home to be buried before he dies."

"The old chief is dying?" Hatcher was surprised. "I had no idea."

"He grows old and has very few days left here with us."

"I figured old Slow Wolf would live forever." Hatcher nodded sadly. "You have my word. When this is over, if you can't take the remains home, I will."

"For this I thank you, my friend."

"You could ride away from this, Jed." Hatcher looked hard at the Arapaho warrior sitting before him. "No one would think the less of you."

"I could, but the Crow Killer cannot." Jed looked over at Red Hawk. "And you know, he would never back down from a challenge."

"Good luck to you then."

As Jed and Red Hawk turned their horses and crossed the creek, Bate Baker pushed his horse up next to Hatcher. "We can't allow this, Lige. It could start a war with the Shoshone."

"Shut up, Bate." Hatcher glared at the trader. "This has nothing to do with us or the Shoshone. This fight is between four magnificent warriors."

"Lige is right, Baker." Wilson spoke as he watched Jed and Red Hawk cross the creek. "This is a fight between those four warriors, it has nothing to do with us."

The piebald and appaloosa had to be tired, but they seemed to know they were going into battle. Arching their necks, the horses pranced as they carried their proud warriors toward the awaiting Shoshone warriors. Hatcher smiled grimly, it was as if he was watching a magnificent play being acted out. Jed and Red Hawk sat their horses proudly, their back's straight, and their magnificent bodies showing scars from other battles. Hatcher could tell the hot-blooded Red Hawk was eager to fight and wanted this. Jed was different, he had been forced to kill many times, but against his will as he was now.

Less than thirty yards apart, the four warriors, two Shoshone and two warriors, one Crow and one Arapaho, sat their horses, nerves on edge with their muscles tensed and ready. All four carried war axes and buffalo hide shields. The two Shoshone were magnificent specimens, probably the cream of the Shoshone Nation. Jed studied the two fighters in front of them and knew this would be a hard fight.

Hatcher watched as the impending battle started. He could tell the Shoshone warriors were enraged, wanting to avenge their dead. Jed and Red Hawk sat their magnificent horses, neither speaking. Hatcher knew Red Hawk was eager for this fight, as he always was. He knew Jed would fight, but he also knew he wasn't eager for more killings as Red Hawk was.

"Do not take these warriors too lightly, my friend."

"Bah, they are Shoshone dogs." Red Hawk spat. "I will kill mine before you kill yours."

Shaking his head, Jed did not take his eyes from the warriors. "Be careful this day, Red Hawk. I do not wish to put you in the bag with the other remains."

In less than a blink of an eye, the two furious Shoshone fighters whipped their horses and charged directly at Jed and Red Hawk. Both were big men, eager to close in with the hated ones in front of them that had insulted them by entering their hunting grounds and killing. Only the banging of war clubs against hide shields could be heard as the four riders clashed hard into each other. Slashing and ducking, all four men were putting on a show. All were expert in horseback warfare. The big difference in the fight was the piebald and appaloosa horses as they were more powerful, heavier, and taller than the Shoshone's. The larger horses shouldered forward quickly, putting their riders on the offensive.

Hatcher, Wilson, and the others watched in awe at the brute power and incredible courage of all four fighters. Hatcher could tell that Jed, with the help of the heavier paint horse, was quickly getting the best of his opponent. Red Hawk fought against an older, wiser warrior, and despite the power of the spotted one, was having difficulty getting through his defenses. Again and again, the war axes clashed as the warriors fought fanatically. Red Hawk let out a shrill war cry as his axe penetrated the shield of his opponent.

Clashing against the Shoshone, with the reflexes and speed of a mountain cougar, Jed lunged from the piebald and dragged the other warrior from his horse. Only the gasp and hot flow of blood splattered on Jed's face and body as his war axe crushed the warrior's head. Quickly swinging on the well-trained piebald standing nearby, Jed started toward the two other combatants when Red Hawk called for him to stay back. Watching his friend and the other Shoshone warrior closely, Jed waited as Red Hawk had asked. For now, he would watch the fight, but he knew he would not hesitate if Red Hawk started losing. The Shoshone had made the challenge, and now, it was two against one.

Back and forth the battle raged as the other Shoshone warriors screamed for their champion to fight harder. They had already watched as Jed killed their other warrior so easily. Jed could tell both men were tiring as their reflexes slowed. Only the stamina of the spotted stallion and the great heart of Red Hawk kept the fight going. Clashing together again, the powerful spotted horse shouldered into the smaller horses knocking him sideways. Like a striking rattler, Red Hawk was atop the downed man, whose leg was pinned beneath his struggling horse.

Ripping the war axe from the helpless warrior, Red Hawk raised his own war axe for the killing blow. Then for some reason, he stepped back and let the man pull his trapped leg free and regain his feet. Tossing the axe at the warrior's feet, Red Hawk grinned and raised his own axe. Nodding with respect, the warrior picked up his axe and faced Red Hawk.

Jed could not believe his eyes. Why did Red Hawk let the man up? Circling each other, the two men clashed together with their great arm muscles bulging, struggling, pushing, and pulling at each other. Flipping backward, Red Hawk tossed the warrior over his head. Springing to his feet, he screamed again and rushed into the Shoshone. The swift crippling blow of the Crow's war axe almost ripped off the Shoshone's arm. The warrior slumped to his knees as his life's blood poured from him. Red Hawk held back and stared down at the dying man.

Jed watched with relief and then curiosity as Red Hawk mounted the appaloosa and rode back to where he sat. Riding to the creek, both men slid from their horses and washed their bodies clean of the blood and brains of the dead men.

"I figured you would scalp him." Jed watched as the Shoshone warriors placed their dead comrades across their horses and turned sullenly back to the north.

"No, he was a brave man." Red Hawk seemed subdued, not like a man who had just fought a great battle with a great enemy. Jed figured he would be bragging about his bravery and killing of the dead one. "For once, I am tired of killing."

Jed nodded. "You have changed, my friend."

"Perhaps, it is time for this one to grow up."

"What happened? You have killed before."

"As he died, I looked into his eyes, as he looked into mine..." Red Hawk swung up on the spotted one. "I did not like what I saw there."

"Come, we will rest here tonight, then ride to Baxter Springs with the new sun." Jed nodded. "I need supplies, then we will go home."

Jed spotted Ellie standing outside her grandfather's office as he rode with Hatcher, Red Hawk, and Wilson into Baxter Springs. A rider had raced ahead with the news of what had happened back at the creek. Like most of the citizens of the town, she waited on the street for the return of the men. Her face seemed relieved as she spotted him riding uninjured into town. She could not help her feelings of anxiety, and despite her words to the contrary, she still loved him very much. Still, she knew her choice had been right for both of them. They would never be happy together. Jed was a fighter, a killer, while she was a life giver. Today, the returning rider who had brought the news of the battle to town, told how magnificently brave he was as he killed the Shoshone. Ellie just could not understand the useless killings and blood that had to be shed between the tribes. She was sad they had gone their separate ways, but glad Jed had found happiness with Bright Moon.

"It is good to see you again, Ellie." Jed looked down at her.

She smiled as she moved over to the piebald. "Are you okay, Jed?"

"I am fine."

"And you, Red Hawk?" Ellie spoke to the warrior in his own language, noticing the warrior appeared subdued.

Red Hawk smiled. "I am fine and you are as beautiful as ever, Medicine Thunder."

"And your father Plenty Coups?"

"He too is fine. He wishes for you to come to see him when you return to the Arapaho people. He hopes you will tell him he can eat all he wants again." Red Hawk laughed.

Ellie laughed at the thought of the huge Plenty Coups. "Has your father lost any weight?"

Red Hawk shrugged. "He is still a large man."

"Then, if he wants to live, he needs to stay on a diet." Ellie used the English word "diet" as there was no such word in the Crow language.

Jed smiled. "She means, my friend, your father still cannot eat."

"Plenty Coups will not like that."

Hatcher dismounted and stood beside Ellie as he looked up at Jed. "Red Hawk offered me this fine spotted stallion for you, my dear."

Smiling, Ellie stroked the neck of the appaloosa. "And what was Rolling Thunder's answer?"

"Well, I think I might just trade with him." Hatcher winked at Jed. "This horse is one of a kind."

Ellie smiled faintly. "Should I get my things?"

Red Hawk turned the horse. "Come, Crow Killer, we must return to our villages."

Jed wanted to laugh, but didn't want to spoil the prank Hatcher and

Ellie were playing on Red Hawk. "Yes, we must return quickly to Slow Wolf."

"Well then, we will talk of this when I come to your village, Red Hawk." The old scout spoke in the Crow language, then returned to English as he spoke to Jed. "Now, I remember who you have there in the bag, it's Iron Breast."

"Yes, it is Iron Breast." Jed was curious. "How did you know?"

Hatcher cleared his throat and looked over at Ellie. "Because I helped Slow Wolf bury him."

"Our chief never told this."

"No, he wouldn't. The less said of a dead person, the better." Hatcher studied the bag. "This one was Ellie and Walking Horse's grandfather. He was considered the greatest Arapaho Chief, and that is why Walking Horse will be chief after Slow Wolf passes."

Jed looked at Wilson. "I will see you in the fall when Hatcher brings you to live in the mountains with me and Bright Moon."

"This time, I'm coming. I'm really looking forward to it." Wilson smiled as he took Jed's extended hand. "I've already sold my place."

"Good, we'll be waiting for you." Jed looked over at the mounted men. "Red Hawk and I thank all of you for coming to save us."

"But, I'm bringing my cow." Wilson laughed.

"Tell my sisters, I miss them and I will come soon." Ellie touched Jed's leg.

A chorus of voices sounded as Red Hawk and Jed turned their horses. Reining in at Wood's Mercantile Store, Jed left the horses with Red Hawk and entered the store.

"Is my credit good, Mister Woods, until I return in the spring?" Jed looked across the counter at the storekeeper.

"Yes, Jedidiah, your credit will always be good here." Woods placed the items, Jed asked for, on the long counter.

Quickly tying the supplies onto the extra horse they had taken from the fallen Shoshone, Jed mounted the piebald. With one final look across the street at Ellie, they kicked their horses into a lope and rode out of town.

"If Medicine Thunder is to be my woman." Red Hawk questioned Jed. "Why did she touch you before we left?"

"Because I am better looking than you are, maybe." Jed grinned.

"But, my friend, you already have a wife."

"And how many does Red Hawk have?"

"None. One such as I cannot tie himself to one woman."

"Uh huh." Jed could tell the warrior's subdued mood had suddenly changed. Red Hawk seemed to be his old self again.

"Tell me, Crow Killer, who would want a wahoo?" Red Hawk had understood what Wilson had said about the cow.

"For milk." Jed looked at Red Hawk. "I thought you had bought a wife for a minute back there."

"You do not think I would trade my great animal for one woman?" Red Hawk shook his head in disbelief. "You know, I was just joking."

"I don't think Rolling Thunder was."

"Yes, and that is a problem. Rolling Thunder will come in the summer."

Jed grinned to himself. It was a good joke. "Maybe, you will be far away, stealing horses."

"Maybe, I will." Red Hawk could not believe Rolling Thunder had taken him seriously. Never would he give his great appaloosa for only one squaw, even if she was the daughter of Hatcher and granddaughter of Iron Breast.

Jed and Red Hawk kept a sharp lookout on the ride back to his cabin. He knew the Arickaree were still out there somewhere and maybe still hunting the ones that had raided their village. The days passed quickly as the miles passed beneath their horse's feet. Finally, the steep descent down into his valley appeared before them. By habit, Jed's eyes searched out the vanishing bright light, but it never appeared as they moved down the trail. His home place was a welcome sight to Jed as they crossed the small creek and rode up to the cabin.

"We will let the horses rest here tonight before heading out for the village." Jed pulled the supplies and rawhide bag from the Shoshone horse.

Stopping suddenly as he started to reach for the door, Jed stared at the leather thong with what looked like a bear's tooth hanging from it. Red Hawk looked over Jed's shoulder as he pulled the thong from the door.

"What is it?" Red Hawk stared at the tooth. "What does it mean?"

Turning the tooth over in his hand, Jed shrugged. "I don't know."

"I believe it is a medicine sign, bad medicine I think." Red Hawk stepped back. "I think it is a warning of some kind."

"Arickaree?" Jed turned the amulet over in his hand.

"No, they would not warn you they were coming."

"Then who?"

Red Hawk shrugged. "I would say it comes from one of your many enemies, one that knows this is your lodge."

Pushing into the cabin, Jed could tell by the way he had set the bar, the cabin hadn't been entered. Unpacking the extra supplies, he and Bright Moon would need for the winter months, Jed started a fire for coffee, then looked again at the bear tooth.

Jed was tired, tired of the constant battles and killings, and he hoped it would one day change. When he was young, it was an adventure to follow Walking Horse, learning the ways of the Lance Bearer. He remembered White Swan's words; there would never be peace for him. His path was the constant threat of death and his duty as an Arapaho Lance Bearer was to protect the people. But now, he had Bright Moon, and he only wanted to live peace, trap in his valley, and be left alone.

Walking to where the teeth of the killer grizzlies hung from the wall, Jed put the tooth up next to them. He could tell whatever bear the tooth had come from had been as big or maybe bigger than the three he had killed. Studying the amulet, he wondered what could the amulet mean and who would come to challenge him next?

With a shake of their hands, Red Hawk and Jed sat their horses on the bank of the Yellowstone. They had somehow survived another deadly encounter and lived to tell about it. In the trials they had endured, the danger and bloodshed, the two men had become closer than brothers, and neither wanted to see the other go.

"Ride with me to the village and meet Bright Moon." Jed tried to talk Red Hawk into riding to the Arapaho village with him. "Little Antelope and Walking Horse would be glad to see you once again."

Looking curiously at his friend, the Crow shook his head. "How is Little Antelope, is she as pretty as ever?"

"Maybe prettier."

"She still touches your heart, my brother." Red Hawk turned the spotted stallion. "Maybe more than Bright Moon."

"Little Antelope is Walking Horse's wife."

"Yes, you have told me this before." Red Hawk smiled sadly. "We are brothers. I can see into your heart."

Jed handed Red Hawk two packages, changing the subject. "The tobacco is for your father, Plenty Coups. The other is for you, my brother, for being a good friend."

"What is in the wrapping?"

"Well open it. Maybe it is a beautiful woman for you." Jed laughed.

Opening the package, Red Hawk held it in front of him and exhaled. "It is the most beautiful knife I have ever seen. Thank you, my brother."

Jed rode into the Arapaho village as the sun was high overhead. The first to see him was Little Antelope, who came running to him, with a smile of relief on her face.

"You have returned to us, my warrior." The slender woman looked up at him.

"I have returned." Jed slid from the piebald and stripped the bridle from the horse, turning him loose. "Is everything all right here?"

Nodding, she motioned at the lodge. "My sister is inside."

"And Walking Horse?"

"He leads the warriors, looking for an intruder."

Jed looked over at the beautiful woman. "Intruder?"

"Come, I will show you." Jed followed her into the nearest lodge.

"What?"

"This." Little Antelope held the amulet out to Jed, then leaned up against him. "I have worried for you, my warrior."

Holding her shoulders, Jed looked down into her dark eyes. "I know you do, Little Antelope, and I worry for you."

Stepping back, she released the amulet. "Go to Bright Moon, my warrior. Ignore my foolishness."

"Foolishness?"

"I am Walking Horse's wife. I must restrain the feelings in my heart for something that cannot be."

Nodding, Jed touched the small tear forming on her cheek. "I know, little one."

Little Antelope wiped her eyes as Jed went through the doorway and disappeared. Walking to the lodge where Bright Moon was, he stopped, taking one last look at the lodge he had just come from. He knew Red Hawk was right. Little Antelope could never leave his heart or his thoughts.

Bright Moon looked up as the doorway darkened, then flung herself into Jed's arms. Smiling, he looked down into her upturned face. Guilt squeezed at his heart as he held his wife. He couldn't help himself, as he still had deep feelings for Little Antelope. Both of them had always fought against their feelings, but both knew they were there. Jed knew that did not make his feelings for Bright Moon less, but his feelings for Little Antelope was imbedded in him since they had first met. It was something he could not easily remove from his heart. Neither he nor Little Antelope had done anything to be ashamed of, and they never would.

"Tell me, what happened in the land of the Shoshone?"

"First, I must go speak with Slow Wolf, then we will have supper and I will tell you everything."

"Did Red Hawk return safely?"

"You know about Red Hawk?" Jed laughed as she wiggled up against him. "Yes, Red Hawk has returned to his people."

Pouting, she looked at the amulet in Jed's hand. "I wanted to meet this Crow friend of yours."

"Red Hawk is a handsome warrior, and he would try to steal you." Jed smiled down at her. "Perhaps, I should keep you hid from his eyes."

"Is he very handsome, as Little Antelope has told me?" Her eyes teased.

Jed nodded, then smiled. "The Crow women say he is the most proud and handsome warrior in their nation."

"Not as handsome as my husband." Bright Moon turned back to her sewing. "Go speak with Slow Wolf, then return quickly."

Stripping supplies and the rawhide bag from the Shoshone horse, Jed turned the animal loose, then walked to the old chief's lodge. The amulet he held in his hand disturbed him. It was the identical amulet as the one left on his cabin door. Setting the bag beside the lodge, Jed bent and entered the doorway.

"You have returned, my son." The old chief stared through the gloom of the lodge.

"Yes, my chief." Jed addressed the old one with respect. "The spirit ones looked over me on this trail."

Motioning to a buffalo robe, Slow Wolf reached for his pipe and tobacco as Jed made himself comfortable. Producing a coal from the small fire, he lit the ceremonial pipe and passed it to Jed. Several minutes passed as the old one went through all the protocol required when smoking the medicine pipe.

"Tell me, my son, has my promise been fulfilled?"

"Yes, my chief." Jed nodded. "The rawhide bag sits outside your lodge as we speak."

"My lifelong pledge has been done." The grey head seemed to sag. "Ask of me anything you wish."

"I wish nothing from Slow Wolf. Only that he lives long and leads our people with the wisdom he has always shown."

Again, the old head seemed to dip. "I wish this could be so, but I fear my time grows short. Tell me of your journey to Shoshone lands."

Jed quickly told the chief everything that had happened on their trail north and how they followed the directions given to them. How their journey had been full of danger and difficulty locating the snake's head. He told about waiting in the dark until daybreak before entering the cave, the battles with the Shoshone, and long race back to the southeast. Also, the challenge of the Shoshone, and the fight that led to the deaths of their two warriors as Rolling Thunder and several whites looked on.

"We killed seven of their people on this trail."

Slow Wolf nodded. "And now we are in Red Hawk's debt again."

"He expects nothing, my chief." Jed looked across at the aged face. "He is my brother."

"I respect the Crow. If it was permitted, I would make him a Lance Bearer."

Jed laughed. "That may be asking a little too much from him."

The old chief laughed. "Plenty Coups would have a fit. Maybe, we should say no more about it."

Jed smiled as he imagined Plenty Coups face turning red when he heard his son was becoming an honorary Arapaho.

"What will Crow Killer do now?"

"I will take Bright Moon and return to my lodge."

"Go with my blessings, but remember the Arickaree and the Shoshone. If the whites from Baxter Springs watched the battle, then they may learn of you killing their warriors."

This had already crossed Jed's thoughts, and he knew Bate Baker was not to be trusted. "I have given this much thought, but as much yelling Red Hawk was doing, they'll blame the Crow."

CHAPTER 7

For three days, Jed stayed at the Arapaho village hunting and swimming with Walking Horse, and then talking late into the night with Big Owl and the other Lance Bearers. Catching his horses, Jed gave Walking Horse the good Shoshone horse as a present, then he lifted Bright Moon onto her horse. The piebald was well rested, prancing for the villagers and well-wishers as he led the little mule from the village. Walking Horse, Little Antelope, and Big Owl accompanied them as they rode along with them to the Yellowstone.

Shaking hands, while the sisters hugged and tried to keep from crying, Jed waved at his escort, then rode the piebald, followed by Bright Moon, into the river crossing. Walking Horse and Little Antelope watched as they hit swimming water and slipped from their horses, swimming alongside them. They all laughed as the little mule outswam the horses with her long ears pointed straight ahead as she exited the river first.

"They are free, my husband." Little Antelope watched the swimming figures.

"Yes, carefree and happy." Walking Horse smiled. "What more could one ask for."

The dark eyes of Little Antelope seemed to cloud over as Walking Horse lifted her onto the horse. Looking over her shoulder, she watched Jed's broad back as he swung up on the black and white horse.

Jed and Bright Moon had hardly topped out of the river bottom to the high ridge that looked down on the crossing when the shrill war cries of several warriors took their attention. Screaming and waving their bows, Crow warriors led by Red Hawk, surrounded Jed and Bright Moon. Jed could only shake his head as the warriors brushed up against him, touching him with their bows.

"What is happening, my husband?" Bright Moon had a hard grip on her rifle.

Jed smiled. "I believe we are being counted coup on."

"Count coup on a squaw?"

"Not just a squaw, Bright Moon, a beautiful squaw." Red Hawk kicked his horse alongside her. "Please do not shoot my warriors."

"Who is this warrior?" The pretty face turned red as she lifted the rifle.

Laughing, as Red Hawk nervously eyed the pointed rifle, Jed introduced the warrior. "This is my good friend Red Hawk, son of Plenty Coups, and a great warrior."

"And very handsome, don't you think?"

"I think someone is very arrogant, is what I think."

Raising his hand, Red Hawk pouted. "She has the same stinging tongue as her sister, Little Antelope."

Bright Moon had been told of this warrior and the time he and Little Antelope had been left in the cave on the riverbank. "My sister said you were very mouthy."

"Again, she brags on me."

Cutting the argument off, Jed looked around at the warriors. "What are you up to this time, my friend?"

"My father, Plenty Coups, wishes for you to come to our village."

"We were heading to our valley." Jed protested.

"You would not disappoint the great Plenty Coups and our people?" Red Hawk looked over at Bright Moon. "He wishes to see the beauty of your woman."

Jed finally relented, knowing he owed the warrior. If Red Hawk had not ridden with him on that dangerous trail, the remains of Iron Breast may not have been recovered.

"Okay, my brother, we will go see my father Plenty Coups."

Watching the proud, straight back of the warrior riding ahead of them on the beautiful spotted horse with his long black hair pouring across his shoulders, Bright Moon looked over at Jed, and teased. "Little Antelope did not speak falsely, my husband. This one is very handsome and proud."

"Yes, he is. There is only one Red Hawk."

"For a Crow." She laughed. "My husband, the great Crow Killer, is much more handsome."

For two days, Jed and Bright Moon were guests in the lodge of Plenty Coups. Jed felt his stomach would burst from all the buffalo tongue and steaks he had consumed at the chief's coaxing. He wondered if he would be able to mount the piebald to ride home.

Shaking hands with Plenty Coups, before they started for their valley, Jed watched the big chief hug Bright Moon.

Nodding at Jed, he smiled. "Be careful, my son, her beauty is beyond compare. Someone we know may try to steal her."

Jed laughed. "Red Hawk thinks more of raiding and fighting than getting married."

The big head nodded sadly. "I may never have grandchildren."

Red hawk hadn't put in an appearance yet as the younger Crow warriors escorted Jed and Bright Moon back to the Yellowstone. Jed was curious, knowing Red Hawk would not let them ride away without a farewell good-bye and he would never miss the chance to badger Bright Moon one last time. For two days, they had fought with each other, worse than he and Little Antelope ever had.

Suddenly, hearing a loud scream, they all reined in and watched as Red Hawk galloped up, leading a two-year-old colt with the identical markings as his great spotted horse. The young horse was beautiful, the spitting image of his sire.

"It took me some time to catch the young one." Red Hawk laughed. "He is already almost as fast as his father."

Jed was impressed with the horse. He indeed was a beauty with the best conformation any horseman would love. The young one was giving Red Hawk and the older horse a fit as he lunged and pulled against the rawhide rope.

"You've got yourself a handful there, my brother."

"Not me, Crow Killer. I am giving this animal to Bright Moon. Now, he is your problem." Red Hawk laughed. "As you can see I have not taught him very good manners yet."

"For me?" Bright Moon was shocked.

"For you, little one." The warrior offered the horse. "If you are to stay up with the paint horse of your husband, you will need him."

"Thank you, Red Hawk." She smiled. "He is beautiful."

"And he needs a beautiful rider." Red Hawk smiled. "When I come in the warm times, we will race him against this one."

"He will win."

"How do you know this?"

"Because the great Red Hawk grows fat."

Looking over at Jed, the warrior seemed to pout. "I thought she might like me a little if I gave her the colt."

"Oh, I like you Red Hawk. I just tell the truth, most of the time."

"Okay, you two." Jed raised his hand and stopped the friendly bantering. "What will you do now, my brother?"

"We ride to the south. Maybe some Comanche horses will follow us home." Red Hawk laughed. "But first, before we part again, we will share our elk meat with you over a good fire."

Red Hawk and Jed led the column of warriors and Bright Moon to a grove of trees where they made camp. "You did not lie, she has great beauty and she is as sharp-tongued as Little Antelope."

"Yes, she is."

Red Hawk nodded thoughtfully. "Maybe, she has turned your eyes away from the mouthy one."

"I told you many times, she is just a friend." Jed assured. "A friend."

"Yes, my friend, you have told me this many times."

Jed shook his head. "But, you do not believe me."

"Yes, I believe you, Crow Killer." Red Hawk smiled innocently. "When I return from this trail, I will ride to your valley and we will hunt."

"Be careful on this trail, my brother, and thank you for giving her the colt."

"He is the best colt we have ever foaled from the spotted one." Red Hawk smiled. "He will carry her for many suns to come."

Jed and Bright Moon watched Red Hawk and his warriors as they disappeared to the south. Raising her hand, Bright Moon waved as the warriors went out of sight.

Looking to where Jed held the fractious colt, she smiled. "Red Hawk acts so proud and brave, but I believe he is lonely."

"No, he just has an adventurous spirit." Jed knew Red Hawk was just too wild to settle down yet. His adventurous spirit kept him riding the war trail. "One day, he will mature and settle down. For a while, back in Shoshone lands, I thought he had."

Jed looked down across his valley at the distant cabin sitting on the far northern end and smiled. They had left Red Hawk and his warriors with the promise the warrior would come for a visit before the cold times came. Bright Moon, like Little Antelope, had sparred constantly with the laughing warrior as they bickered over one thing and then another. Their parting this time had seemed sad. Jed loved his valley and Bright Moon, but he still missed the camaraderie of his friends, Walking Horse and Red Hawk.

"We are almost home."

"It is good to be home." Bright Moon was glad to be back in the valley. "I like going, but I like returning to our lodge."

"Yes, it is."

Bright Moon looked over at the spotted colt. He finally had settled down and learned to lead. "Your friend Red Hawk is a good man. I like him, even if he is a Crow."

"Well, now that's a surprise, after the way you two fought."

"A Cheyenne could not let a Crow get the best of her."

Jed laughed. The way they had argued, anyone would think they were enemies. "No, I guess not."

Finally, Jed had everything he wanted. Perhaps now, he would find peace and happiness in the mountains, alone except for his new bride and the wild ones who roamed the valley and mountains. This time he hoped it would be so, all he wanted now was his valley and Bright Moon.

The summer had been spent breaking the spirited spotted colt. A new corral had been built to keep the horse where he could be handled and worked with every day. The colt, like his sire, was highly intelligent and easy to work with. In just a few weeks, Jed knew he would have the colt broke, backing up, and working like an old horse.

Finishing his supper, Jed looked over at the open door. "It's time for the colt to be ridden."

Bright Moon smiled. "He is a very strong horse and he is strong-minded."

"Yes, he is." Jed nodded. "With the new sun, I will ride him."

Raising her eyebrows, as she cleaned up the dishes, Bright Moon looked over at Jed. "Be careful, he does not ride you."

"I'll be careful. I aim to cheat him a little."

"Cheat him?"

"Tomorrow."

At the break of day, Jed was already running the colt around the corral not letting him stop. With the flick of a rawhide rope, he kept the horse moving until a sweat started to pop out on his spotted hide.

"The Cheyenne would just climb on him and ride."

"And get thrown off, how many times?"

Bright Moon laughed. "Many times."

Mounting the piebald, Jed led the colt down to the deeper part of the stream. Standing in belly deep water, Jed reached over and tightened the rawhide rope he had tied around the colt's withers. The horse lunged several times from the water as he felt the unfamiliar rope tighten around his girth. Catching the colt, as he quieted and stood still beside the piebald, Jed looked to where Bright Moon sat her horse.

"If he throws me, catch him as he leaves the water." Jed left a long piece of rawhide hanging from the colt's halter. "Don't let him get by you."

"You are going to get wet, warrior."

"You're probably right, maybe many times today."

Easing from the piebald onto the spotted one, Jed felt the power of the colt as he lunged and bucked in the chest deep water. With a death grip on the rawhide rope and clinging onto the colt's flanks with his legs, Jed rode the colt for several jumps before being thrown into the water as the horse slipped on the gravel bottom.

Bright Moon laughed as Jed came sputtering to the surface looking for the young horse. Catching the frightened colt as he pushed up against the piebald, Jed mounted his horse and again slipped across onto the colt. Finally, after bucking Jed off several times, the young horse stopped and started responding to the rawhide reins as Jed moved him about in the creek.

"That's enough for him today." Jed petted the wet neck, then eased back on the piebald.

Leading the colt back to his corral, he tossed the horse some dry grass from the barn and stood back admiring the animal.

"When will you let him run with the others?"

"Soon. I will ride him a few more times and then we will turn him out." Jed fastened the gate. "Then it will be your turn to ride him."

"In the water?"

'No." Jed laughed as he grabbed her. "I will lead you on him a few times. Then, young lady, you should be able to ride him by yourself."

Winter was once again upon the beautiful secluded valley Crow Killer had discovered and claimed for his own. Many battles with deadly enemies, both man and beast had been fought to win this harsh, wild land. Under the soft doeskin shirt covering him, his body was covered with old scars that carried many memories, mostly sad. Known as Jedidiah Bracket to the whites back in the settlement and as Crow Killer to his adopted Arapaho Tribe, the tall, dark complexioned man stood quietly staring out across his beloved valley. The heavy snows had not come yet this year to blanket the valley and mountains, but soon, very soon they would blow their cold breath across the land. In time, the north and west winds would come with a vengeance to hurl its cruel winds across the abundant grassy fields, covering both with powdery snow. Later, the heavier snows would fall, blanketing the already dead brown grass and timber along the valley's edge. Soon, it would be time for him to set his traps. With the cold upon the land, the fur bearing varmint's coats would quickly thicken to protect them from the harsh winter that lay ahead.

Over the warm summer, Walking Horse, Little Antelope, and a few warriors had visited Jed and Bright Moon. Only a few days later, after they had departed, Red Hawk and his warriors showed up to sit around and smoke their pipes, bragging about the raid on the Comanche. Red

Hawk brought in two full-grown elk as he rode up to the cabin. Red Hawk bragged on the spotted colt as Bright Moon paraded him around the cabin. He also said he had only loaned Bright Moon the horse and that he would take him when he departed, causing a battle of words until Jed finally broke them up. Now, with everyone back at their villages to prepare for the meat taking times, both Jed and Bright Moon felt alone.

Bright Moon stepped from the warm cabin and took the tall man's arm. "What does my husband think about this morning?"

Smiling down at her small olive face, he pulled her to him. "I'm thinking about taking a bath."

"You speak crazy, my husband." The slender woman laughed lightly, making her snow-white teeth sparkle in the morning sun. "It is far too cold to go into the water."

Grabbing the shrieking girl in his arms, as if she was a feather, he started toward the small stream below the cabin. "I will let my beautiful bride test the water."

"You would not dare." She struggled as he neared the water. "If you get me wet, I will get even with the mighty Crow Killer."

Setting her down softly, he ran his strong hand across her face. "No, I wouldn't dare. I like to eat too much."

"Uh huh." She laughed as she ducked away from his reaching arms. "No more of this silliness. Come, your breakfast is waiting."

Following the woman back to the cabin, Jed turned, taking one last look across the flat valley, then followed her. Stopping momentarily at the corral, he patted the neck of the powerful paint horse and spotted colt while looking over the other horses. It had been many months since Wet Otter and his Pawnee warriors or any others had come to the valley to raid and kill. Still, even though every enemy had been defeated or killed, including the killer bears, Jed always kept his horses in the large corral at night. The words and warnings of Walking Horse still lay heavily on his ears. The tall Arapaho Lance Bearer had warned him, always be vigilant and stay alert.

Since bringing Bright Moon home in the early summer after his journey with Red Hawk to the Shoshone lands, the days in the valley had remained peaceful. They had been happy and content, roaming the mountains, swimming in the clear, cold streams, spending the days in each other's company. With the pure bliss of youth and love they had enjoyed each other over the summer. Riding across the valley on the piebald and now broke spotted horse, they would chase anything, deer, elk, or rabbit, that would run before them. Still, out of habit, or maybe fear of unknown enemies riding against him, Jed always kept his horses corralled at night. Many times over the past year, during the long nights, he would wake up from the slightest noise of a nightwalker and go check around the cabin. Bright Moon would scold him for being so suspicious, but Jed could not forget Walking Horse's words to always be alert.

Not only Walking Horse, but his other good friends, Blue Darter the Blackfoot and Red Hawk the Crow, had all warned him many times to stay alert and never let his guard down. Maybe their dire words of warning were the reason he was so watchful, unable to sleep as soundly as he once had. Now, he had the young and beautiful Cheyenne woman, Bright Moon, to protect. Jed knew the ways of the tribes, and any warrior seeing the young woman's beauty would want her for themselves. The Hawken rifle was always in his hand or nearby when he went outside. He had relentlessly taught Bright Moon the ways of the smaller thirty-caliber rifle and how to reload it quickly. She had become an excellent shot, almost as good as Jedidiah.

High in the mountain valley, he could never be sure what each day would bring. Only a foolish man would let his guard down. Many tribes knew this was the hunting grounds of Crow Killer the demon, the man who could turn himself into a bear. Some, such as Squirrel Tooth the Nez Perce, swore they had actually seen him change into a bear right in front of them. Most warriors avoided the valley, scared of the spooky, eerie tales that were told around their campfires of the legendary bear killer. The old medicine men of the tribes warned the ghosts of the ones that had died at Crow Killer's hands might still walk the land at night. Still, Jed worried there was always the possibility of attack from the young and wild hot-blooded warriors of the warlike tribes.

Many whites also knew Jedidiah Bracket lived somewhere high in the remote valley, but few knew the mountains well enough to find it. None dared to venture into the forested mountainous terrain for fear of the wild tribes and animals living there. Some of the older trappers knew of its location, but they also knew of Jed's hatred for anyone trespassing on his domain. They dared not chance their lives by venturing into the high meadows. Most of the ones that knew the valley's exact location were dead. Lem Roden and the brothers, Seth and Billy Wilson, were all gone now. Leaving only Lige Hatcher, the one the tribes called Rolling Thunder because of the noise his Hawken made when they first heard it. Lige was a friend and no threat, and he was also the father of Ellie, the medicine woman he once intended to marry.

For three years, everyone in Baxter Springs or at Bridger's Trading Post had seen the heavy bundles of pelts he had brought out of the mountains. However, furs were not enough to entice them to trespass into Jed's high mountains. Most whites, though none would admit it, were scared of Crow Killer and the rumors of his battles with the killer bears. None, not even other mountain men, were willing to risk their lives for furs. There was plenty of game in other mountain valleys to trap without provoking the rage of the Crow Killer, by encroaching into his hunting grounds.

Early the next morning, Jed held back one of the Blackfoot horses as he let the others through the gate. He smiled as the small herd splashed across the cold stream and laughed as they kicked up their heels, racing across the valley floor. The little black mule, that Silent One always rode, led the small band of horses as they bucked and cavorted out across the valley floor. The little mule always brought back memories of the Assiniboine lad, the Silent One. Some were sad thoughts, most though, were of the earlier, happier days they had spent together in this place. Fastening the gate, Jed entered the cabin and felt the warmth of the cabin and the smell of cooking biscuits and elk meat frying on the hearth.

Finishing his breakfast, Jed pulled down his heavy fifty-caliber Hawken rifle and examined the weapon closely. Bright Moon glanced over to where he sat at the log table. She knew well what weighed on his mind. The weather was changing, turning colder, and the meat taking time was near. It was time to hunt for the buffalo meat they needed to get them through the harsh winter. They could subsist on elk and deer, but a good buffalo tongue or chewy steak was a delicacy. Plus, they needed the heavy hides for the coats they would sell to the traders at Bridger's. The little woman smiled as she studied him. Her first spring and summer in the valley had passed so very fast. Bright Moon and Jed had worked tirelessly through the summer. The barn was packed full of dry grass for the horses, and the traps were all oiled, ready to be set. Split firewood was stacked high against the cabin walls, far more than enough to see them through the coming winter. Throughout the summer months, they had ridden the valley and studied the game trails. When the cold winds came from the north, Jed would know exactly where to set his traps and snares.

Picking up his plate from the table, Bright Moon studied the rifle. "We will go for buffalo meat soon, my husband?"

"Yes, we must hunt soon." Jed nodded, absorbed in his work. "It's almost time for the storms to come, bringing snow and closing the smaller passes."

"I will ride with you?"

"Yes." Jed smiled over at her as she sat down across from him.

He could not forget his friend's last words of warning before departing, "Be watchful and never leave her alone." Walking Horse had said with a wave, when he left with Little Antelope and his warriors, as they headed back to their village. No, he would never leave Bright Moon alone. He had left Silent One behind and had always blamed himself for his death at the cabin door. The youngster had been killed by Seth and Adam Beale while Jed was away trading his pelts. Even Lem Roden had come close to being killed, alone at the cabin, by the killer grizzlies. Never, would he chance leaving Bright Moon behind, alone and unprotected.

In the valley, the temperature was falling as each night passed, and Jed knew it was time to ride to the lower valleys for buffalo. Gathering the horses and little mule, he needed to carry the heavy hides and bundles of meat home, he checked their feet for any lameness. He swore, as he carved on a broken chip in a hoof, this year after he sold his pelts, he would buy nippers and a file from the old blacksmith, Otis McGraw. Then, he would have the right tools to work the horse's feet properly. Jed smiled, as he knew the old thief would probably ask for the little mule in trade for the valuable tools. He couldn't figure why McGraw wanted the mule so bad. She was small and kinda ugly, and she definitely had a mule's disposition. Jed had refused McGraw's offers for the animal many times. Thinking of Silent One, he just couldn't part with her. Plus, she was invaluable as a watcher against any enemy, human or otherwise.

Jed knew Bright Moon was already prepared to leave. Earlier, he had told her they would be traveling light to Turner's Hole, taking only their rifles, sleeping blankets, and fire making utensils. Anything they needed to eat would be supplied by the wildlife along the mountain trails. They would not have the comforts of the cabin, but this was a hunting trip, nothing to be enjoyed. Jed studied the dark sky overhead, knowing it was time to depart, he could wait no longer. This time of year, in the high mountains, timing was of the utmost importance. The weather had to be cold enough to keep the meat from spoiling. Their timing also had to be right so they could return through the passes before getting snowed in.

At daybreak, the piebald, spotted horse, and five others stood ready for the trek to the lower valleys. The little black mule stood quietly beside the piebald with her ears drooping as usual.

Lifting Bright Moon onto the colt's back, Jed smiled. "Don't let him buck you off this morning. The ground might be a bit hard for you to land on."

"He will not buck with me this morning, my husband." Bright Moon held a firm grip on the reins.

"Don't know about that, he sure can buck when he's a mind to." Jed laughed, remembering the horse pitching Bright Moon into one of the ponds that dotted the valley. "Let's head out."

The trip across the mountains and down the long trail to Turner's Hole had been an uneventful and enjoyable ride. The colt hadn't given Bright Moon any trouble, behaving like an old broke horse. Jed caught fish out of the Snake for their supper one night and furry fat rabbits were cooked over their campfire at the next campsite.

For a week, after arriving in Turner's Hole and dropping several young buffalo, Jed and Bright Moon feasted on buffalo steaks and tongue. The work was hard, skinning and preparing the many bundles of buffalo tongue, hams, and hides for their transport back to the cabin.

Jed also kept a sharp lookout across the valley as they worked, remembering the French Canadians he and Lem Roden had killed.

The north winds had set in and the temperature kept falling for several nights, freezing the small stream that fed the valley. Still, Jed lingered in the small valley working over the meat and hides as he studied and frowned at the graying skies.

"Soon, a big storm will come, my husband." Bright Moon looked up at the darkening clouds as she heated their breakfast coffee. "We have to leave now."

Jed heard the warning in her voice, and he knew she was right. "I will catch the horses and we'll leave this morning. Forget the coffee."

Five pack animals and the black mule stood packed and ready to head for the high valley. The heavy packs of meat and hides were equally divided between the horses and mule. The piebald and Bright Moon's spotted horse were standing ready with the sleeping robes and rifles tied to their withers. Lifting Bright Moon onto her horse, then swinging on the paint's back, Jed took one last look at the clouds. Quickly, he turned the horse back up the narrow mountain trail that led out of the valley. He swore lightly under his breath as he looked worriedly at Bright Moon. Perhaps this time, he had been greedy and stayed too long. He wanted the extra buffalo hides for the valuable coats they would make. Hopefully, they wouldn't pay for his greediness by getting caught in the first storm of the year.

"The storm will not strike today, my husband." Bright Mood could see the worry in his face. "But, soon it will reach us."

Jed knew she spoke the truth, and they had to hurry. The worst of the steep, narrow passes were ahead of them, a day's ride away. The cabin lay due west, a little better than two days, and all uphill. The horses were heavily loaded and they would tire easily on the upward pull if he hurried them along too fast. He knew he had to stay at a steady pace. Listening to the beginning of the moaning winds, it was hard not to push his horse into a faster trot on their homeward journey as they tried to outrun the storm.

Bright Moon looked over her shoulder from where she brought up the tail end of the string of horses. The Pawnee horses were strung out tail to tail in a line by rawhide thongs. They were used to following a lead horse so they rarely gave any trouble. Her dark eyes narrowed as she took in the billowing dark clouds, she knew a heavy storm was building. She looked ahead at Jed's broad back, then sunk deeper into her heavy parka. She had faith in her warrior that he would lead them safely through the passes. Bright Moon was Cheyenne, and had lived all her life through the fierce storms during the cold times. However, the Cheyenne had always been snug in their warm lodges under heavy buffalo robes when the winds struck and the snow and icy pellets beat down against the hide lodges with a fury. In these narrow passes, they were at the mercy of the storm with nowhere to seek shelter. The passes were high and narrow, with no respite from the bitter winds and stinging ice pellets.

Instinctively, she could sense a bad storm was approaching, as the trees started to sway and the winds slowly picked up its volume and velocity. The heavy snow hadn't started falling yet, but Bright Moon knew the icy sleet would precede the heavier snows as it had already started stinging her face. They had traveled all day and long into the night, feeling their way along the narrow trail before Jed called a halt to let the horses blow. Dropping the reins of the paint horse, he walked back to where Bright Moon eased to the ground, trying to bring life back into her legs.

"Perhaps I waited too long to head home to our lodge." Jed listened to the wind moving the limbs. "The storm will hit soon."

"Yes, my husband. The cold will drop before morning and the snow will come." She nodded up at him. "But, first the icy pellets will come down harder and sting us."

"You got any ideas?"

"No, my husband, there is no shelter here. We must move on."

"It will be dangerous traveling these rocky passes in the dark."

"Yes, but we have no choice." Bright Moon smiled up at him in the dim light. "If we stay here, we will freeze."

"Or get snowed in." Jed added. "We will give the horses a few minutes, then we will move on.

"Let the little mule lead us through the night." Bright Moon suggested. "She is too mean to let a mere snowstorm keep her away from her warm lodge."

In spite of the cold and wind, Jed had to chuckle. "Perhaps you are right."

"It is all we can do." Bright Moon touched his arm. "I have faith, you will see us safely to our lodge."

Helping Bright Moon back on her horse, Jed wrapped a heavy trade blanket across her legs and around her shoulders. Patting her on the knee, he moved back to the head of the line. Untying the mule, he placed a loop of rawhide around her small neck and put her in front of the piebald. She had led him out of bad places before, and he had faith in her instincts. He knew once again, she would lead them safely across the high places to their valley. In some ways, a mule's senses were much keener than a horse's, Jed knew some would argue that, but Jed had faith in her. The little mule would not lead them blindly into a steep crevice or over an unseen drop off. Jed chuckled to himself, Bright Moon was right, the little animal was too mean to let a little storm stop her.

An hour later as the night completely engulfed them, Jed once again stopped the string of horses and dismounted. The ice was slowly starting to pelt his face harder as he walked back to where Bright Moon was waiting. Helping her to the ground, Jed led her back up the line to the piebald and raised her up on his horse.

"I will walk behind the mule." Jed turned, after wrapping her in their sleeping blankets.

"How far is the high ridge, my husband?"

Jed knew she spoke of the pass above the cabin where the bright light always revealed itself. "If we can travel all night and tomorrow, we will be home by dark."

"The horses need rest." Bright Moon yelled above the screaming storm. "They are tired."

"We have no time to rest them. We must hurry before the worst of the storm reaches us." Jed could barely make out her silhouette in the gloom and icy mist.

Sliding from the paint, Bright Moon yelled through the wind. "I will walk. We can put some of the hides on our horses."

"You can't walk in this." Jed shook his head.

"I am Cheyenne. I can walk as good as an Arapaho Lance Bearer."

"Have it your own way." Jed shook his head, then quickly pulled the frozen hides from the overloaded Pawnee horses and redistributed them on her spotted horse and the paint. "That'll lighten their loads alright."

After tying a light piece of rawhide around Bright Moon's waist, Jed secured it to his belt and started the pack train forward. The black mule seemed eager to be moving, as she sensed ahead there was a warm shelter and dry hay waiting. For two hours, they moved up and down the dirt and rock passageways, then stopped to rest where they were temporarily out of the wind. It was almost pitch black along the trail, and only Jed's faith in the little mule kept them moving forward.

All night, as the storm intensified and the snow began falling heavier, Jed kept them moving, only stopping in short intervals for rest. The snow was heavy and getting deeper beneath their feet, but at least it was blowing in from the northeast against their backs and not into their faces. Jed knew some animals would turn and move away from the wind, but he still had faith in the black mule. Also, the trail was mostly steep uphill, skirted with timber, so it would be hard for them to climb out or get off the trail. Holding on to Bright Moon, he supported her as the trail started to become slippery in places from the snow and ice. He could feel her weight leaning against him, as she was tiring.

Their journey up from Turner's Hole had been fast paced, hard even for a man. Jed knew if they rested the horses too long they would cool down and their muscles could tie up. He had heard the old-timers speak of pack animal's muscles bunching up, causing the animals to refuse to move forward. He couldn't take the chance, as he needed the horses to get the meat safely back to the cabin. Clucking to the mule, he nodded grimly as she took up the slack in the lead rope. She was a handful at times, but he had to admit the little animal was all heart. She didn't hesitate to move forward.

The first eerie rays of sunlight started lifting the darkness from the rocky trail. Jed thought he knew where they were by the feel of the trail beneath his feet. As the sun lit the trail, he knew his guess had been accurate. Already, a foot of fresh snow had fallen on the trail under them. Jed knew exactly where they were. Ahead, less than a mile, they would have to cross a small creek that he had named Black Creek, from the dark rocks that lay beneath the shallow stream.

Stopping at Black Creek, to break the forming ice and let the animal's water, Jed hoisted Bright Moon back onto the piebald's back, behind the packs.

"I can walk, my husband."

Ignoring her protests, Jed wrapped her up snug while letting the horses drink a little water from the creek. Before sending the mule across the knee-deep stream, he eased up on her back. As she started into the water, he hoped she wouldn't decide to dump him as she had done to Silent One on many occasions. The winds were blowing heavy snow about them and the temperature was well below freezing. This time he had to trust the mule. He couldn't afford the time it would take to wade the creek and dry his wet feet, to keep them from freezing.

Sliding from the mule, he patted her neck and thanked his good luck he hadn't swapped her to McGraw at Bridger's Post. He swore the little mule would have a home forever if they all got back to the cabin safely. The dangerous passage through the dark, stormy night made him think back to his flight from the grizzly sow across the mountains. They weren't home safe yet, but with the coming light, he knew they were over the roughest part of their ordeal.

"How much farther is it?" Bright Moon stretched her stiff legs as Jed lifted her from the piebald.

"If we can travel all day, we will be home by nightfall."

"I will walk now, my husband." She looked up at Jed. "The horse has enough to carry."

"For a little ways then."

Jed examined all the horses. The steep trails had taken their toll as they were exhausted and couldn't carry their heavy loads further. He had no choice and was forced to leave several bundles of meat lying beside the trail. He hated to abandon the meat, but the animals were done in from the heavy weight and the cold, blustery winds. He had to lighten their loads if they were going to make it back to the cabin before they balked and froze on the high pass. He doubted the meat would go untouched by the wolves or other meat eaters. He would return for the bundles after he got Bright Moon home safely and saddled fresher horses. There were still two Pawnee horses left at the cabin, and he would ride them when he returned for the meat.

Mile after mile, up and down the narrow trail, the little mule plodded onward, leading the string of horses toward the pass above the cabin. Jed had to admire the animal as she never once turned aside or stopped while she hurried them homeward.

Stopping the mule, he looked back along the string of tired horses. "We will let them rest here for a spell. When we top out the summit of this hill, we will be able to see our lodge."

"We are almost home." Bright Moon was relieved, as she was half frozen even under her buffalo coat and the horses were exhausted. "I am glad, my husband."

"You can sleep before a warm fire for two days." Jed quipped between cracked lips.

"I will."

Starting to lift her onto the piebald's back, Jed felt her hands push him away.

"I will walk."

The last few miles, Jed supported her as they clung tiredly to the little mule and staggered forward through the heavy snowstorm toward the cabin. Almost in a daze, they didn't even feel the cold that gripped their feet as they crossed the stream below the cabin. Jed shook his head as the mule stopped and the string of horses eagerly pushed forward to the corral gate. Wiping the snow from his eyes, he blinked in surprise, not two feet away was the gate of the enclosure and the safety of the cabin.

"We're home, Bright Moon." Jed called out hoarsely as he pulled her to the cabin door. "We're safe."

His hands were so stiff, that he could hardly work the cabin's latch. Sitting Bright Moon stiffly into the elk hide chair, Jed struggled to work the flint striker to light the fire. Luckily, he had put kindling and small firewood in the cabin before they had left for Turner's Hole.

"Can you keep the fire going while I see to the horses?"

Nodding, she pulled the frozen coat from her shoulders. "I will warm the cabin and fix us some biscuits, maybe."

"First, you get dry moccasins on." Smiling, Jed pulled on dry leggings and moccasins, then turned to the door.

The horses had pushed their way through the gate and were chewing on the small bit of hay they found in the bottom of the feed trough.

Leading each horse to the barn door, he quickly unlashed the bundles of meat and hides, then removed the packsaddles. Rolling the buffalo meat and hides into the barn, Jed piled several arm loads of hay into the manger and retreated to the cabin.

Bright Moon stood before the fire where she had a pan of biscuits cooking and several deer steaks on the spit.

"Them steaks still good, girl?"

Smiling, she flipped the meat. "I would not poison you now."

Early next morning, after a good night's rest and after admonishing Bright Moon to stay alert and in the cabin, Jed returned over the mountain where he had left the bundles of meat. Somehow, the buffalo meat hadn't been touched by night varmints. Jed did not know how, but the sharp-nosed night critters never smelled the frozen bundles. Loading the fresh horses, Jed turned the piebald back toward the cabin.

Somewhere, far off on the east ridge, the lone howl of the big grey wolf sounded out across the valley. Jed had never seen the wolf up close, only from a distance, but for some reason the wolf seemed like a friend. Many times before, when the killer bears or enemy warriors had attacked or had come close to the cabin, the wolf had called out his warning. Maybe it was only in his mind, but like the strange light, the call had not been his imagination.

Unloading the horses, Jed smiled as Bright Moon came from the cabin with a steaming hot cup of coffee. The storm had blown itself out, but not before blanketing the valley and mountains in snow. The temperature remained below freezing, but the high winds had subsided. After stacking the meat in the barn, Jed thanked her for the hot coffee and moved back into the warmth of the cabin.

"It is good, the meat was not touched." Bright Moon smiled. "We will eat well during the cold times."

"Tomorrow, we must raise it into the trees." Jed sipped his coffee greedily. "It'll keep the little varmints from ruining it."

Two days later, after resting and thawing out, Jed curried the little mule down and placed a packsaddle on her back. Hanging the steel traps on her, he led the spotted horse out of the corral and turned the other horses out on the snow covered meadow below the cabin. This morning, he chose the spotted horse. He wanted to keep the young colt ridden so he wouldn't turn wild over the winter months.

"Is not the snow too deep to set the traps, my husband?"

"No, I believe the fur bearers will be hungry." Jed shook his head. "I'll give them a try anyway."

"You will be back when the sun is high?"

"At dinner." Jed smiled down at her. "I will set the south end of the valley today and the north tomorrow."

"Are you sure there is not too much snow?" She wanted him to rest another day. "Maybe you should wait one more sleep."

"No, not for these." Jed tapped the traps and reassured her. "I will return when the sun is high."

CHAPTER 8

The first storm of the winter in the high meadow had subsided, but in places the heavy snow still lingered, glistening across the landscape. The trees along the mountain slopes were covered in snow with their limbs heavily laden and drooping. Jed moved slowly from pond to pond and along the beaten game trails that showed where the varmints had been traveling in their search for food.

The fur trader, Bate Baker, and fur buyers at Bridger's Fort had said they would not pay a good price or even buy beaver plews this season. The beaver hat lost its appeal to the rich in the east and had been replaced with something new. Now, the silkworm was desired over the heavier and bulkier beaver hats. Jed didn't care, he would trap for the flat tails anyway. He knew they would be reluctant, but they would buy the beaver if they wanted the other valuable furs especially the heavy buffalo coats. Coats the immigrants heading west desired and needed so badly.

The weather was cold, but Jed knew the first cold snap would abate and free up the streams for a month yet. The temperature remained below freezing, just enough to preserve the meat he had pulled into the trees, but not cold enough to freeze the ponds solid. Beaver in the far southern part of the valley were plentiful and he had plenty of traps for both beaver and other land mammals. The money was in silver fox, muskrat, bobcat, mink, and other animals, but the beaver plews would pay for the staples they would need for the coming year.

Jed finished setting forty traps and turned the spotted one back to the north and the hot dinner he knew would be waiting. Wading through the wet land and knee deep in the ponds, his feet were soaked clean through, and a dry pair of moccasins would be warm and welcomed.

Approaching the opening where he had the spotted horse and black mule tethered, he stiffened as he noticed both animals had their attention focused down the valley, further south. Checking the priming on his rifle, Jed eased up beside the black mule and watched the far tree line. Something or someone, high on the pass, was holding the animal's attention. Following the mule's eyes and ears, Jed could tell whatever she was focused on was making its way down the southern mountain trail. Swinging on the horse, Jed led the mule in a hard lope across the flat meadow to intercept the trail that led out onto the valley floor.

Quickly tying the animals out of sight, Jed slipped behind a mountain cedar and squatted above the trail. Above on the heights, something was definitely moving, and he could hear it coming down the trail. Jed hoped the horse or mule wouldn't call out and give his position away. Finally, he could hear the muffled hoofbeats on the snowy trail as two horses approached his position. He was curious, who would be riding the high country in this wintry weather? Jed remembered the many times enemy warriors had ridden down the same trail in search of him. Rechecking the Hawken's priming and his war axe, Jed moved closer to the edge of the cedar so he could get a clear view of the trail.

From where he waited, Jed could plainly see the markings on the horses, identifying them as Blackfoot. Two warriors, wrapped in trade blankets, slowly rode their horses in plain sight down the slippery trail. Pulling up as they neared the cedar tree that hid Jed, both men raised their hands slowly.

"If you are out there, Crow Killer, we come in peace." The rider mounted on the bay horse called out. The speaker looked over at the other warrior, then lowered his hands.

"Maybe, he is not here."

"Blue Darter says the Arapaho will always be waiting here somewhere when unknown warriors enter his valley."

The second warrior studied the valley then pointed excitedly. "He is here. There, do you see the tracks in the snow?"

Both warriors shuddered when Jed stepped out with the Hawken pointed at them.

"We have come in peace, Crow Killer." The first warrior raised his hands again. "Blue Darter has sent us to you."

"Why did Blue Darter not come himself?" Jed lowered the rifle slightly.

The first warrior shrugged. "I am his younger brother, Tall Wind."

"And I am Swift Arrow."

"Tell me, why are you here in my valley?"

Tall Wind looked at Jed. "Blue Darter has sent us to warn you."

Jed raised the rifle. "Why didn't Blue Darter come?"

"Blue Darter is Chief of the Piegan Blackfoot now and must stay at our village to protect our people."

"And protect his leadership, maybe?"

"Yes, there are ones that would take over if he were not in the village." Tall Wind admitted. "Blue Darter is not a hereditary chief and can be replaced."

"You men look cold and hungry."

"The mountains are cold up high, and yes, we are hungry. We have come far with little time to prepare food." Swift Arrow nodded stiffly.

"Your trail must be important for you to ride so far in this cold weather without eating." Jed remarked.

"Blue Darter says we must ride here to seek you out as fast as our horses could carry us."

Jed believed the two warriors. If they came here to raid, they would not be so foolhardy, riding into his valley in plain sight. "Come, we will ride to my lodge."

Bright Moon stepped back, startled as Jed led the two Blackfoot warriors into the cabin. She was ashamed, busy cooking their meal, she never heard their horses approach the cabin. No Cheyenne would let an enemy get this close without seeing them.

Raising his hand, Jed calmed her, introducing the two warriors. "This is Tall Wind and Swift Arrow."

"Blackfoot warriors!" Bright Moon stared hard at the warriors. "They are enemies."

"No, they were sent by Blue Darter, my friend." Jed hushed her. "They will have your respect, woman. These men are guests in my lodge."

Jed ushered the two Blackfoot to the table and placed hot cups of coffee in their cold hands. Sitting down at the table, across from the warriors, he poured himself a cup. He could see Bright Moon was still upset.

"Your squaw is Cheyenne." Tall Wind nodded at the woman. "She thinks we are your enemy."

"She is Cheyenne alright." Jed grinned proudly over at the woman. "Sure can't deny that."

"Cheyenne are bad enemies."

Jed studied the tired faces before him. "Tell me, brothers, why has Blue Darter sent you to me in the dead of winter?"

Tall Wind downed his coffee and set the cup down. "We have bad news for Crow Killer."

"We will eat, then you will speak of this." Jed knew it was bad manners to sit in council before offering a guest food.

Bright Moon wasn't happy about feeding her food to tribal enemies, the Blackfoot. Worse yet, the warriors she didn't trust were in her lodge. She knew it was bad manners to treat a guest with distrust, but these were Blackfoot warriors, the most savage of the tribes.

Finished with their meal, Tall Wind thanked Bright Moon as she poured them another cup of coffee, then turned to where Jed waited. The Blackfoot studied the inside of the cabin and watched as Jed moved about the room. Blue Darter had told them many times of the Arapaho Lance Bearer, the killer of his enemies and killer bears. Tall Wind knew Blue Darter had spoken the truth. The Crow Killer moved with the grace and agility of a mountain cat. Underneath the soft deerskin shirt, the muscles rippled even though they could not be seen. Tall Wind knew this Arapaho could become a truly dangerous enemy.

"My brother, Blue Darter, has sent us with a warning for Crow Killer." The warrior set his cup down. "A bad warning."

"He should have come himself." Jed studied the warrior. "You could have been killed before I knew who you were or what you wanted."

"We thought this too, but my brother said you would not kill, even an enemy, without giving him a chance to speak."

"This is so." Jed admitted. "At least I haven't so far."

"Blue Darter sends this word." Tall Wind continued. "Bear Claw, the eldest son of Lone Bull, brother of Deep Water and Standing Bull, will ride here against you."

"Bear Claw? Haven't heard of him before."

"No, you would not have." Tall Wind continued. "Now, this warrior has a new name."

"Blue Darter can't stop him?"

"My brother sent word to his village for him not to ride here, but this one seeks revenge against the demon that killed his father."

"Bear Claw." Jed uttered the name again. "A fitting name if he is to challenge me."

"He has earned the name." Swift Arrow spoke up. "He will come alone to this place."

"He will come alone, with no warriors to help him?"

"This is the word he sent to Blue Darter." Tall Wind sipped on his coffee. "He does not come to raid, only to kill you."

"Do not be fooled. This one is young as you are Crow Killer, and he too is a great warrior." Swift Arrow warned him. "He had a vision. He thinks he is invincible, and yes, he will come here alone to challenge you."

"A vision?" Jed shook his head. "So there is another warrior with a vision and a desire to kill me."

"One of our medicine men, a seer had this vision and foretold of his greatness." Tall Wind shrugged. "He has seen the power of Bear Claw in the smoke."

"Tell me of this vision."

"This warrior was named Squirrel as a child, then his father Lone Bull, just before you killed him, gave him the name Coyote Man." Tall Wind explained. "After Lone Bull and Deep Water were killed and Blue Darter returned as Chief of the Piegan Blackfoot, the warrior Coyote Man returned to his own village. With the death of his father, Lone Bull, he now is the hereditary chief of his people. After purifying his body in the sweat bath, the medicine man of his people, named Twisted Robe, held council with this warrior for two days. After the council, this one who had not eaten for many days disappeared into the mountains alone."

"Then what happened?" Jed was becoming curious.

"Coyote Man went off alone into the forest." Swift Arrow swallowed more coffee. "After several days, when he did not return, Twisted Robe sent warriors to track him."

"They find him?"

"Yes." Tall Wind nodded. "He entered a bear's lodge armed only with a knife."

"You mean a cave?"

"Yes, they found the warrior lying beneath the dead body of a huge bear. The bear was a giant grizzly. He had ripped Coyote Man into many shreds with his long claws."

"And?"

"Riders came to us with word that he killed the huge bear with only his knife, exactly as the seer predicted." Swift Arrow continued. "The medicine man called a huge council of elders and gave him the new name, Bear Claw."

"So, now he thinks he is invincible and can kill me?"

"Yes, the seer said he has taken your medicine from the dead bear, and now, he will be able to challenge and kill you, Crow Killer."

"Many have tried." Jed shook his head. All he wanted to do was live in peace, but now, a new menace may come against him. "When will he come?"

"They say his wounds are bad and he is still weak." Swift Arrow shrugged. "I do not know if this is true. I believe he will ride here soon."

Jed stood and walked toward the open hearth. "I do not wish to kill this one."

"Do not underestimate this one, Crow Killer. He is a mighty warrior and fears nothing." Tall Wind warned. "He wears the claw necklace of the one he killed."

"As were his cousin Small Mountain and Lone Bull his father." Jed sat back down. "Tell him not to come to this place. I do not wish to kill him."

"No, we will not do this." Tall Wind shook his head. "If Bear Claw knew we came here to warn you, he would seek us out and kill us."

"You fear this warrior, that much?" Jed looked at the men. "Then, why did you come?"

"Blue Darter asked us to do this thing. He is your friend."

"For this, I thank you. Do you really believe this warrior will come here to this place?"

"Yes, we believe this."

"Why would he come alone?"

"Crow Killer has not seen this one's eyes." Swift Arrow spoke. "We think he is possessed. He is evil and he hates you above all others."

"Is he a worse hater than Standing Bull?" Jed asked.

"We journeyed to his village before we came here, and yes, he is much more dangerous than Standing Bull." Tall Wind remembered his uncle Standing Bull.

"As we said, Bear Claw is still recovering from his wounds, but already he dresses like a bear." Swift Arrow seemed to shudder. "He wears the bear's teeth across his face and the claws around his neck."

"He wears bear skins across his body." Tall Wind added. "We believe he is touched by the spirit people."

"But, he did not appear that weak to us."

"And now, he is the chief of his village?" Jed questioned.

"Yes, his people are all in awe of him."

"Or fear." Swift Arrow hissed. "I would not like to meet this one in battle."

"When will you return to your village?"

"With your permission, we will let our horses rest two suns, then we will leave."

"You have it." Jed nodded. "You will rest here until the weather brightens."

"Thank you, Crow Killer." Swift Arrow stood up. "I will take care of our horses."

"Wait, tell me, would Bear Claw have left these as his warning to me?" Jed put the two amulets on the table before the warriors.

"Where did you get these?" Tall Wind stared at the teeth attached to the leather thongs.

"One was left at the Arapaho village of Slow Wolf." Jed pointed out the tooth. "The other, I found on the door of my lodge when we returned from the village."

"I have seen them, or some like them, hanging from Bear Claw's neck."

Swift Arrow shook his head. "How could this be? The warrior we saw as Bear Claw was far too weak to ride here for many suns yet."

"Maybe this Bear Claw plays games. Maybe, he was faking, trying to trick you into telling me he was weak."

"Why would he do such a thing?"

"It could have been to try to put a scare into me." Jed studied the amulets. "Or to make me think he was still hurt and couldn't come for me yet."

"Thank you, Bright Moon." Tall Wind placed his empty coffee cup on the hearth. "Heed our warnings, Crow Killer. I say this because you are Blue Darter's friend. There has never been a warrior like the Blackfoot Bear Claw."

"What would you have me do, Tall Wind?"

"Leave this place quickly."

"And go where?"

"Return to your white people's village." Tall Wind opened his hand. "There, he cannot challenge you to combat."

"You mean you think when he finds me, he will challenge me to a fight?" Jed shook his head. "Just this lone warrior and me?"

"This is what he said he will do, no matter where you are." Tall Wind explained. "This one truly believes he is a bear now."

Jed knew if Bear Claw came to the Arapaho village and challenged him, no warrior could interfere. It was against the Lance Bearer's code to ask or receive help from any other warrior as long as Bear Claw came alone.

"Tell my friend, Blue Darter, I will come to visit him sometime next summer."

"My brother would like that." Tall Wind nodded sadly. "I pray the great spirits will help you, Crow Killer, against this evil one."

"Thank you, Tall Wind."

"I have looked into this one's eyes. I think he is touched by the spirit people." Swift Arrow warned.

"Even some of his own warriors fear this one." Tall Wind added.

Two days later, Jed watched the two Blackfoot warriors disappear back up the mountain trail they had come down. He had presented them with presents, sending Blue Darter gunpowder and shot for his long rifles. Riding out with them to the mountain trail, Tall Wind told Jed he had no way of knowing when the warrior Bear Claw would come, but he was as sure as the rising sun, the warrior would come here soon to challenge Crow Killer. Again, he warned Jed not to take the threat lightly. Jed could tell the two warriors were afraid of Bear Claw, not because of his prowess in battle, but because the seer had predicted he could not be killed by mortal man.

"I fear for you, my husband." Bright Moon was holding her small rifle when he entered the cabin. "If this warrior comes here, I will kill him."

Jed laughed lightly. "We cannot worry about a big wind before it blows."

"We are so happy here in our valley." She stepped closer to him. "Why can't they leave us in peace?"

Jed remembered White Swan's earlier visions as the old medicine man sat before his small fire and cast the bones, then stared sadly into his fire. The old one had predicted Crow Killer would fight many battles against many enemies and he would never be killed by mortal man. The same vision this Blackfoot medicine man had predicted for Bear Claw. Jed smiled as he thought of White Swan and his visions. Perhaps, this Bear Claw was not mortal. At any rate, Jed knew one of the medicine men had to be wrong. If they met in combat, one would surely die, but which one?

"I will run my traps." Jed had the little mule and the piebald caught and bridled. "We will speak no more of this matter."

The coming of the cold times was Jed's fourth winter in the high country. It was still early, but already storm after storm had blown across the tall mountains, filling the passes with snow, blocking anyone from entering or leaving the valley. The valley was blanketed in snow, covering the cabin, barn, and the surrounding trees and slopes. Busy digging out his traps and tending to the horses, Jed had no time to worry about the threat of the Blackfoot warrior, Bear Claw. Even with the bad storms and cold, the small barn was already full of drying hides ready to be packed into bales, as they prepared for the trader's store come breakup. This season, the snow had been deep, but the fur bearers needed to eat so they hunted the heavily traveled trails where Jed had his traps set.

Despite the hard work, Jed and Bright Moon had time to enjoy the winter wonderland that engulfed them. Dragging a stiff elk hide up a smaller hill and using it to slide downhill at a fast pace until they ran out of momentum and stopped on the valley floor. Laughing, Bright Moon shoved Jed back into the deep snow as he tried to rise from the hide.

"One more time, my husband." She begged. "Let's ride the hide once more."

"Don't you ever tire?" Jed pulled her playfully against him and laughed.

"I am not tired, but I am not as old as the great Crow Killer."

"Oh, really."

Finally, after several trips up and down the slope, they returned to the cabin cold and exhausted, ready for a hot meal and coffee. Many days, as the winter deepened, they enjoyed passing the time, riding the elk hide or snowball fights. The valley was like a giant toy with so much work to do, yet they still made time for fun. Racing their lunging horses through the heavy snow, they would laugh when one would fall from their horse into the deep cushioning snow. In the summer months, they had the clear streams to swim and fish in, and there was always plenty of game to hunt. Yes, Jed smiled, the valley and his mountains were at times a winter wonderland and always a wonderful place to live. Now, he had a beautiful and loyal companion to share it all with him. Jed looked at her as they returned to the cabin, thinking why couldn't everything stay as it was now? All he wanted was Bright Moon, his warm cabin, and the peace he longed for.

Three weeks later, Bright Moon turned from her cooking as Jed entered the cabin. "The days grow longer, and soon the passes will clear. We must be watchful."

"Do you still worry about the Blackfoot?"

"I worry for you, my husband." Bright Moon placed food in front of him. "The Blackfoot are dogs, not to be trusted. I would kill them all."

"Not all of them." Jed remembered his friend Blue Darter. "They are the same as us, some good and some bad."

"I have never seen the good in a Blackfoot, any Blackfoot."

"Are all Cheyenne good?"

"They are not Blackfoot."

"You did not answer my question."

Bright Moon shrugged. "It was a bad question, my husband."

Many suns passed with the turning of the seasons, and the days lengthened and warmed. Finally, the day came when Jed brought in all his traps and started packing the bundles of furs to carry to Bridger. With the warmer days, the snow would be gone and the deep rivers would lower. Soon, as the spring waters run off, he would take Bright Moon and trade his pelts, then visit her brother, He Dog, and the Cheyenne people. Afterward, they would take the southern trail on their way home so they could visit the Arapaho village of Slow Wolf. It had been many days since Jed had last seen his adopted people, his friends, and the lands of the Arapaho. He wondered if the great Chief Slow Wolf still walked the land. On his last visit, Walking Horse had said the old one was becoming weaker.

He knew even though she was happy in her new home, Bright Moon looked forward to seeing her family. Now, with the additional worry of the Blackfoot, Bear Claw, she wanted to be near the safety of the Cheyenne village.

Jed was worried. When he had left the settlements, after the Shoshone fight, his stepfather, Ed Wilson, had promised to come to live in his valley. Lige Hatcher had promised as soon as he returned to Baxter Springs, he would guide him back into the deep mountains. Jed wasn't sure, but he figured as soon as the heavy runoff receded and left the mighty rivers passable, there was a possibility they could show up. His furs were prime, and soon he would have to travel to Bridger's Fort. However, after the Blackfoot warning, he was reluctant to leave the valley without warning Hatcher about Bear Claw.

Jed had no way of knowing when or even if the warrior would come to his valley as Tall Wind and Swift Arrow had warned. As bad as he needed to take his pelts to Bridger, he could not leave without warning

Hatcher and his stepfather, and let them walk into a trap. Jed only had the two warrior's words to go on. He had no way of knowing if the threats were real or just threats, but he didn't want to take any chances. He had lost too many of his friends to warriors from other tribes, and he did not want to lose anymore. Worse yet, he had no way of knowing when Lige would be coming to the valley. Jed was in a quandary, whether or not to start for Bridger's Fort. Still, he knew he couldn't let his furs spoil in the heat, so he had to go.

"We will leave soon, my husband?" Bright Moon was finishing the last of the heavy buffalo coats. "I will finish with this one tonight."

Jed ran his hand softly over the beautiful hair coat. "Your coats are sewn much better than mine."

"As they should be, my husband." Bright Moon held up the coat. "It is a woman's place to do this work, not a warrior's."

"No, Bright Moon, we work this valley together." Jed picked up a beaver plew. "Share and share alike."

"The fighting too?"

"No, fighting is for warriors, not women." Jed thought of Sally Ann, and there was no way he would place Bright Moon in any danger. "You do the cooking and I will do the fighting. Providing there is any fighting."

"I fear where Crow Killer walks, there will always be fighting."

"Not if I can avoid it." Jed looked off across the valley. "All I want is for us to live a peaceful life."

"Little Antelope says the old one, White Swan, looked into his medicine bones and told of the battles and hardships that were to come for Crow Killer."

"Just the talk of an old man."

"I know how much you thought of White Swan. To you, he was not just an old man." Bright Moon folded the coat. "The coat is finished."

"It will bring much at Bridger's." Jed nodded as he examined the coat. "It is a beautiful coat."

"When will we leave for the trader's post?"

"Soon." Jed thought about his stepfather and Hatcher. He still hoped to warn them of this new threat.

"I will prepare for our journey."

The days were warming, and Jed could no longer wait. Hatcher and Wilson hadn't come to the valley, but hopefully he would meet the old scout on the trail if he was bringing Ed Wilson to the mountains. He stared at the cabin as he finished lashing on his last bundle of furs. Everything of value had been hidden in a small cave above the cabin. He hoped Bear Claw wouldn't come to the valley while he was absent, but he had no way of knowing. In the high mountains, there was no way of guessing what the future would bring. Perhaps, if White Swan still lived, he could look into his smoke for the answer.

Jed took one last look around the cabin before latching and barring the cabin door, then lifted Bright Moon onto the spotted horse. Five loaded horses, including the little black mule stood tied, head to tail, waiting in a line, ready to head out. Bright Moon brought up the rear of the pack train, watching the horses closely until they got the freshness out of their systems. Most of the horses hadn't been used all winter, making them frisky in the briskness of the cool morning air.

Topping out on the flat ground, high above the cabin and valley floor, Jed took one final look down at his paradise while the horses regained their wind. The first steep pull up out of the valley, loaded with heavy bundles of furs, was hard on the animals that were soft from not being used. The other horses, except the piebald and Bright Moon's spotted horse, were all stout, hardy mustang type animals. Jed had no idea where the piebald came from, but he didn't show mustang blood. He was just too large and muscular of a horse. Most horses belonging to the tribes, like the Pawnee, were smaller in stature and showed their pedigree going back to their Spanish mustang ancestors. These little horses were stout and hardy, but they did not carry the muscle mass or strength of his piebald paint horse. Jed always wondered where Black Robe, the Nez Perce, had acquired the beautiful piebald. He had heard of the great Appaloosa of the Nez Perce people, so he knew where the spotted one got his breeding. All were in good flesh, thanks to the hay they had put up to keep them fed through the long winter months.

Motioning at Bright Moon, Jed nudged the piebald forward and led the string of horses across the saddleback that would lead to the downward trail. The rocky pass followed the mountain passes, down to the lower valleys and up again crossing another mountain range, then finally back down to the crossing at the Snake. This time he would not cross the river, but follow its banks upstream to Black Horse Crossing. Bridger's Trading Post was two days ride from the crossing. Jed remembered the last time he had crossed with the wounded warriors on their long ride home. Looking back at the small form of Bright Moon, he smiled, as she was enjoying the beautiful scenery. She was having fun, completely content traveling to Bridger's.

With every step of the piebald, Jed strained his eyes and ears, hoping to pick up the sound of approaching horses. Somewhere ahead, if he was lucky, he would come face-to-face with Hatcher and his stepdad. Jed was worried, since both Lige Hatcher and Ed Wilson were getting older. Hatcher was an experienced Indian fighter, who had made his way in the high country for many years, learning from Bridger, Beckworth, and many others. He was a good scout and trapper. Perhaps, if he knew of the Blackfoot and was ready for trouble, he and his rifle just might be a match for the young warrior. But, not knowing anything about the one Tall Wind and Swift Arrow had described, Jed worried he wouldn't be ready.

Tall Wind had said the warrior was only coming to these mountains for the Arapaho, Crow Killer. Perhaps, he wouldn't attack the two white men if he did find them on the trail. It was a thought, but Jed could not be sure. Somewhere ahead, he hoped to meet up with the two men. The thought struck him as the piebald navigated the rocky trail that he could cross the Snake and pick up the immigrant road, then veer east on to Bridger's Post. The trail would be almost two days longer turning north, but it would give him the chance to find Hatcher if he was on the trail headed for his valley.

Reining in the horses at sundown, Jed unloaded the packsaddles and tethered the tired animals on the lush spring mountain grass that grew abundantly in the small valley they were crossing.

"Is a fire safe, my husband?" Bright Moon asked as she started gathering small sticks to start a fire.

"Yes, we will put it out before full darkness comes." Jed studied the trail closely as the sun began slowly setting in the west.

"You worry about Rolling Thunder?" Bright Moon pulled flint and steel from a pouch around her small waist. "I see your eyes follow the trail all day."

"I wish I knew if Rolling Thunder had left for the valley yet or if he was still coming this spring."

"Your father Wilson said he would come." Bright Moon struck the steel, igniting a small handful of squaw wood and dead crumpled up grass. "Will he not do as he says?"

"He said he would come to this place if Rolling Thunder would bring him here." Jed shrugged. "I don't even know if Hatcher is in these parts."

"Rolling Thunder spoke of staying in the white village until the snows melt."

"Yes, then he would meet up with Chalk Briggs train and lead them west."

"Would he not bring his friend to our lodge first, then take the southern trail to Arapaho Country?"

"He would do this, but he should have been to the cabin many suns ago." Jed shook his head.

"You worry too much, my husband." Bright Moon added larger sticks to the fire. "They will be safe."

"You know this huh?"

She smiled and looked over at him. "I know this. No lone Blackfoot can harm Rolling Thunder, no matter what his name is."

"I wish I had your confidence, Bright Moon."

"I have never seen my husband, the great Crow Killer, worry so much." Bright Moon made a face. "Worry will make you an old man quick."

"I guess I do worry too much." Jed checked his rifle and reclined against the fur packs. "I've seen too many of my friends die."

"I know my husband does not worry for himself." Bright Moon handed him a plate of meat and dried bread. "I will always be here, husband. Do not worry for me or Rolling Thunder."

Jed thanked her for the food and again turned his eyes down the trail. Tomorrow, when they reach the Snake, he would turn north, if he hadn't come upon Hatcher. Bright Moon scolded him for worrying too much, but this was different, something troubled him. In the past, all he had was himself to look out for or worry about. Now, he had a wife, but he couldn't help think of his first wife. Sally Ann had died in his arms and there was nothing he could do to save her. Her death had been so senseless. Now, he had Bright Moon to worry about and he vowed nothing would happen to her.

At daybreak, the animals were packed again and ready for the trail leading to the Snake. The horses were fresh and eager to travel in the early morning as the high country was always cooler than the lower valley. The air was thinner on the mountains, but so pure one could clearly smell the pine, cedar, and even the smell of the rushing streams that crossed their path. The horses were stepping out at a good pace as they traveled down the rocky trail.

Jed had traveled this trail many times, and he remembered most of the landmarks as he passed. He thought of the terrible ordeal as he packed the wounded High Horn and One Bull over this same trail. Then his mind turned to the hurried race with Ellie in their rush to return to his cabin to save Walking Horse.

His mind returned to the horses as their hard hooves echoed in places against the mountain wall as they walked along the rocky path. By nightfall, they would be on the bank of the Snake River where he intended to turn north, if Hatcher hadn't been sighted. The north trail was his only choice, and a couple days did not matter if he could make sure Hatcher and Wilson were safe.

Almost at noon, Bright Moon swung lightly to the ground as her spotted horse came even with the piebald. Digging into a par fleche bag, she pulled out pieces of jerky and dried biscuits.

"We are almost to the river." Jed bit into the meat. "We will cross in the morning."

"The water will still be cold."

Jed thought of the raft he had hidden on the riverbank and smiled. "You, my lady, will cross high and dry."

"Has the river lost all its water?"

"It hasn't as far as I know." Jed smiled. "Come, we go."

Nearing the Snake crossing, Jed reined in the piebald suddenly and studied the sandy banks of the slow moving river. Again, the little mule warned him with her long ears pointing straight at the tall cane growing along the riverbank. She had sensed something ahead at the river's edge.

Slipping from his horse, Jed handed Bright Moon the rein and moved forward cautiously.

The river was quiet, and not a sound came from the tall trees along its banks on either side. No birds sang and no squirrels barked out their warnings. Only the ripples of the moving water as it crossed over snags and tree trunks in its path, made any sound in passing. Jed could sense something was wrong. Something lurked about the canebrakes covering the river's sandy banks. He moved forward silently, studying every foot of the riverbank before moving closer. Suddenly, he spotted what he sought, a dark hand moved as it reached out from the tall cane, pulling at the ground, trying to crawl toward him.

Searching the riverbank, Jed moved ahead cautiously and stood over the bloody body. Turning the warrior over, Jed studied the face closely. Hearing something in the tall timber above him, Jed lunged sideways behind a tree as a rifle went off. Feeling the bullet clip his sleeve, Jed turned his full attention to where the rifle had sounded from. From the other side of the Snake, another rifle roared, causing a howl to come from above him. Whirling as he heard a noise behind him, Jed stepped sideways as the wounded man was flung almost onto him as he fell. Bright Moon stood only a few feet away, holding her smoking rifle.

Several minutes passed as they crouched listening, then up river, Jed heard the sound of three horses racing away to the east. Looking to where Bright Moon was reloading her rifle, he held up his hand as she started toward him.

"Stay there, Bright Moon, hide yourself." Jed knelt behind a small tree. "There may be more across the river."

"The one on the ground was just pretending to be hurt, my husband." Bright Moon pointed her rifle at the dead man.

Jed could see the long skinning knife that had dropped from the man's hand. "I believe you, thanks."

"Someone moves over there." Bright Moon nodded across the river.

"Don't shoot, Jedidiah. It's me."

"Lige." Jed was shocked to see Hatcher walk from the cover of the trees and hold up his hand.

"It's me. Now, Jed, don't let Bright Moon go shooting over this way." Hatcher yelled across the river again.

"I'll keep her under control." Jed looked back at Bright Moon. "Come on across."

Jed and Bright Moon watched as the scout swam his horse across the Snake. The river's early winter snow melt off had receded, lowering the water to its normal level. Still, the horse was swimming against the current, soaking the man.

"We better get a fire going." Jed looked at Bright Moon. "Old Lige is sure gonna be cold when he comes out of there."

"I will get wood."

"You okay?" Jed looked down at the body.

"That one is a Ree. Maybe, worse Indian than Blackfoot." Bright Moon shrugged. "Him make good Indian now."

Jed smiled. "Do you like anybody?"

"Bright Moon like Cheyenne, Arapaho, and maybe a few whites."

Shaking his head, Jed turned to where the horses waited. "I'll get rid of your friend here, then unsaddle. Do you want the scalp of this one?"

Making a face at Jed, Bright Moon started gathering firewood. Minutes passed, then Hatcher came splashing out of the river and shook hands with Jed. The scout was soaked, wet up to his shoulders as he looked down at the dead body.

"Ree." Hatcher bent over the warrior. "I saw him lunge at you, but got busy watching the others. I saw your woman do for him with her rifle."

"She did for a fact. Bright Moon done for him."

"Bright Moon, and she's just a child." Hatcher looked over at the young woman and shook his head. "But, I wouldn't want that child shooting at me."

"I am not a child, Rolling Thunder." Bright Moon frowned as they talked about her. "I am eighteen summers, a woman."

Hatcher laughed. "Reckon she told me."

"Bright Moon is not your normal woman, Lige." Jed smiled. "She's got more spunk than most."

"Shucks boy, she's Cheyenne." Hatcher pulled a dry blanket from his pack. "Possibly the meanest tribe there is."

"I wouldn't let Bright Moon hear you say that, Lige." Jed whispered. "That's if you want supper tonight.

Hatcher sat wrapped in trade blankets with his buckskins propped drying over the cook fire. Jed moved away, leaving the warmth of the fire, disappearing into the trees that had concealed the men who had waited in ambush across the river. He found the small ledge where the men had waited, observing the trail below. Up high on the ledge, Jed could plainly see Lige and Bright Moon sitting around the fire below. Jed knew he and Bright Moon had been lucky today as the ambushers had a clear and close field of fire from up there. They owed their lives to Hatcher.

"What did you find, Jed?" Hatcher looked up as Jed returned to the fire.

"You hit someone up there." Jed took the coffee from Bright Moon. "There's quite a bit of blood and signs of three men."

"Then I was lucky with my shot." Hatcher nodded. "I never could get a clean look at them."

"Warm yourself with this." Bright Moon handed Jed his sleeping robe.

"Well Lige, you saved our necks today." Jed took the robe from Bright Moon. "Thank you."

"I was just lucky." Hatcher looked out across the river. "I was sitting over there thinking about whether I wanted to swim the river right then or wait until daybreak. That's when I spotted four men riding down the riverbank on this side of the river. Three white men and an Indian."

"They must have ridden here from Bridger's Post." Jed added. "They probably crossed the Snake at Black Horse Crossing."

Hatcher laughed as he looked across the fire. "I watched as the Indian nicked his horse's neck and rubbed blood all over his face, then laid himself down in the cane breaks. The others wiped out their tracks and retreated up into the trees on that ledge."

"Pretty smart of them. If you hadn't been waiting, they had us dead for sure." Jed admitted.

"They had a good ambush set for you alright." Hatcher nodded. "It was pure luck, I just happened to be sitting over there when they rode up."

"Yes, it was lucky for us." Jed agreed. "They were probably watching us come down the mountain from up on the ledge."

"Appears they were."

"I was hoping to meet you on the trail before we reached here." Jed looked over at Bright Moon.

"I got a late start for your valley." Hatcher poured himself another cup of coffee. "I meant to bring your pa and Ellie with me two weeks ago."

"What happened?"

"Your pa's horse fell with him, broke his leg. Ellie stayed behind to help him recover while I rode on up here to tell you what was happening."

"Broke his leg, is he alright?" Jed asked.

"He's got a good doctor."

"I thank you for seeing after him."

"You should thank Ellie." Hatcher looked over at the bales of furs. "Looks like you had a good catch this winter."

"Yes, we had real good luck this year." Jed looked at Bright Moon. "We both worked hard over the cold times."

"She's a dandy." Hatcher smiled. "Known her since she and Little Antelope were children. Both of them gals are workers."

"I know one thing, if she hadn't killed that Ree when she did, he'd of opened me up like a ripe melon for sure."

"The others took off to the east toward Bridger's."

"You figure they'll be waiting ahead at the crossing?"

"I figure."

Jed shook his head. "They'll have to make a try at us when we reach Black Horse Crossing."

"How's that?"

"Bridger don't put up with any shenanigans close to the post."

"Maybe." Hatcher poked at the fire. "But those rules are for Injuns. We're dealing with white men."

"Does that make a difference to Bridger?"

"No, not to Gabe, but white men can trade anywhere." Hatcher patted one of the bales of hides. "But, they sure can't get plews like you got here anywhere."

"I reckon you're right there."

"Come morning, one of us will have to ride point until we reach Bridger's."

"Reckon that'll be me." Jed reached for the plate of food Bright Moon handed him. "Thought you would be heading back to Baxter Springs?"

"Nope, was headed to visit Walking Horse, Little Antelope, and to check on Slow Wolf, but I reckon that can wait a spell now."

"Are you scouting for Chalk this season?"

"Told him I would. Gave him my word on it."

"He should reach Bridger in late spring."

"Should, or early summer at the latest." Hatcher nodded. "Tell me, Jed, why were you looking for us so hard?"

Jed looked across the fire. "I may have more trouble coming at me, Lige. I sure didn't want you and Pa to get caught in the middle, without knowing about it."

"What kind of trouble?"

"You ever heard of a Blackfoot warrior named Bear Claw?"

Hatcher looked up fast as the name was pronounced. "Yep, forgot all about him with all this business going on. I was gonna tell you about him when I got here."

"You know him?"

"Not personally, just what Squirrel Tooth the Nez Perce told me." Hatcher nodded. "He was in Bate Baker's store couple weeks back."

"What did he tell you?"

"Just that he'd heard about a Blackfoot named Bear Claw killing a huge grizzly with only a knife. Claims this warrior has broken your bear medicine."

"That's it?"

"Yep, that's all he said. Why?"

"Two Blackfoot warriors were sent to my cabin by Blue Darter to warn me that this Bear Claw was coming to challenge me."

"Squirrel Tooth didn't say anything about that."

"He wouldn't." Jed shook his head. "He would like this Blackfoot to kill me."

"Yeah, I've heard how you shamed him."

"Squirrel Tooth shamed himself." Jed shrugged.

"Indians are superstitious, not cowards." Hatcher smiled. "I couldn't blame him for being a feared of you."

"I reckon you're right." Jed nodded thoughtfully. "I've never met an Indian that was a coward."

"What else?"

"They said the grizzly mauled Bear Claw real bad. Figured it would take him a while to mend up and regain his strength."

"After he healed up, he would come after you?" Hatcher pulled on his coffee. "Is that the way of it?"

"That's about it." Jed replied. "I didn't want you and Pa to run into him without being warned."

"Well, I do appreciate you thinking of us." The old scout nodded. "This one sounds like a bad one for sure."

Jed looked into the fire. "I don't believe he's hurt as bad as Blue Darter or Squirrel Tooth think."

"How's that, Jed?"

Quickly telling of the two amulets that had been left in the Arapaho village and on his cabin door, Jed knew it had to be the work of the Blackfoot. Also, the warrior couldn't have left both amulets so far apart if he was hurt as bad as he had been told.

"Well, there's one thing for sure, somebody's lying." Hatcher pointed out. "Well, I'll be trailing along with you come sunup."

"Company is always appreciated, thank you." Jed smiled and knew Hatcher worried about him and Bright Moon.

CHAPTER 9

Daylight found Hatcher and Bright Moon riding east with the pack-horses loaded up and lined out between them. Hatcher smiled as he noticed the hard look on Bright Moon's face and the rifle lying across her horse's withers. He could tell her look was genuine and she wasn't bluffing. Hatcher had lived with the Cheyenne and Arapaho for many years. He knew the women could be just as hard as the warriors when they were protecting their young or family.

"I expect you got that spotted horse from Red Hawk." Hatcher pointed at the young horse and laughed. "You steal him?"

Bright Moon frowned. "He was a gift."

Hatcher had to tease her. "I never knew a Crow to give a horse like that away, especially to a Cheyenne."

"Red Hawk is a friend of my husband."

"That he is, madam, but he is still a Crow."

Jed left an hour earlier to scout the trail ahead for any unwanted visitors or another ambush. The trail along the Snake River was heavily covered in trees and brush. Jed could plainly see the tracks of the ones that tried to ambush them in the soft sandy dirt of the trail. The horses were being pushed hard as their tracks were spread wide as they ran. The river wasn't crossable at this part of the trail as the mountain across the river was impassable. Jed knew the men would not try to hide their tracks if they couldn't cross over. Although, as heavy as the foliage was, one of the men could drop off anywhere along the river to try another ambush.

Drops of blood showed on the trail for over two miles and then disappeared. Jed figured the man somehow got the bleeding stopped or he had bled out and died. He knew the man must be dead since no sign showed of anyone dismounting to bandage the wound. The blood had been steady so Hatcher's shot had hit the man pretty hard. Jed kept the piebald close to the timber so he could duck out of sight, in case someone showed themselves or tried another shot. Yesterday, he had been very fortunate since the first shot had been close enough to put daylight in his shirt, but hadn't struck his hide.

Late afternoon found him at Black Horse Crossing looking out across the river. He remembered another time when he had crossed here, when Ellie was with him on her way to help Walking Horse. It seemed like years ago, but actually it was only two seasons. Dismounting, Jed examined the tracks of three horses as they moved across the sandy river's edge and into the water. All the tracks were cut deep into the sand showing the horses were carrying riders, whether alive or dead he couldn't tell which. He knew it would be easy to dump a man into the water when they reached midstream and let the body float downstream with the current.

It was late in the day, and they had been traveling steady all day without resting. Tonight, Jed would set up camp on this side of the river and cross over, come morning. At least the river would be between them and the ones that tried to ambush them back at the crossing on the Snake. Jed ground tied the horse and looked around for logs to make a makeshift raft to ferry the pelts across. This was the first time he had brought his furs across Black Horse Crossing. The first couple years, he had crossed at the first crossing and took the trail leading to Baxter Springs. The raft he had cached at the Baxter Springs Crossing on the Snake was of no use to him here at Black Horse Crossing. Here the river wasn't too deep, but still deep enough to swim the horses and get his prime furs wet.

Two hours later, as Jed drug suitable logs close to the river with his horse, Hatcher and Bright Moon came riding up. With a smile and a wave, she reached for him as he helped her from her horse. Relieved to see her, Jed hugged the girl to him. He knew she was safe with Hatcher, but still, he worried. He had thought Sally Ann was safe behind the board walls, but he had been wrong. He had no choice but to bring Bright Moon with him to Bridger, and he would do everything he could to keep her safe. Once they reached Bridger, he would send for He Dog and his warriors, then nobody would dare attack them.

Leading Hatcher to the riverbank, he showed the old scout the fresh tracks. "I believe they're all carrying men."

"Peers like they are, the prints are all deep."

Looking across the flowing water, Jed shook his head. "They could be waiting over there when we try to cross, just like before."

"I'll cross first and take a look around, then you can pull Bright Moon and the plews across." Hatcher studied the far bank.

The land had changed upstream along the river as they traveled east. Now, trees covered both sides of the river with heavy cane and thickets. Hatcher pointed at the bleached horse skull peering at them from high on his perch in a tree.

"He's watching over us from his bird's-eye perch." Hatcher laughed. "At least I hope he is."

"You want me to cross first?" Jed questioned.

"No, the paint is the strongest swimmer. He'll be needed to tow the raft across and he'll respond better with you riding him."

"Okay."

"Make sure Bright Moon keeps down low behind the bales."

"I'll keep her safe."

Hatcher rubbed his whiskered chin. "I don't think they'll attack the raft in midstream."

"Why not?"

"They don't want to get them furs wet, no more than we do." Hatcher squinted at the crossing. "No, sir, they might take me, but they'll not risk them furs by shooting you."

"Let's eat. We'll worry about the crossing come morning."

Hatcher sat puffing on his pipe beside the fire Bright Moon had built out of sight of the river. As soon as supper was finished, Jed again disappeared back out into the dark.

"He's just out there looking around, lass." Hatcher assured her.

"Tell me, Rolling Thunder, why is there no peace for him?" Bright Moon clutched the small rifle and stared off into the dark. "He only wants peace, but his enemies keep riding against him."

"It was foretold that this would be his destiny." Hatcher shrugged. "White Swan looked into the smoke and foretold this."

"So that is the way it will always be?"

"Are you sorry you married him, child?"

The dark eyes flashed fire across the space between them. "I am the luckiest woman in the Cheyenne and Arapaho Nation to have one such as Crow Killer. No, I am not sorry, I am proud."

"I didn't figure you would be."

"My sister, Medicine Thunder, was a fool not to marry him."

"No, Bright Moon. My daughter may be half Arapaho, but she was raised in the white civilization. Her white upbringing made her too soft for our way of life. I'm afraid she is not like us."

"You mean she does not like killing?"

"She is a healer and doesn't understand the killing of an enemy."

"If I had not killed that one yesterday, my husband would surely have been killed." Bright Moon stared across the fire. "Sometimes, one has no choice."

"I understand that and Jed understands."

"But, Medicine Thunder does not?"

Hatcher smiled sadly. "No, I'm afraid my daughter doesn't."

"Would she have let the Ree kill my husband?"

"I don't know the answer to that." Hatcher shook his head. "I surely don't."

Two hours later, Jed slipped silently back into the firelight and sat down. "A hot cup of that coffee would sure go down good, Bright Moon."

"You have been across the river." She could see his wet hair and the wet spots on his shirt.

"Find anything, Jed?"

"Nothing. It's as quiet over there as a dead possum." Jed blew on his steaming coffee. "I believe they've pulled out."

"Then, we'll still cross as we planned."

"Sounds good to me."

Birds called in the early morning quietness of the Snake as Jed finished loading and rechecking his log raft. Each log was laced tight with rawhide strips and securely anchored.

Bright Moon snuggled down, out of sight, behind the bales of furs.

Making sure the girl was not looking, Hatcher quickly shed his buckskins and mounted his sorrel horse. Jed grinned as the old scout hit swimming water and had to slide off into the cold water. His Hawken rifle was securely tied into the horse's mane to keep it high and dry.

"His skin is so white, where the sun does not reach." Bright Moon giggled. "Why is your skin not white?"

"Bright Moon, I'm gonna paddle your bottom." Jed shook his head. "Or Rolling Thunder will if I tell him you looked."

"You know I have brothers."

"I doubt he'll care if you have brothers."

"You would not tell, would you, my husband?"

Jed laughed as he watched Hatcher wade from the river and disappear into the trees. A few minutes later, after scouting out the trail, the old trapper reappeared fully clothed, motioning Jed to cross.

Pushing the raft into the water, Jed quickly swung on the piebald and started across the Snake. As the big horse hit swimming water with the rawhide rope looped around his neck, Jed slid from his back. Stroking powerfully beside the swimming horse, he tried to help the horse tug the heavy raft across the smooth water.

Bright Moon peeked her head above the furs and laughed. "Your skin is dark, my husband."

Shaking his finger at the girl, Jed kicked hard with his legs, looking back occasionally to make sure the raft was keeping upright and balanced. Feeling the gravel beneath his feet, Jed slid back on the wet horse and drug the raft up on the bank. Quickly redressing, Jed looked to where Bright Moon was stepping from the raft.

Hatcher pointed north, up the small trail. "Their tracks showed they are still headed away from us."

"Good, then let's get packed and hit the trail." Jed pulled on his moccasins. "Bright Moon, do you have anything you want to tell Rolling Thunder?"

Beneath her dark face, she blushed. "Only that I'm glad he made it across safely."

"Well, thank you for worrying, Bright Moon." Hatcher smiled.

Only a deep frown of warning came from the girl, telling Jed he had said enough. Laughing, he turned then cinched up the pack animals.

"Come look at these tracks, Jed." Hatcher motioned to three sets of horse tracks leaving the water.

Kneeling, Jed examined the tracks closely. "One is not carrying any weight."

"Exactly." Hatcher nodded. "The one I shot must have gone under and they dumped him in the river."

"They must be pretty green to think I would fall for that trick." Jed shook his head. "I wonder who you killed."

"These two don't know I'm here with you, Jed. Probably young whites thinking they could pick up some easy money by stealing your plews."

"I reckon they got some bad information somewhere."

Hatcher studied the trail leading off to the north. "We're still a day's ride away from Bridger's so we best stay alert."

Helping Bright Moon repack the horses, Jed helped her on her horse. "I'll take the lead. Give me an hour's head start."

"We'll just poke along for a while, and that will give you time to get ahead of us."

Watching Jed ride away, Hatcher looked over at Bright Moon and her prize horse. "I hope that thing you're riding can last until we get to Bridger's."

Bright Moon smiled pleasantly, knowing Rolling Thunder just teased her. "One day, we will have a race, your horse against my spotted one."

"No, thank you." Hatcher knew he wouldn't stand a chance against the appaloosa in a race.

Riding all day to the east toward Bridger's, Jed's senses and nerves had been taut as he checked the trail they followed. The three sets of horse tracks were still visible and heading east, but nothing else showed anywhere on the trail. With dark coming on, Jed slid from the piebald beside a small stream and started gathering wood for a fire.

Setting a slow pace so Jed could scout out the trail leading to Bridger's, it was almost dark when Hatcher and Bright Moon finally caught up to Jed at their night camp. Hearing the noise the packhorses made as they moved closer, Jed waved and walked out to meet Hatcher and Bright Moon.

"How was your day, Jed?"

"Nothing, Lige. Quiet all the way here."

"What about the tracks?"

Jed pointed east. "They're still headed to Bridger's like they don't have a care in the world."

"They will when I get there." Hatcher swore. "You take a good look at those tracks out here on this sandy ground."

"Why?"

"One of their horses has a loose shoe which has twisted almost off."

"I didn't notice." Jed studied the track. "You're right."

"We'll be there in the early morning. Then, we'll take a look around for that horse."

"And if you find him?"

"He tried to kill you, didn't he?" Hatcher's face turned red as he studied the track. "Maybe, I'll repay the compliment."

Jed looked over to where Bright Moon was fixing their supper. "You know they may not be our only problem when we get to Bridger's."

"What are you saying?"

"The Arickaree, they could cause trouble when they see me."

"Yeah, I forgot about what you told me about the raid."

"We'll just have to keep our eyes open."

The night passed quietly as the hobbled horses grazed through the night and were fresh and ready to push on to Bridger's Post with the coming of day. Jed noticed the old post hadn't changed any as the three riders and loaded horses trailed under the uprights of the gates. Reining in at the trader's store, Jed slid from the piebald and helped Bright Moon down. The head clerk at Bridger's, informed of the great Crow

Killer's appearance at the post and knowing of the wealth of furs he brought, hurried out to greet Jed.

"It is good to see you again, sir." The clerk did not know whether to call him Jedidiah or Crow Killer. "I hope you are well."

"We are well, Mister Caldwell."

"How is old Gabe doing, Alex?" Hatcher asked as he dismounted.

"He is doing well, Lige." Caldwell smiled, eyeing the bundles of furs closely. "And you, sir?"

"As well as an old man can do, I expect." Hatcher laughed.

"Are you here to sell your plews, sir?" Caldwell looked at Jed.

"That's why we're here alright."

Motioning for his hired help to unload the horses, Caldwell invited Jed, Hatcher, and Bright Moon into the store's kitchen for breakfast. Warning the clerks not to open the bundles until his return, Jed followed Caldwell into the store.

"I will open them when I return." Jed looked hard at the clerks.

"As you wish, sir."

"We have business at the livery, Alex." Hatcher nodded at the clerk. "We'll return shortly."

"You do not want breakfast?"

Hatcher shook his head. "We'll have to decline. We've already ate."

"I will leave my wife here to rest within your walls." Jed looked over at Bright Moon. "Will you see that she is fed and rested?"

"I know, Bright Moon. She is the sister of Yellow Dog, the Cheyenne." Caldwell smiled at the girl. "She will be made most comfortable, I assure you, sir."

"Good." Jed started to follow Hatcher from the store toward the blacksmith shop, then stopped to face the clerk. "You do know Yellow Dog is dead?"

"No, I had not heard he was dead." Caldwell looked across at Jed. "But, you know Injuns do not speak of their dead."

"Have any Cheyenne been here to trade recently?"

"No, I doubt the Cheyenne would come here after the raid on the Ree village." Caldwell looked at Jed. "Did Yellow Dog's death have something to do with the raid?"

"So the Arickaree know the Cheyenne were responsible for the raid?"

Caldwell nodded. "They know, but they think another tribe south of here helped them."

"You mean the Arapaho?"

"No, it was another tribe they described to Bridger."

Jed turned away. Apparently, the Ree did not hold the Arapaho responsible for the raid. He could not understand the Arickaree's mistake. Their tracks had led straight back to the valley of the Crow Killer. The travois' tracks cutting deep into the trail would not be difficult for the Ree to track. He just couldn't see how they could blame the Paiute for the raid.

Hatcher turned his head slightly and whispered at Jed. "Did you see the Arickaree warriors when we rode in?"

"Yes, I seen them alright."

"I doubt they'll try anything here at the post, but keep on your toes."

"I don't think we've anything to worry about, Lige." Jed shook his head. "They don't know anything about the Arapaho being involved in the raid."

"They don't?

"No, leastways that's what Caldwell said."

Seeing the two men walking toward his stable, McGraw greeted them in front of his shop. "It is good to see you, my friends, welcome."

Shaking hands with the old blacksmith, all three retreated inside the shop, out of sight of the Indians gathered around the stockade.

"It is good to see you as well." Jed greeted McGraw.

"Did you bring the little mule this trip?"

Jed grinned. McGraw hadn't forgotten the black mule. "She's here, but I couldn't do without her."

"Still not for trade, I reckon?" McGraw laughed loudly. "I'm willing to make a better offer this year."

Hatcher didn't know what the men were talking about. One mule wasn't something to haggle over. Either she was for sale or she wasn't. Interrupting the friendly bantering, Hatcher looked about the shop. "We're looking for a horse with a crooked left front shoe."

"There are lots of horses here at Bridger's, Lige."

"Not with a crooked front shoe." Hatcher knew the horse still carried the loose shoe as they had tracked it to the gates of Bridger's Post. Whoever rode the horse was stupid and didn't even know the shoe was crooked. Any blind man could track the animal with his eyes closed. Nevertheless, very few horses were carrying shoes there anyway as Indian ponies were never shod.

McGraw hesitated, employed as the post blacksmith, he didn't want to get involved with any quarrels. Bridger didn't tolerate any fighting within the walls of the post. He remembered, last year when Jed had killed two whites and several Rees just outside the post. Bridger hadn't been happy with the incident, cussing and staying in a black mood for days after he had returned. He was even more disgusted that Jed had left the post before his return.

"Gabe won't be happy that you've returned." McGraw clucked his tongue, as he looked over at Jed.

"His head clerk Caldwell was."

"Is Gabe at the post?" Hatcher looked around the grounds.

"He is, or at least he was last night." McGraw looked about. "Ain't laid eyes on him since I turned in, around dark."

"And the horse with the crooked shoe?" Jed questioned. "You laid eyes on him?"

"Nope, ain't seen hide nor hair of him neither."

"You sure?" Hatcher looked hard at the old man.

McGraw spit a stream of tobacco. "I'm sure."

Turning, Hatcher walked from the shop without looking back. "I believe you just made an enemy, Mister McGraw."

"I know, but I have to live here." The blacksmith explained. "And Bridger don't put up with idle talk."

"The man that rides that horse tried to kill me and my woman."

"She's not hurt, I hope."

"Is the horse here?"

"He's here, so you be real careful if you go snooping around, boy." McGraw warned. "The man that rides him is a rough one."

Jed smiled. "Why, Mister McGraw, I'm always careful."

"So I've heard." The old man spit again. "This time, you be extra careful, you hear?"

Catching up to Hatcher as he entered the trader's store, Jed grabbed the old scout by the arm. "McGraw says he's here."

"He say who rode the horse?"

"No."

"Let's get your furs sold, then we'll question Bridger himself."

"You think that's wise, Lige?" Jed looked about the store. "Any man in the place could be the rider of the horse. I don't know if you noticed, but we're kinda outnumbered here."

"Like I said, let's get your furs sold, then we'll see."

Jed cut the rawhide bindings from the bundles of furs, then turned to where Caldwell waited with his figuring pencil. Every plew in the bundles were prime. Every fur the trader picked up and blew on were soft and shiny.

"These are the best furs I have seen this year." Caldwell nodded over at Hatcher. "Just magnificent."

"Then, they should bring top dollar, Alex?" Hatcher questioned him.

"They will." Caldwell confirmed.

"Then again, maybe they won't." The voice came from a well-dressed figure standing in the doorway. "I assume this is the legendary Crow Killer?"

"Who's asking?" Hatcher interrupted Caldwell, who started to answer.

"The name is Jean Leblew."

"French Canadian?"

"My father was French. My mother... she died when I was born." The tall man shrugged his shoulders.

"Leblew." Hatcher nodded slightly. "I've heard of a man by that name. He was a knife fighter in New Orleans."

"Monsieur, I am just a simple storekeeper."

Hatcher looked at the heavily muscled man. "Leblew was one of the deadliest fighters in Louisiana. He had killed several men in duels."

"Mon ami, I think you have mistaken me for someone else." Leblew smiled innocently. "Now, who is this gentleman?"

"His name is Jedidiah Bracket." Hatcher admitted. "Or Crow Killer if you want."

Leblew stepped further into the room. "Aha, a man of exceptional talent for killing, I hear."

"I have killed." Jed looked closely at the well-dressed Frenchman.

"You know Bridger's laws about intertribal fighting anywhere near this post, and yet you ignored them." Leblew smiled coldly at Jed.

"Hard to ignore a man coming at you with a loaded rifle, Leblew." Hatcher interjected.

"Let this young gentleman answer for himself, Monsieur Hatcher."

"Since when is it any business of yours what I do here?"

"Since I have bought into this little fort and gone partners with Mister Bridger." Leblew stepped closer to the counter.

"Then Bridger won't be buying my furs?"

"No!"

Motioning for Bright Moon to stand behind him, Jed started retying the bundles of furs. His mind on the furs, he ignored Leblew as he stepped closer to the counter where the pelts lay.

Caldwell placed his hand on the retied bundles. "Mister Bracket, do not be hasty. I will buy your pelts. This is my store too."

"Sell your pelts half breed, then leave this post and do not return." The voice was harsher this time as the Frenchman spoke. "Or we will take up your part in the killings last spring."

Jed turned on Leblew, his dark eyes blazing with rage. "My pelts are no longer for sale to you, mister."

The store clerk was amazed as Jed gathered up a bundle of furs under each arm. Caldwell knew each bundle weighed close to one hundred pounds and the man hefted them like they were feathers.

"Wait, Jed, let me find Gabe and straighten this out." Hatcher placed his hand on Jed's arm. "Give me a chance, please."

Jed set the bundles back on the counter, as Hatcher propelled Caldwell outside, out of earshot. The younger clerk moved up to the counter and reopened the bundles. With another clerk's help, they counted and separated the hides. Jed watched as the two men stood in awe as they made their count.

"The pelts are still not for sale yet." Jed watched the men. "We will wait for Bridger."

Leblew walked around Jed and looked at Bright Moon, then smiled. "Perhaps, we can do business, Mister Crow Killer."

"What do you propose?"

"I will buy your pelts, but I will need a little something extra thrown in to boot."

Bright Moon could tell the words were about her and quickly started tying the bundles back together again. Taking up a bundle, she turned for the door when Leblew knocked it from her grasp. Springing forward, Jed knocked the Frenchman backward into the counter. One of the clerks raced from the store yelling for Bridger and Caldwell.

Leblew held out his hand and smiled. "We will fight, Indian, but as gentlemen not heathens."

Jed touched Bright Moon's face to make sure she was okay. "You are not a gentlemen, Frenchman, and yes, we are going to fight."

"Splendid, sir, splendid." The Frenchman touched the hilt of a foot long rapier he carried on his side. "This will be my weapon."

"And this will be mine." Jed touched the war axe stuck in his belt.

"The axe is a formidable weapon." Leblew nodded. "Is it the one you killed my brother with?"

"Brother?" Jed questioned. "What brother?"

"Jock Bedeaux. You killed him two years ago in Turner's Hole." Leblew hardened. "Curasenay the Delaware witnessed you killing him without giving him a chance."

"He got what he deserved." Jed argued. "I killed him alright. He was a murderer and thief."

"These things are true, monsieur." Leblew smiled coldly. "But, he was still my brother."

Caldwell followed by Hatcher and Bridger entered the room. "I will buy your pelts, Mister Bracket."

"That will have to wait, Caldwell. Monsieur Crow Killer and I have business outside, providing this half breed is not a coward." Leblew laughed.

"What's this all about?" Bridger stepped forward.

"An easy question, monsieur." Leblew smiled cruelly at the old mountain man. "This one killed my brother and his partner as well, you know. Now, sir, I demand satisfaction."

"Satisfaction?" Bridger looked over at Leblew. "You know I do not allow fighting here."

"I have challenged this half breed mongrel, let us say, to a contest of wills." Leblew laughed, then looked over at Bright Moon. "What you allow and do not allow means nothing to me. When I am finished with him, I will come back for his woman."

Jed lunged forward as the Frenchman moved behind the counter. Jed was livid with rage and fury as he glared at the man. "You want to fight Frenchman? Quit the talking and let's fight."

"Do not be crude, monsieur." Leblew smiled. "I would rather you call it a duel or shall we say a contest of wills. Either way, you are a dead half breed."

"Don't count on it." Jed pointed at the door. "Let's get to it."

"I am dissolving our business relations as of now." Leblew bowed slightly at Bridger. "I am sorry, I did enjoy my time here."

"That's fine with me." The old mountain man frowned. "Caldwell will pay you what you've got coming. I believe you've overstayed your welcome."

"I stayed long enough for this gentleman to come here for my convenience."

Somehow, the Indians inside the stockade already knew about the upcoming fight between Leblew and Crow Killer. Wagers were already being made as the warriors moved closer to the trading store. Hatcher was stunned when he followed Jed and Leblew from the store to find at least fifty warriors from different tribes assembled around the store.

"I will not allow fighting within these walls." Bridger called for several of his men.

Hatcher knew after the insult to Bright Moon, there was no way he could stop Jed from fighting the Frenchman. "Let them fight in the stables, Gabe. Leastways it'll be fair."

Bridger looked over at the two men and nodded. He always forbade any kind of fighting in the post grounds or anywhere near it. Fighting was bad for the trade business. He could not let so many tribes gathered inside and outside the post keep their tribal feuds aflame. The simplest way to prevent unwanted warring on one another was to withhold trading privileges to any tribe breaking the truce. Nevertheless, for this one time, he knew it would be best to honor Hatcher's request.

Nodding, Bridger pointed toward the open ground around the stable. "There, if they want to kill each other, let them spill their blood there."

Bright Moon pulled Jed by the arm as she followed him from the room. "No, my husband, he did not hurt me. It is not worth it."

"Would you have me let him insult you, wife?" Jed looked down at her. "I should let a man slap you?"

"It would be better than you fighting."

"A man has his honor." Jed shook his head. "You know better, Bright Moon. I cannot allow this man to insult my wife and still look you in the eyes."

"I know, my husband. I just worry for you." Bright Moon looked up into Jed's eyes. "Be careful."

Hatcher stopped Jed on the porch. "If this is the Leblew from New Orleans and I believe it may be, he's a real killer with that pigsticker of his."

"Any suggestions, Lige?"

"Just be faster than he is." Hatcher looked at the broad back of the Frenchman. "Kill him quick, if you can."

"I'll try my best."

"Jed, he's not the sweet gentleman he seems." Hatcher added. "He is deadly and very dangerous."

"I believe you, old friend."

The gathered warriors encircled the two opponents as the men waited twenty feet apart in front of the stables. The Frenchman and Jed stripped to their waists. Hatcher hadn't been wrong, Leblew was indeed a magnificent figure as he stood in front of the crowd. Long, well-muscled arms and a deep chest foretold the power he carried in his broad shoulders. Jed could see why he had the qualities to be such a deadly knife fighter.

Bridger had refused to watch the fight so Caldwell had been elected to start the battle. Jed held his war axe, while Leblew waved his sharp-pointed dagger. The blade was made for both stabbing and slashing, so either way it touched his opponent, the blade would cut deep. Just as Caldwell started to drop his arm, the crowd was pushed aside as several mounted warriors rode into the circle.

Jed was shocked as he glanced over at the warriors. He was surprised to see the Cheyenne and Arapaho warriors as they sat their horses, staring at the circled watchers. He Dog, Crazy Cat, Walking Horse, and Big Owl, along with several other warriors sat their horses stoically glaring at the crowd. Walking Horse and He Dog slid from their horses and walked to where Jed waited.

"What is wrong here, my brother?" Walking Horse could see there was fixing to be a fight.

"What are you doing here?"

"We came to trade, and meet you and my sister."

"You know the Arickaree blame the Cheyenne for the raid on their village."

He Dog laughed as he looked around at the gathered warriors. "There are not enough Ree here to fight a real warrior."

"It is good to see you." Jed looked to where Leblew waited. "To answer your question, this one insulted my wife and your sister."

"And you will kill him."

"He says I killed his brother and challenged me to fight." Jed picked up a handful of sand and rubbed his hands. "Wouldn't you kill him, my brother?"

"Half breed, are you gonna fight or talk all day?" Leblew fidgeted.

"Let us help you kill him."

He Dog raised his war axe and whirled on the crowd, causing the gathered warriors to pull back from the menace of the Cheyenne.

"These dogs of men will not fight." The Cheyenne jeered at the warriors. "We will help you kill this one."

"No, I cannot let you do this!" Jed exclaimed. "It is my wife, he insulted."

"Be careful, my brother." Walking Horse looked across at Leblew and laughed. "Kill him quick so we can go have a good meal of buffalo tongue."

He Dog whispered to Jed. "This one looks powerful, my brother."

"That's the story going around alright." Jed smiled. "If this doesn't work out well, you have my permission to kill him."

"You have our word, this one will not leave this place alive."

Jed could hear the excited chatter of the gathered warriors as many were scared of the newly arrived Cheyenne and Arapaho warriors. Still, none would miss the fight they knew was fixing to take place. They all had heard of Crow Killer, but few knew of Leblew. They had only heard the words the Delaware warrior, Curasenay, had been spreading as he slunk around Bridger's Post. Every warrior among the Ree knew the Delaware had scouted, stole, and killed with Leblew's brother along the northern border and Canada for several years.

Caldwell called the two men together, then quickly retreated as he dropped his arm. Leblew was faster than he looked as he rushed forward and ripped with his long knife. A loud shout went up as the crowd thought Leblew had drawn first blood in the fight. Jed had sensed the Frenchman's charge, moving faster he slipped sideways out of the rapier's reach. Again, Leblew leapt forward, and again, Jed avoided the reaching knife. Circling, Leblew toyed with the sharp knife flicking it out, touching Jed's war axe lightly, then slipping back. Both men had already learned to respect each other's speed.

Once again, Leblew charged expecting Jed to retreat. This time, Jed leapt upward landing a hard kick to Leblew's rib cage, knocking the attacking man sideways. Jed knew he had damaged the Frenchman's ribs. With the power of the kick, he knew the man had to be hurt. Jed hadn't come away unscathed, a thin trickle of blood showed along the leg that had kicked out. Taking a long breath, Leblew circled to Jed's left, away from the powerful leg kick.

The heated fight was taking its toll on the combatants as both men were bleeding and limping. Leblew was breathing in short breaths as his damaged ribs made it difficult to pull air into his lungs. Hatcher had been right, the Frenchman was a dangerous adversary. The man was fast and accurate with the long blade. Several cuts appeared along Jed's arms and rib cage. The war axe had been effective in keeping Leblew at bay, but still, the speed of the man's knife arm was like a striking rattlesnake. Jed had never fought a man with Leblew's speed. For his part, Jed's deadly leg kicks had done most of the damage in the fight.

Blood seeped from the man's mouth, and Jed figured a broken rib had penetrated Leblew's lung. Several times during the fight, Jed had landed a wicked kick to the Frenchman's rib cage. Each blow had cost him as the keen blade of the Frenchman had found its mark. Along with his arms, both of Jed's legs were covered in blood. The cuts were not deep, but the blood still flowed freely causing concern among Jed's followers.

He Dog nudged Walking Horse. "He will kill this white man."

"Perhaps, they both will die." Walking Horse shook his head concerned.

"I will be proud of my brother if he dies." He Dog spoke up.

"He will not die, he is Crow Killer." Crazy Cat raised his arm. "Any warrior that can kill the bears cannot be killed by a mortal man."

"White Swan seen in his smoke that Crow Killer cannot be killed by a mortal man." Walking Horse spoke out as the fighter's separated. "Let us hope this is so."

Jed moved around Leblew, keeping the exhausted Frenchman circling, giving him no time to regain his breath. The sharp knife had lowered, the man was losing his great strength. Suddenly, Jed lunged in with a vicious downstroke of the war axe, breaking the knife arm of the Frenchman. A roar went up from the watchers as they knew the battle was finished. Leblew switched hands with the knife cutting a deep slash in Jed's stomach. Retreating, Jed shook his head. The man might be his enemy, but he was a brave fighting man.

Jed knew his loss of blood was weakening him. He had to end the fight quickly and kill this enemy. Feinting a rush, Jed whirled to his left and buried the axe in Leblew's back. Sinking to his knees, the Frenchman looked up at Jed.

"You are as they said, a great warrior." The dark head sagged. "Finish it, mon ami."

Hearing the words, Jed lost all hate for the Frenchman. Still, the heavy war axe descended upon the lowered head almost spitting the Frenchman's skull in two pieces. Pulling his own skinning knife, Jed ripped the dark hair from the man's bloody head. Waving the hair for all to see, Jed tossed the scalp to the ground. Turning weakly, Jed smiled as he looked at Little Antelope standing beside Bright Moon.

Rushing to Jed's side, He Dog and Walking Horse ushered him into the trader's store and laid him down. "Bring your white medicine doctor quickly."

Caldwell stood white faced before the Cheyenne. "We have only a horse doctor here at Bridger."

"Bring him, quickly!" He Dog threatened. "Crow Killer must not die."

Rushing to Jed's side, Bright Moon started stemming the flow of blood from his many wounds. Most of Jed's wounds were superficial, but the stomach wound was laid wide open and would need sewing up.

"Be strong, my husband. Do not die." Bright Moon pleaded.

"I will not die. I have too much to live for." Jed smiled up at her.

"You were brave, my warrior." Little Antelope held a towel across Jed's stomach trying to stem the flow of blood. "You are a great warrior."

"I don't feel great right now, Little Antelope."

Later in the day, Hatcher traded Jed's furs to Caldwell, and then purchased the supplies Jed would need to see him through the coming year. Loading the Pawnee horses and the black mule, Hatcher stood out on the trader's porch with Caldwell as the blacksmith McGraw walked up.

"Old Doc Gruber says he will make it just fine." McGraw looked at Hatcher.

"He's gonna be sore for a while, but thank your horse doctor for us. He patched him up with no leaks."

McGraw cleared his throat. "You were asking about a crooked shoe."

"So?"

"Leblew was the man who rode that horse." McGraw was embarrassed. "I should have told you before."

"Yes, you should have." Hatcher frowned at the man. "Who rode in with him?"

McGraw looked about the enclosure. "Right there's your man."

"Who are you looking at?"

"The Delaware who rode with Leblew. His name is Curasenay." McGraw spit. "He's a bad one, a killer."

"Delaware?" Hatcher had somehow mistaken Curasenay for a white man. "These eyes of mine must be getting old. I coulda swore he was the third white man."

"What'd they do?" Caldwell followed Hatcher's eyes.

"There were four of them, two whites and I reckon two Injuns." Hatcher spit. "They tried their best to kill Jed and Bright Moon."

"You said there were four."

"That's right, Mister Caldwell. Now, there's only one left." Hatcher looked at the bag of coins and supplies. "Just make sure my horses aren't touched. I'll be right back."

Turning from the trader's store, Hatcher located the Delaware and started in an about route to intercept the warrior. McGraw and Caldwell watched as Hatcher calmly walked up to the Delaware and stuck his skinning knife into the warrior's stomach. Curasenay never knew what happened to him as he slipped slowly to the ground dead. Every warrior seeing the killing, quickly deserted the post without looking back. Wiping his knife on the dead man's shirt, Hatcher spit on the body and walked back to where McGraw waited.

"I reckon that'll do for him." Hatcher looked at both men. "You see who killed him, McGraw?"

"We never seen a thing." The blacksmith shook his head. "Did we, Alex?"

"No, not a thing."

CHAPTER 10

Both warriors and women closed in on Jed's travois as it passed slowly through the gates, flanked by Cheyenne and Arapaho warriors. Many wanted to touch the great Crow Killer or touch his litter. Many were his enemies, but all had great respect for the man who had the reputation of being a demon. All who saw him defeat Leblew, now believed he was invincible. The name, Crow Killer, became a famous name around the campfires of the tribes. Today, as Jed passed beneath the gates at Bridger, he was quickly becoming a living legend.

Bridger stood watching with McGraw as the travois disappeared through the gates. "He's quite a man. We sure could have used him back in the shining times."

"His time is still shining, Gabe." The blacksmith nodded. "Will you trade with him next year?"

"Why not? Leblew started the fight and paid for it with his life."

Walking up, Caldwell laughed. "You just remember that next year, Gabe. We sure don't want to lose those pelts he brings in."

"In the shining times, mine were better." Bridger bragged. "Much better."

"I doubt that." Caldwell shook his head. "They don't get any better than his plews."

"Yes, they're good furs." Bridger admitted. "But, we brought in more."

"Yes, that you did." Caldwell laughed again. "Tell me, Mister Bridger, how many trappers were in your hunting brigade?"

For three weeks, Bright Moon fussed over Jed as he was recovering from his many wounds. Hatcher wanted to go after Ellie, but Jed told him no. He only wanted Bright Moon and Little Antelope to tend to his wounds. Walking Horse had sent his warriors home to their village as he and Little Antelope remained in He Dog's village while Jed recovered. The early spring weather turned warmer, and Bright Moon had spread Jed's soft blankets beside the cook fire as he requested.

"You should not stay out in the night air, my husband."

"You will lay beside me to keep me warm." Jed was recovering, still weak from loss of blood, but he was recovering.

Snuggling beside Jed, completely exhausted, Bright Moon quickly fell into a deep sleep. Unable to sleep, Jed lay looking into the fire, deep in thought. His body still ached from the many stitches the horse doctor had used and a slight fever was still with him.

Sensing somebody close by, Jed rolled his head slightly to the side. "Who are you?"

"You are Crow Killer, the bear demon?" The voice was kept low, so not to wake up Bright Moon.

"I am Crow Killer."

The huge warrior stepped closer. The glow of the small fire revealed his disfigured face, painted all black. "I am Bear Claw."

"I have heard of Bear Claw."

"I have killed the grizzly and have taken your power over the bear." The voice was calm, no brag. "Now, I will kill you."

"Kill me then, there isn't much I can do about it now."

The voice hissed. "I am Bear Claw. I would not kill a helpless warrior."

"Then why are you here?"

"I came here to find you." The warrior spoke again. "I watched while you fought with the one at Bridger's. He was a great fighter, a worthy foe."

"He cut me up some at that."

"I feared he would kill you and deny me that honor."

"Is it such an honor to kill?"

"I will return when you have healed." The warrior pointed at Jed. "Then, you and I will see who has the greatest power."

"How are Bear Claw's wounds?"

"I am strong again." The black face nodded. "I was not hurt nearly as bad as everyone thought. Still, I am sore, but I am strong."

Jed looked at the dim face. "Tell me, Bear Claw, how did you find me here?"

"Your friends, Tall Wind and Straight Arrow, told me you traveled to Bridger to sell your furs." Bear Claw seemed to laugh. "I rode hard coming to the crossing of the river."

"Did you kill Tall Wind and Swift Arrow?"

"No, they still live." The warrior shrugged. "I do not make war on my own people."

Jed nodded in relief. "Help me to my feet and we will finish this here and now."

"No, Crow Killer. When you die, I want every warrior to know you were strong, not weak like a child." Bear Claw looked down at Bright Moon. "She will know and the Arapaho will know who is the greatest of warriors."

"I will be strong again soon." Jed waited for a response, but none were forthcoming. "I wouldn't count me out too quick, if I were you."

Bear Claw started to leave, then turned. "The Delaware dog that set the trap for you back on the river was with the one you killed at the fort. He is dead now too."

"Leblew was the one who tried to ambush us?" Jed realized why McGraw wouldn't say who owned the horse with the crooked shoe.

"Him, two others, and the Delaware."

"Were you there?"

"Yes, I rode the trail from Bridger, looking for you." Bear Claw added. "I watched the cowards as they set their ambush."

"Did you kill Curasenay?" Jed asked.

"No, your friend Rolling Thunder did for him at the white man's fort."

"Hatcher?" Jed couldn't believe it. "How did he know?"

"I do not know how he knew about this one, but he killed the Delaware." Bear Claw shrugged. "Your friend, Rolling Thunder, is a mighty warrior."

Jed thought Bright Moon was sleeping through the whole confrontation, but seconds after Bear Claw left, she rose up, uncocking her rifle that lay hidden beneath the blanket. Jed laughed quietly as she looked off into the dark.

"You were not asleep, my wife?"

"You think me a child, husband?"

"No, you are not a child, Bright Moon." Jed smiled. "Tell me, why didn't you shoot him?"

"Bear Claw is our enemy, but he is an honorable warrior." Bright Moon leaned on her elbow and looked down at Jed. "I would not kill an enemy who held your life in their hands and let you live, not even a Blackfoot."

"You are a good woman."

"No, my husband, I am Cheyenne." Bright Moon smiled. "I no longer worry about Bear Claw or any other. The great Crow Killer cannot be killed by mortal man."

"I can't huh?" Jed was curious.

"The one at the fort proved that." Bright Moon snuggled next to Jed and fell asleep.

"You are Cheyenne, little one." Jed looked down into her calm face. "That you are."

Jed thought back to his conversation with Bear Claw. He had underestimated the Blackfoot. Bear Claw was a dangerous enemy. Any enemy warrior, who had the stealth and courage to enter a Cheyenne village alone to find his enemy, deserved the greatest respect. In the future, he would have to be more alert than he had ever been. Even more alert than when the bears stalked him. Bear Claw may seem human, but Jed wondered. He shook his head, had the superstitions of White Swan finally rubbed off on him?

As Jed recuperated, Hatcher stayed close by, visiting with Walking Horse and He Dog. After hearing of Bear Claw coming into the village, none of the three would let Jed out of their sight. Slowly, he recovered as he limped around the village with Bright Moon. Finally, Hatcher could no longer delay his departure. Chalk Briggs sent word by an Indian runner that he would arrive at Bridger in a short week. Hatcher feared for Jed in his condition, but he had given his word to Briggs to lead his train west. He had to choose between a man that was almost a son to him, and his word he had given Briggs.

"Go, Rolling Thunder. We will protect Crow Killer with our lives." Walking Horse assured the old scout. "I will take him back to our village and he will be safe there."

"What about sending warriors to kill this Bear Claw?"

"Never, this we cannot do. To kill this one would shame Crow Killer and the Arapaho." He Dog flattened his hands.

Walking Horse nodded in agreement. "Bear Claw acted honorably when he came into our village."

"You know he will be waiting out there somewhere to challenge him."

"We know this. We will protect our brother until he has healed and strong enough to defend himself against this enemy."

"Rolling Thunder knows Crow Killer is invincible." Walking Horse looked across at Hatcher. "When he is strong again, he will kill this warrior himself. Look how easily he killed the great Frenchman."

"I hope you're right." Hatcher nodded sadly. "Because I fear, until Bear Claw is killed, he will stalk your brother through these mountains."

"Just as the grizzlies stalked him, and they are all dead." Crazy Cat laughed.

"Bright Moon told us what he spoke of." He Dog added. "He will challenge Crow Killer to battle, but he will not attack without warning."

"Can you be sure of this?"

Walking Horse nodded. "Bear Claw wants power. He wants Crow Killer's power and he wants all to know he has defeated Crow Killer in battle."

"It will be a fair fight." He Dog predicted. "This warrior will have it no other way."

"Does he have a chance against this Blackfoot?"

"We have never seen this one." He Dog shrugged. "But, we have seen Crow Killer, the greatest of warriors."

"Yes, but he has been grievously wounded so many times." Hatcher shook his head. "He carries many wounds on his body."

"White Swan foretold he would lead a dangerous life, but he would never die by man's hand."

"I hope you both are right." Hatcher rose from the ground and shook hands with the two warriors.

"Do not worry for our brother. We will protect him with our lives." Walking Horse assured him.

Waving, as he led his packhorse from the village, Hatcher reined in beside Jed and Bright Moon where they stood waiting at the edge of the village. Clearly, Jed was still weak from his wounds.

"How long will you remain with the Cheyenne?" Hatcher dismounted and stood before Jed.

"Only a few more days, then we will ride with Walking Horse and Little Antelope to Arapaho Country. We will remain there with our people until I am strong again."

"Be careful, Jed."

"Do not worry, Rolling Thunder. I will protect my husband." Bright Moon smiled over at Hatcher. "My brother, He Dog, will send warriors with us on our journey."

"Good, I'll see you in the fall." Hatcher shook hands with Jed. "Tell Slow Wolf, I will come to see him then."

"We never did have our horse race." Bright Moon smiled.

"This fall, young lady."

Jed and Bright Moon watched as Hatcher disappeared on the trail heading for Bridger's. The old scout turned and waved one last time as he dropped from their sight.

"He is a good friend." Bright Moon nodded.

"Yes, he is like a father to me."

Walking Horse led the small group of women and warriors as they crossed over the mountainous trails, leading west to the Arapaho lands. Cheyenne scouts were in front and back of the main body as the riders made their way through the timbered country. Jed rode the piebald in the center of the procession. His strength was returning, but he was still sore from where Leblew's blade had bit into his stomach. He knew he had been fortunate to survive the fight. The Frenchman had been a dangerous enemy and a formidable foe.

"How are you feeling, my warrior?" Little Antelope moved up beside Jed.

"I am fine."

"I will have my husband stop and let you rest, if you want me to."

"No." Jed shook his head. "I am getting stronger. We can continue."

Little Antelope looked to where Bright Moon was talking with her brother, He Dog, then asked Jed. "Does my sister make you happy?"

"Yes, she makes me very happy."

"I am glad. You deserve a good woman." The small woman smiled over at Jed.

"And I deserve a good friend." Jed looked deep into her eyes.

"Crow Killer has many friends among the people."

"I mean a special friend, a very special friend."

"I will always be here for you, my warrior, always." Little Antelope glanced quickly at Jed. "It can be no other way, Jed."

"Thank you, little one."

"It seems so long ago when we first met."

"Yes, it does." Jed agreed. "But, it actually wasn't that long."

Little Antelope dropped her head. "It has been for me, Jed."

"I know."

Kicking her horse, Little Antelope moved up beside Bright Moon and He Dog. Jed could hear them laughing, but not what they were saying. He studied both sisters, so much alike and yet so different. He could sense the feelings Little Antelope held for him, feelings that could not be turned off. Jed felt the same, but she was Walking Horse's wife and now he had Bright Moon for his wife. Neither would dishonor themselves, so they were destined to be just friends, and only friends.

Three days later, Walking Horse led the small caravan across the last stream and entered the Arapaho village. Crossing the water, Crazy Cat held up his hand and said his goodbyes to Walking Horse and Jed.

"We will meet again, my friends." Crazy Cat looked over at Little Antelope and nodded. Jed knew the warrior still had strong feelings for the comely woman that had not been forgotten. "Now, we must return to our people."

"Thank you, my friend, for seeing us safely home." Jed shook hands with the warrior and watched as the Cheyenne warriors, led by Crazy Cat, disappeared from sight.

The thundering bedlam of women screaming, dogs barking, and warriors racing their horses back and forth alongside the returning people caused pandemonium in the village. The noise was deafening, until Slow Wolf raised his feathered lance, putting a halt to the jubilant cries. Easing to the ground, in front of the aging Slow Wolf, Jed took the hand of the old one.

"It is good you have returned, my son."

"It is good to be home, my chief."

Slow Wolf could see Jed was sore, as the pain in his face was starkly visible. Ushering Jed and Walking Horse into his lodge, the chief motioned them to seats around his small fire. "Crow Killer has been in a fight?"

Walking Horse quickly recounted the fight at Bridger's and the meeting with Bear Claw. "It was a bad fight, my chief."

"All fights are bad." Slow Wolf added. "Again, as White Swan has foreseen, he has survived."

Walking Horse shrugged. "The Frenchman was a dangerous foe, but now, we have this Blackfoot stalking Crow Killer right into our own camps."

"This one comes for revenge?"

Jed nodded. "Yes."

"Blackfoot lands are so far from here." Slow Wolf looked into the fire. "I wish White Swan was here to interpret the meaning of this warrior."

"The meaning is simple, my chief." Walking Horse spoke slowly. "This one comes to kill my brother. We will not allow this."

"And if he openly challenges Crow Killer to fight?"

"Then I will take up his challenge." Walking Horse spoke.

Slow Wolf shook his head. "This cannot be, as long as Crow Killer lives. You cannot dishonor him by taking up his fight."

"Slow Wolf can see for himself, my brother is still weak."

"From what you say, I do not think this Bear Claw will return until Crow Killer has time to recover from his wounds."

"I hope Slow Wolf is correct. It will be many suns before my brother is strong enough to take on this warrior's challenge." Walking Horse shook his head.

"Go now, let Crow Killer rest." Slow Wolf dismissed them. As Jed exited the lodge, Slow Wolf took Walking Horse by the arm. "Send for Red Hawk."

"Red Hawk?"

"I will not lose Crow Killer while he is defenseless."

Walking Horse looked at the old chief curiously. "But, you said we could not interfere as it would dishonor the Arapaho."

"Red Hawk is Crow, not Arapaho."

Walking Horse smiled. "So he is, so he is."

Bright Moon studied the deep slash across Jed's stomach as she applied the creams the horse doctor at Bridger had given her. The horsehair stitches would have to be removed soon.

Looking down into his eyes, she smiled. "Your wounds are mostly all healed, my husband."

"The soreness is still there." Jed remembered the doctor telling him the wound was deep and would take several months for it to completely heal inside and out.

"Yes, but the rest of your smaller wounds are all closed. There will be many small scars."

"Just add them to the rest." Jed smiled.

Bright Moon frowned. "I will get Little Antelope to help me with the stitches."

"Tomorrow, will be soon enough." Jed stretched out his hand. "Come to bed now, little one."

Walking Horse waited near the river with Big Owl as several Crow warriors descended to the water's edge on the other side. Hand signaling to the Crows for permission to cross, the two Arapaho kicked their horses into the deep river.

Six young Crow warriors sat their horses watching as the two Arapaho swam the river and exited dripping wet from the water. None moved, only sat stoically watching as the warriors remounted their horses. Walking Horse took in the Crows, and all were young warriors. The traditional forelocks, stiffened with bear grease, stood up proudly on each man's forehead. None were painted for war, but each was armed with trade rifles and bows.

"What do the Arapaho wish here?"

"Chief Slow Wolf has sent us here."

"Speak. Tell us, why do you cross the river into our lands?"

Walking Horse bristled, as the voice of the young Crow made his temper flare. Seeing the color come up in Walking Horse's face, Big Owl raised his hand.

"Our chief wishes for Red Hawk to come to our village."

"Why does he wish this thing?"

"Tell Red Hawk, his brother Crow Killer needs his help."

The young warrior glared across at the two Arapaho. Every Crow warrior knew of Red Hawk's friendship with Crow Killer, and some resented it. Still, it was not wise to make either Red Hawk or his father, Chief Plenty Coups, mad.

"Tell us, why does Crow Killer not come here himself?"

"Crow Killer is hurt and cannot travel." Walking Horse spoke. "Tell me, Crow, what is your name?"

The dark eyes of the young warrior stared unblinking at Walking Horse. His mind seemed to be thinking, but still, he made no move. "I am Long Leaper, son of Wild Wind, the warrior Crow Killer killed."

"We are sorry for your loss, Long Leaper."

"I do not ask for your sorrow, but I will do as you ask. I will tell Red Hawk." The warrior nodded. "He is in the south, raiding the Comanche for their horses."

"When will he return?"

"We do not know this."

"We thank you, Long Leaper." Walking Horse nodded at the youngster. "We'll be expecting him."

"You go now, to your side of the river." The Crow pointed his rifle. "We will send runners to Plenty Coups for his advice in this."

"I will have someone there to meet Red Hawk when he comes." Walking Horse pointed across the river.

"It may take several sleeps for our young chief to return."

"Thank you, Long Leaper." Walking Horse nodded. "There will be a watcher across the river."

"The young Crow warrior is not so friendly." Big Owl muttered as he turned his horse back to the river. "I feel he wants to take my pretty hair."

"No, I doubt that one would be." Walking Horse replied. "I doubt you would be too friendly either if you were asked to help the man that killed your father."

After swimming across the broad river, Walking Horse looked back over his shoulder in time to see the Crow warriors disappear over the high bluff.

"Come, Big Owl. We will ride to our village and tell Slow Wolf what has happened."

"Why does our chief wish to speak with Red Hawk?" Big Owl asked.

"Our old chief is cunning, my friend." Walking Horse smiled to himself. "If Red Hawk, a Crow, kills the Blackfoot, no one can blame the Arapaho for cowardice."

"This is a good plan." The big warrior chuckled. "A very good plan."

"I hope so."

"You know, Red Hawk may want many horses to do this thing."

"No, he will do it for Crow Killer."

"It would be worth many horses." Big Owl shrugged.

Walking Horse checked the powder in his Hawken and smiled. "Yes, providing Red Hawk kills the demon Blackfoot."

"Red Hawk is a mighty warrior." Big Owl laughed. "For a lowly Crow."

"He is that, for a fact. He and his warriors almost finished me last year." Walking Horse remembered his battle with the Crow. "But, I fear this Blackfoot leads a charmed life."

The smoke holes, of the Arapaho village, filled the clear air with smoke that drifted into the tall trees bordering the village. As their horses splashed across the small stream that ran the length of the village, people looked at them with pride. The stream ran pure and clear, meandering across the valley, providing fresh water for the people and their livestock. Walking Horse's chest swelled with pride to see the village, knowing the Arapaho people were safe and protected. He knew his beautiful wife, Little Antelope, would be waiting near their lodge and would be with him soon.

Sliding from his horse, Walking Horse thanked Big Owl for riding with him, then turned the tired sorrel horse loose. Entering the lodge of Slow Wolf, he greeted the aging chief, taking a seat before his fire.

"You have seen Red Hawk, my son?" Slow Wolf leaned forward weakly.

"The Crows have sent runners to bring him to the river."

"Good." Slow Wolf nodded his grey head.

"What has happened, my chief?" Walking Horse could see the worry in Slow Wolf's face. "What is wrong?"

"The Blackfoot has been here while you were gone."

"Here in the village, when?"

"Yes, in the village." Slow Wolf replied. "Perhaps last night or early this morning before the sun showed itself."

"How does my chief know this thing?"

Tossing a bear's tooth into the warrior's lap, Slow Wolf hissed. "He left this tied to the lodge of Crow Killer and Bright Moon during the dark time."

"What?" Walking Horse was confused as he looked at the amulet. "For what reason would the Blackfoot come here?"

"The piebald horse of Crow Killer is missing from the herd." The chief shook his head. "We believe the Blackfoot took the horse and left this amulet for us to find. He wants us to know who is responsible for the theft."

"Does my brother know of this?" Walking Horse studied the bear's tooth.

"No, his woman, Bright Moon, has kept him close to his lodge all day." Slow Wolf looked across the fire at Walking Horse. "We were afraid if he knew, he would try to go after the thief."

"You are right." Walking Horse agreed. "He thinks much of that horse, but he is still too weak to ride."

"He grows stronger and he walks every day to the horse herd to check on the animal." Slow Wolf poked at the small fire absently. "I do not know how Bright Moon kept him from learning the horse is missing."

Walking Horse stood up. "I will have to tell him. I cannot keep a thing like this from him."

"Yes, but I fear he will not listen to words of caution now."

"As I do."

Walking Horse stood outside the lodge hesitating to enter. He did not want to keep secrets from his friend. He knew he had to tell of the theft of the horse. What words should he say to Crow Killer to keep him from following the horse thief? Crow killer was a brave and savage fighter, but not now in his condition, he was still too weak. He needed to wait and regain his strength before challenging the Blackfoot. Looking about the busy village, he was about to lift the lodge flap when Bright Moon came through the opening.

"My brother Walking Horse has returned." Bright Moon smiled. "Will Red Hawk come here?"

"You knew I went after Red Hawk?"

"Yes, Slow Wolf told me when he found out the horse was gone."

"He will come soon, I hope." The warrior tried to look through the doorway. "Is Crow Killer awake?"

"Yes, but he has made me promise to walk with him today to see the black and white one before we retire to our sleeping robes."

"Then, he does not know about the horse being gone?" Walking Horse whispered.

Bright Moon dropped her eyes. "A wife should never lie to her husband, but I could not tell him."

"You did right, Bright Moon."

"I hope he will not hate me."

Walking Horse smiled down at the woman. "He will not hate you. I know my brother's feelings for you. He likes the piebald, but he loves you, my sister."

"Will you tell him now?"

"Yes." The warrior nodded sadly. "Has your sister been here?"

"Little Antelope just left. We removed the horsehair from my husband's stomach."

"How is his wound?"

"It has closed and my husband grows stronger every day."

Walking Horse looked one more time around the village before entering the lodge of Crow Killer.

The night was already coming on, bringing the colder air with it. It had been a pretty day outside. The birds called to one another, and the squirrels barked and scolded down from their lofty perches, high in the oak trees. The younger boys of the village stalked the tree dwellers with their blunt arrows and sometimes scored a direct hit with no effect. A squirrel had a compact body and could fall from a thirty foot limb without being harmed. No small arrow with a blunt point could harm them. Now, the early spring air was becoming colder as night neared and the lodge was inviting.

Forcing himself to go forward, Walking Horse ducked through the flap into the warm lodge.

"My brother, sit down." Jed greeted the warrior. "Bright Moon was just fixing to walk with me to go see the piebald."

"It is getting dark and the air cools." Walking Horse shook his head. "Stay here, I must speak with you."

Jed laughed. "It is but a short walk."

"Yes, a short walk." Walking Horse nodded. "But, maybe you should wait until the sun brings its warmth again."

Jed could sense something bothered the Arapaho. "What is wrong? Speak, my brother."

Walking Horse did not know how to break the bad news because he knew how much value Crow Killer placed on the horse. The piebald had become bonded with Crow Killer. In battle, they were like one, and no warrior or horse could stand against them. To lose one such as him was a bad omen and a bad loss.

"There is no good way to tell you this, my brother." Walking Horse shrugged.

"Speak, Walking Horse." Jed knew both Bright Moon and Little Antelope were just there, so it couldn't be one of them. "Tell me, what is wrong?"

"The piebald is gone from the herd."

"Gone? You mean raiders were here?"

Walking Horse shook his head. "No, it was not raiders."

"Then, who took the horse?" Jed rose up on his elbow.

"The Blackfoot was here again." Walking Horse laid the bear tooth and thong in Jed's hands. "He left this on your lodge flap."

"He was here outside my lodge?"

"Yes, he left his bear medicine for you to find."

Slowly rising, Jed pushed through the doorway and walked out into the fading sunlight of the day. Rage shook his body as he realized his own house had been violated. How did the Blackfoot know he was here and how did he know the exact lodge he slept in? The warrior must have been watching from the trees down closer to the stream, that was the only answer. "Are you sure the piebald is gone?"

Walking Horse followed Jed from his lodge. "Yes, if he was not, the bear tooth would not be tied to your lodge. Slow Wolf sent boys to search the herd."

Turning to Bright Moon, who was still waiting outside, Jed questioned her. "You knew the horse was gone?"

"Yes, my husband." The woman dropped her eyes. "I knew."

"Why didn't you tell me?"

"I waited for Walking Horse to return."

"She was told by Slow Wolf not to speak of it until I returned." Walking Horse intervened. "It was not her fault."

"No, it was not her fault, it was mine." The rage slowly ebbed from Jed. "When was he taken?"

"It must have been last night. Bright Moon found the bear tooth when she went to start the cooking fire this morning."

"As I lay asleep like a baby." Jed shook his head in rage. "I am ashamed."

Walking Horse watched as the warrior looked about the village. "He is a mighty warrior to come here again alone."

"No, he is a superstitious fool and a thief in the night." Jed swore.

"I have sent for Red Hawk to come here. He is on his way."

"Red Hawk?" Jed looked questioningly at Walking Horse. "Why is he coming here?"

"Slow Wolf sent for him."

"Why?"

"You are weak yet, my friend." Walking Horse shrugged. "You cannot challenge the Blackfoot in your condition."

"No, but I can kill him!" Jed exclaimed. "I have grown stronger."

"No, my brother, you cannot even ride a horse without hurting."

Nodding slowly, Jed sat down against the lodge. "So I have stooped to letting my friend, Red Hawk, fight my battles?"

"Just until you grow stronger, my husband." Bright Moon sat down beside him. "That will be soon."

The Blackfoot warrior, Bear Claw, laughed lightly as he stroked the sleek neck of the piebald. It had been so easy to take the horse of the great Crow Killer. The amulet with the bear tooth had just been an extra touch to madden or maybe even frighten the bear killer. It had been so simple. He even looked into the lodge where the warrior and his woman slept like babies. Bear Claw grinned as his medicine was mightier than the Arapaho's. His confidence in his medicine was so strong and powerful that he knew he could never be defeated in battle. The warrior smiled arrogantly, laughing at the mighty Arapaho people. They were a weak people, letting an enemy enter their village so easily. He had made his own camp less than five miles from their village. His horse, the stolen horse, and the small camp lay hidden in a small draw right under their noses.

However, Bear Claw was worried as something else nagged at him. He was now the head chief of his village, but he had been away from his village far too long. He needed to return to his people to see to their welfare. The warrior hesitated to leave this place. He had sworn to kill the Arapaho demon, the evil one who had killed so many of his people, including his father and uncles. Still, he knew as chief, it was his responsibility to return to his village and see about them. He knew there were warriors in his tribe that would remove him from being their chief if he stayed away too long. The Blackfoot may think him dead so he had to return soon, before anything bad happened.

Bear Claw gritted his teeth as his blood burned for revenge, but still, his conscience called him to check on his people. The huge warrior thought of his father, whom he had sworn to avenge. His mind turned to the traitors of his father and the Blackfoot people. In time, Blue Darter was another one he would seek revenge against, but not until Crow Killer was defeated. Then the dog, Blue Darter, and his followers would fear the one they knew was invincible. Eventually, they would know he would be coming for his revenge against them. He wanted them to quake in their robes as they slept. The gods had showed him his path, as the old medicine man, Twisted Rope, of the Blackfoot had told him, and now, he would follow that path to the end.

Bear Claw studied the black and white paint horse, wondering if the theft of the animal would bring Crow Killer from his lodge. Thinking the horse would not be enough, he thought back to the beautiful woman who was lying next to the warrior as he slept in his robes. The evil grin came back across his scarred countenance, the face of death. Looking up at the night sky, the warrior quickly gathered his weapons and closed the small opening, leading into the walled place. He would not leave this land until he was certain Crow Killer would follow. Bear Claw laughed, what better way to strengthen his medicine than to kill this mighty warrior in front of the Blackfoot people so he had to lure this enemy back to his village.

Hitting a dog trot, the warrior crossed the short distance to the village. He did not like being afoot, but this way he would leave less tracks and the horse would not be discovered by the night herders. Slipping beside a large elm tree that stood alongside the village, Bear Claw sat down to wait for his quarry. He knew there was a possibility the woman would not leave the lodge until daybreak when she started the breakfast fires. If he tried to enter her lodge and take her, something could go wrong. If the Arapaho woke up, he would have to kill him there and that is not what he wanted. The Blackfoot people must see him kill this demon, for them to fully believe in his powers. He could not take the chance of being captured or killed, so he had to wait patiently.

No moon showed as darkness and heavy fog engulfed the village with only the dying embers from the cook fires emitting any light. Slipping closer to the lodges, Bear Claw tried to distinguish which lodge was the one Crow Killer slept in. Two nights ago, there had been a full moon and no fog, so when he lurked in the shadows, he had observed the warrior and his woman entering and leaving their lodge several times. Passing several lodges in the dark, he finally settled on the one he believed belonged to his enemy. Covering himself with a trade blanket, the Blackfoot sat back against a lodge and waited. He was surprised, that the village dogs could smell him, but no alarm was sent out. He nodded, this proved his medicine was strong and he would be invincible in battle.

Twice, he was alerted as the warrior came from the lodge to relieve himself. Sitting back down, he almost laughed in disgust. To kill this weak one would be so easy. No, he would not kill tonight, he would wait. The Arapaho must die in battle against the Bear Claw so all would know who killed him and who now held the greatest medicine. He wanted to see the Arapaho on his knees, begging for his life, pleading for the great Bear Claw to finish him. Then, it would be Blue Darter's turn to feel the Bear Claw's revenge. As he waited in the darkness, hate seemed to drip from his thoughts, like venom from a snake's fangs.

Again, a figure passed through the lodge flap and started his way. Instantly on his feet, he reached out as the woman came close, unaware of his presence. His huge arms enveloped the small frame as she passed. Muffling her screams as the woman struggled, the powerful warrior quickly bound and gagged her. Tossing her over his shoulder as if she was a feather, he stealthily moved to the lodge flap and placed another amulet on it. Fighting back the desire to go into the lodge and kill Crow Killer, the Blackfoot passed back along the creek and returned to where the horses waited.

Taking the gag from the coughing woman's mouth, Bear Claw placed his huge hand across her face. "If you yell, woman, I will cut your throat."

Removing his hand, the warrior untied her hands and feet so she could stand. Quick as a wink, the red-hot taste of her sharp blade passed across his ribs as Little Antelope struck at him.

Wrestling the skinning knife from her grasp, Bear Claw felt his side. "The wife of Crow Killer carries a sting like her husband."

"Why have you taken me, warrior?" She could barely make out his image in the dark, but Little Antelope knew he was huge.

"You do not know who I am, woman?" Bear Claw laughed as he placed a covering over his wound. "I want to make certain the great bear killer will come after you."

"He would have come after the horse." It was dark in the canyon, but Little Antelope could smell the odor of nearby horses. "You did not need me."

"Perhaps it was your beauty that I desired to take."

Little Antelope glared at the warrior. "Touch me, and I'll claw out your eyes."

"You may just be worth my eye."

Little Antelope did not dare let this one know he had taken the wrong woman, not the wife of Crow Killer. He thought with her as his captive, he had the reason that would bring Crow Killer after him without hesitation. "My husband will kill you."

"You would not mourn for me?"

"You are not funny, Blackfoot."

"So you do know who I am." Bear Claw laughed as he caught the horses. "If you try to escape, I promise I will hamstring one of your legs. You would not be so pretty to your husband, hobbling around with a crippled leg."

Little Antelope shuddered, this warrior was crazed. "I will not try to escape. I want to be there when Crow Killer catches up to you and carves out your heart."

"For a woman of your beauty, I know he will come." Bear Claw sneered. "Yes, woman, your beauty will bring him to me."

Little Antelope knew Jed would come for her, but she hoped he wouldn't. She would rather be in the hands of this crazy one, than see her warrior get hurt again.

CHAPTER 11

Early morning, Walking Horse woke up to find Little Antelope missing from their sleeping robes. He ran frantically to Jed's lodge, threw back the flap and stepped into the dim light from the small fire's dying embers.

Jed rose from his robes. "What is wrong, my brother?"

"Little Antelope, I look for her."

"My sister is not here." Bright Moon wiped her eyes. "What do you mean, you look for her?"

"She is missing from my lodge."

Jed pulled on his hunting shirt and followed Walking Horse from the lodge. Holding out a bear tooth amulet, he had found on his lodge, Walking Horse groaned.

Jed could only feel the amulet in the dark, but he knew what it represented. "He left another bear token for us to find."

"I did not want Bright Moon to see it." Walking Horse whispered.

"When did you miss her?"

"I believe only a few minutes have passed." Walking Horse paced back and forth. "I was asleep."

"This bear amulet is his sign." Jed felt the bear tooth. "The Blackfoot has taken her."

"We must go after her."

Jed knew the torment the warrior was feeling. "We can't leave until the sun comes again. We don't want to disturb any tracks he might have left."

"I cannot leave her in his hands."

"We won't. Gather the warriors and horses. Prepare for a long trail." Jed took the arm of the frantic warrior. "We will find her with the coming of the day."

"If she is alive."

"She will not be harmed. It's his way of luring me to him." Jed explained.

"Can you be sure, my brother?"

"Yes, I have seen into this warrior's heart." Jed assured him. "She will not be harmed unless I do not follow him."

"Tell me, is this one touched by the evil ones?"

"He believes he cannot be killed, but I think he just seeks revenge against me." Jed didn't know for sure. "For what he has done this night, I will kill him."

"You are still weak."

"Now, I will kill him." Jed squeezed the amulet hard. "Hate makes a man strong."

Bright Moon watched as Jed prepared his weapons for the days ahead. She put together food for his journey and wept for Little Antelope as she worried for her sister. She knew he was still weak from his wounds, but he had to go after Little Antelope. Her words could not stop him because this time it was different, she didn't want to stop him. "I will go with you, my husband?"

Wiping the tears from her face, Jed kissed her lightly. "Not this time."

"Then ride my spotted horse, next to the paint, he is the strongest horse in the village."

Jed hated to take her horse, but to save Little Antelope and catch up to the piebald, he knew he needed the powerful animal. "Thank you. I will ride him."

"It is the only way I can help my sister."

Bear Claw had made no attempt to hide his tracks as he departed from the village. Jed and Walking Horse, with several Arapaho warriors, easily followed the Blackfoot to the canyon where the horses had been hidden. Jed quickly picked up the tracks of the piebald as they headed northwest toward Blackfoot Country.

"He returns to his country." Jed pointed at the tracks. "If he gets there before we catch up, he will wait and challenge me so his people will know his power."

"We must hurry."

"No, the warriors must return to the village."

Walking Horse looked over at Jed. "That leaves only you and me to follow this trail."

"If you want Little Antelope to live, it must be this way." Jed nodded slowly. "Somewhere ahead, he is watching his back trail. Even the great Bear Claw would not be foolish enough to lead so many Arapaho warriors back to his village."

"Do you fear this Blackfoot?"

"I fear for Little Antelope, my brother. If we do not go alone, I believe he will kill her." Jed warned him.

Walking Horse nodded slowly. "Perhaps Crow Killer is right."

"But, I do respect this warrior as an enemy." Jed looked across at the sad face of Walking Horse. "I believe he will not do harm to her if we come alone."

"Then it will be as you say." Walking Horse agreed. "My mind does not think clearly in this."

Walking to where Big Owl and the warriors were waiting, Walking Horse spoke briefly with them. Grumbling, they turned back to the village.

"We have a hard trail ahead." Jed swung stiffly up on the spotted horse. "We will try to catch up, but we must be careful not to ride into a trap."

Walking Horse looked over at the appaloosa. "We will catch up. We have to."

Jed nodded. "Yes, somewhere at the end of this trail, we will find her."

Two days later, making a patrol on the Arapaho side of the Yellowstone, Big Owl and his warriors stopped and watched as warriors approached them on the trail. Thinking it might be the Blackfoot, waiting ahead to ambush them, they waited. Recognizing the rider, Big Owl let out with a loud yell and kicked his horse forward in a lope. Red

Hawk and two Crow warriors sat their horses as the Arapaho warriors thundered up.

"Red Hawk, it is good to see you here." Big Owl nodded.

The handsome warrior sitting the spotted appaloosa nodded. "It is good to see Big Owl."

"You have come to help Crow Killer?"

The dark eyes of the young chief looked back down the trail. "Where are my brothers, Crow Killer and Walking Horse?"

"Crow Killer and Walking Horse follow the trail of the Blackfoot." Big Elk explained. "He sent us back to the village. He wishes only for him and Walking Horse to follow the Blackfoot's trail."

"We met your warrior who watches at the river." Red Hawk shifted on his horse. "He says my brother is very weak."

"This is true. Crow Killer is weak from wounds he received in a fight at Bridger."

"The Pawnee told us of this fight." The Crow looked hard at Big Owl. "Why did you let him go alone?"

"Walking Horse will soon be our chief. We dare not disobey his words."

Red Hawk knew the warrior was right. To disobey the leader on a raid was a bad thing. "Why do they follow this Blackfoot into his lands?"

Big Owl quickly told him about Little Antelope's abduction, the theft of the piebald horse, and the amulets that were found. He explained how Crow Killer figured the warrior was trying to lure him into Blackfoot lands. Red Hawk listened quietly, knowing Jed's feelings for the woman. He knew Crow Killer would follow the Blackfoot for as long as it took to get her back, no matter what danger he encountered.

"How far ahead are they?"

"At least two suns." Big Owl replied. "Crow Killer thinks the Blackfoot travels to the northwest toward his village."

Speaking quickly to the warriors with him, Red Hawk nodded at Big Owl and kicked the great spotted horse down the trail, following the tracks that were left behind. Big Owl watched as the rider disappeared, and shook his head.

"What is wrong?" Long Leaper the Crow asked. "Why do you shake your head, fat one?"

Whirling, Big Owl pointed his rifle at the young Crow warrior. "You have a smart mouth for one so young, Crow."

"Tell me, why do you shake your head?" The young warrior was not backing down.

"I think they are all dead men." Big Owl responded. "I believe this Blackfoot, Bear Claw, has strong medicine."

"Why do you think this?"

"He came into our village twice without being seen or heard, that is why." The fat warrior shrugged sadly. "He took a woman and horse from under our noses. Our night herders think he is a ghost."

"Then we should go after them."

"No, we were told to go home."

"You do not give me orders, Arapaho."

"No, I do not." Big Owl declared. "Go if you wish."

Long Leaper shook his head. "No, I will do as my chief orders."

For three days, the two warriors followed the tracks of the piebald paint and another horse. Bear Claw had made no attempt to cover his trail. Several times, Walking Horse yelled in rage and fear after seeing the tracks of Little Antelope around a still warm campfire. Jed felt the same way as Walking Horse, Little Antelope was dear to him too, but he dared not rush forward and run into an ambush. The cat and mouse game had gone on for three days and they hadn't closed the gap on the Blackfoot in the least. The piebald was strong, and Jed knew the big powerful horse would be hard to run down. Jed figured the Blackfoot rode the piebald, placing the lighter woman on his horse. If he rode hard, the spotted horse he was riding might catch the Blackfoot, but then the crazed one might kill Little Antelope if cornered.

"We must hurry, Crow Killer." Walking Horse was frantic. "We have to catch up with them before they reach Blackfoot lands."

"We cannot kill our horses, my brother." Jed warned. "We cannot be afoot. I promise we will catch up when he makes a mistake."

"I do not know what he has done to her." Walking Horse replied sadly. "My heart speaks instead of my brain."

"I understand, my brother." Jed agreed. "I feel the same way."

"Why did he take Little Antelope?"

"I think he meant to take Bright Moon and took Little Antelope by mistake." Jed figured Bear Claw had seen Little Antelope enter his lodge several times and thought she was his wife. The Blackfoot had no way of knowing he had the wrong lodge in the dark of night.

"They do look alike." Walking Horse frowned.

"Little Antelope probably knows this too, but if she told the Blackfoot he had taken the wrong woman, the crazed one might kill her."

"You are right."

Red Hawk rode the spotted stallion hard, crossing many miles of valleys and mountains in his haste to catch up with Jed and Walking Horse. Looking down at the valley below, he spotted his friends crossing a small meadow. Starting the spotted horse downhill to cut them off, he reined in quickly, then turned his eyes to the upper valley. Turning the great horse back to the northeast, he took a gamble. Somewhere, the Blackfoot moved just ahead of his pursuers. Several times Red Hawk had found the tracks of the Blackfoot as he doubled back on his trail, keeping a close watch on Jed and Walking Horse as they followed his trail. He hadn't caught sight of the warrior and Little Antelope yet, but he felt the Blackfoot was near. Perhaps, he could get ahead of the warrior without his knowing and set his own trap. Red Hawk knew the warrior was smart, trying to keep ahead of his pursuers, just enough to stay out of sight, but still know how close they were. Red Hawk also knew this one was deliberately luring Crow Killer and Walking Horse into Blackfoot lands.

Kicking the appaloosa into a short lope, Red Hawk covered several miles, letting the horse slow down and rest at intervals. As day broke, he climbed back over the switchback and eased down into the lower basin. He had to be careful, as the Blackfoot could be anywhere in the jumble of trees and brush. If only he could surprise the warrior, he might get off a shot before he was discovered and this pursuit would be finished.

Bottoming out on the valley floor, Red Hawk quickly checked the trails leading through the meadows for any sign of horses passing.

Finding none, he found a small knoll covered in thick cedar with a clear view of the entire valley. Hobbling the horse, he sat back to watch the valley from his vantage point. If he had guessed right and was lucky, sometime soon, the Blackfoot and Little Antelope would pass below where he sat. If he had guessed wrong, then he would still have time to catch up with Crow Killer and Walking Horse.

Red Hawk had no way of knowing when the Blackfoot would arrive or even if he would come that way. He had never ridden this far north, but as large as the mountains were, he figured there were other passes leading away from where he sat. He could only wait and watch, hoping he had picked the right valley. Red Hawk looked at his horse. The spotted one was powerful, but the last few days he had been ridden hard. The animal was tiring and had little run left in him.

Bear Claw sat the piebald and studied the valley behind him for almost an hour. Shaking his head, he looked over at Little Antelope. "Maybe your great warrior does not want you back."

The hideous scarred face of the huge warrior made her shudder, not so much at his appearance, but the pure crazed look that came from his eyes. Beneath the black paint, scars crossed his face, leaving white marks down his cheeks and eyes. How the bear hadn't blinded the warrior, she could not understand. Little Antelope had seen many wounds, but the Blackfoot's face was so disfigured, it was hard to look at. One eye seemed lifeless, white in color, but she could not be sure.

"My husband is wounded and weak." Little Antelope lied. "He cannot come."

"Then, you will be my woman." Bear Claw laughed.

"I would rather be dead, Blackfoot."

"Death is so permanent, woman."

"Death is better than being your woman." Little Antelope looked away. "Kill me now, Blackfoot!"

Bear Claw looked out across the valley. "He follows us, as we speak."

"How do you know this?"

"Because woman, the medicine seer of my village foretold that I would defeat this Crow Killer in battle and take his medicine, and to do this, he has to come here to Blackfoot lands."

"Never, Blackfoot. Never!" Little Antelope shuddered. "Crow Killer will never be defeated by the likes of you."

"We will see."

"Yes, we will see." Little Antelope argued.

Jed studied the tracks on the trail he and Walking Horse followed, then looked over at the warrior. The tracks were still fresh. The winds hadn't blown any dust into the clear hoof prints.

Walking Horse looked over at Jed and pointed down at the tracks. "The Blackfoot plays with us."

Jed nodded. "He sure isn't trying to hide his trail or make any time."

"I do not believe he is too far ahead of us."

"I think he watches us now." Jed looked across the valley. "I believe he has been watching our every move."

"You give this warrior too much credit." Walking Horse shook his head.

"No, he is out there, right now." Jed disagreed. "I can feel him."

"I'd rather we see him, than feel him."

Red Hawk figured Crow Killer and Walking Horse were only hours behind him, maybe riding into this valley even now. The warrior scanned the valley trails continually for several hours. He knew there was little or no way of spotting his hiding place from below. He also knew the Blackfoot must come soon, if he was planning to cross this valley. The meadows in this valley were long, taking at least an hour to cross, then ride out of sight of any pursuers. If the warrior did not cross soon, he would be taking a chance that Crow Killer and Walking Horse might spot him out in the open.

Red Hawk just started to give up his vigilance, thinking the Black-foot had taken another trail, when the appaloosa pricked his ears. His dark eyes moved down the valley. He finally spotted what he had been waiting for so long. The piebald was unmistakable, even from a mile distance. Out on the valley floor, the Blackfoot with Little Antelope following close behind came into view. Holding the spotted horse's nose, Red Hawk watched as they rode straight at him. Red Hawk grinned, the spirit people were with him this day, handing the Blackfoot into his hand as the man and woman passed almost directly below where he waited. One hundred yards down the trail, Bear Claw rode the piebald into a heavily wooded area and dismounted. From where he was watching, the heavy brush and trees obstructed his view, Red Hawk could not see what the warrior was doing.

Red Hawk could not believe his eyes as the warrior mounted on the piebald and raced back up the trail in a hard lope. The paint was running too hard for him to get a clean shot. He did not want to miss and give the warrior a chance to race back where he had left Little Antelope. The spirit people were surely with him, as they handed Little Antelope into his hands without having to fight the Blackfoot. Red Hawk was not afraid to confront Bear Claw, but Little Antelope's safety came first. If he could rescue her while the Blackfoot was looking for his pursuers, it would be better, then she would be safe. Quickly seizing his opportunity, Red Hawk mounted the spotted horse and hurried down to where he had last seen the Blackfoot and Little Antelope. Riding into the heavily wooded area, he spotted the bay horse, then the little woman herself. Bear Claw had bound her hand and foot to a small tree, making sure there was no way she could get free and escape while he was away.

Dismounting, the Crow quickly released her and helped Little Antelope to her feet. "Oh, Red Hawk, you have come for me."

"Yes, but now we must hurry from this place before the Blackfoot returns." The warrior looked out across the valley.

"He goes to see if Crow Killer still follows." Little Antelope nodded. "This one is evil, touched by the spirit people."

"You believe that?"

"Hurry, Red Hawk. Take me from this place before the crazy one returns." Little Antelope pleaded.

"If he returns, I will kill him."

"No, I do not think he can be killed by man." Little Antelope placed her small hand on Red Hawk's arm. "You have saved me twice now, my friend. Promise me, you will not try to fight the crazy one."

"You do not think I can defeat the Blackfoot?"

"It is not you I doubt, Red Hawk. No man can stand against the spirit people and their strong medicine." Little Antelope touched his arm. "You are a good friend. I do not want you hurt."

The warrior was about to laugh and tell her she was just being superstitious, but then just minutes ago he had said the same thing. He remembered thinking the spirit people were with him this day. Still, there was no use tempting the medicine people. He would take Little Antelope and flee this place.

Bear Claw spotted Jed and Walking Horse coming over a mountain pass from where he had hidden in some mountain cedars. The piebald smelled them as he tried to nicker out a greeting. Holding the horse's muzzle, the Blackfoot studied the two for several minutes as they neared.

"Fools! They follow me right into the land of the Blackfoot." The warrior grinned evilly. "From here there is no escape. Now, you will die, Crow Killer, then your friend."

Kicking the piebald into a hard lope, Bear Claw quickly returned to where he had left Little Antelope and the bay horse. Hair stood up on the back of his neck as he stared at the vacant area where he had left the woman. Sliding from the piebald, he quickly examined the ground and the cut rawhide thongs he had tied the woman with. Cussing, he whirled, his face a mask of rage. He knew the two Arapaho were following him, he had seen them, so who had taken the woman of Crow Killer? One rider had come in and released his captive, his tracks were all about. Studying the tracks carefully, tracing them out with his finger, the scarred face hardened. Now, there were three enemies in his land.

"Crow." Bear Claw whispered the word. The tracks were plain to see. The warrior who had taken the girl was a Crow. The seams and the rolled toe of the moccasin track were the trademark of the Crow squaws. Bear Claw had heard rumors of the friendship between Crow Killer and the Crow Red Hawk. Until now, he thought they were just that, rumors. Glaring from crazed eyes, as he studied his back trail, the warrior shook his fist in rage.

He had been a fool playing games with Crow Killer far too long, and now there were three warriors against him. Three warriors were following his trail. Three were coming here, so now, he would have to fight. Too many, the Blackfoot knew his medicine was powerful, but against three experienced and hardened warriors? No, he would have to ride to the Blackfoot people and get warriors to help him fight these interlopers who followed him. His dark eyes glared. This changed nothing, he would still challenge Crow Killer to personal combat. His warriors would only be there to keep the other two out of the fight. Bear Claw grinned again, thinking after he killed the Arapaho, he would kill the other two. Then, he would take the beautiful Arapaho woman for his squaw.

For now, he had no choice. Even the great Bear Claw was no match for the two warriors who followed and the one that had taken the woman. In his rage, he wanted to follow the Crow and kill him, but he knew there was no way to catch up with the warrior before the others found them. To stay in this place longer or to follow the Crow could be the death of him and his plans.

Jed and Walking Horse followed the clear trail into the wooded place where Little Antelope had been tied. Sliding to the ground, both warriors studied the ground closely. Jed gasped as he spotted the rounded hoof print of the appaloosa.

"What does Crow Killer see?" Walking Horse studied the soft ground.

"It is the track of the spotted horse of Red Hawk." Jed pointed to the deep tracks. "He has been here."

"Are you sure, my friend?" Walking Horse questioned. "Many horses leave the same track."

"I'm sure. I would know the spotted one's track anywhere." Jed explained. "I followed it for many days after Billy Wilson stole the animal."

"What has happened here?" Walking Horse searched the ground. "If Red Hawk and the Blackfoot had fought, there would be blood or signs of struggle."

"I think Red Hawk has taken Little Antelope from the Blackfoot." Jed walked about searching out every track. "The piebald goes north, and the spotted horse and another horse go back to the south and east."

"Are you sure of this, my friend?" Relief covered Walking Horse's face. "How are we to know for certain?"

Jed knew Walking Horse worried about Little Antelope and was too exhausted with grief to read the signs so plain on the ground before them. "The Blackfoot rides for his own country."

"And Red Hawk?"

"He hurries to the south to bring Little Antelope back to you safely." Jed was just guessing, but the tracks were easy to read. "The Blackfoot knows he cannot fight all of us. If he had followed Red Hawk, we would be right behind him."

"So he will no longer seek you out?"

"Oh, he'll be coming for me alright, but next time, he will give no warning before he attacks me." Jed explained.

"What should we do?" Walking Horse was eager to find Little Antelope, but he did not want to abandon his friend if he was needed.

"You will follow the track of Red Hawk and Little Antelope." Jed looked across the meadow. "They are headed for the Yellowstone."

"And you, my friend?"

"I go after the piebald." Jed nodded. "To finish this."

"I cannot let you go alone." Walking Horse argued.

"It is my wish." Jed replied. "You must go to Little Antelope and keep her safe."

"She is safe and in good hands." Walking Horse looked out across the valley. "Red Hawk will see her safely back to the village, as well as I could."

"No, my friend, you will follow them."

"Is Crow Killer strong enough to challenge the Blackfoot?"

"Go Walking Horse, find her." Jed smiled. "And if you catch up with Red Hawk, be careful as you approach him."

"Now, you are teaching the teacher?" Walking Horse laughed. "I will be careful."

Jed swung up on the spotted horse. "Tell Red Hawk not to come back after me."

"He is your friend. He will not listen to an Arapaho."

"If I kill the Blackfoot, his people will take it as a bad omen and let me go in peace." Jed assumed. "If he kills me, it will not matter."

"What will I tell Bright Moon?"

"Tell her, someday I will return to her."

Shaking hands with the warrior, Jed kicked the spotted one and followed the tracks of the piebald. Walking Horse could only shake his head in sadness as he watched his friend ride away. He wanted to follow, but for some reason Crow Killer wished to ride this trail alone. Turning his tired horse, he took a straight course back to the Yellowstone.

Red Hawk scanned his back trail, then kicked the spotted horse into a fast trot. Throughout the day, they traveled hard to the south, stopping only to let the horses drink and graze for a short spell. He did not believe the Blackfoot was following, but no one could tell what a crazed person might do.

"You said Walking Horse and Crow Killer would follow our trail." Little Antelope could see the worry in Red Hawk's face and the way he watched their back trail. "Why do you worry so much?"

"They follow, but I fear the Blackfoot, riding the powerful paint, could catch up to us before they do and steal you back."

"I know he would have to kill you first."

"You said this one is touched by the evil ones."

Little Antelope gripped the skinning knife Red Hawk had given her. "He will not take me alive again."

Red Hawk laughed lightly. "Walking Horse would be mad at me if I let you kill yourself."

"Then Crow, you better keep us ahead of the Blackfoot."

"I see why Crow Killer thinks so much of you." Red Hawk grinned. "You are a strong woman for a Cheyenne."

"You read too much in what you see, Crow."

"My eyes are not blind, woman." The warrior explained. "I have seen the feelings you have for each other. Your eyes do not lie either."

"I have a husband." Little Antelope looked straight at Red Hawk. "Crow Killer is only my friend."

"Crow Killer thinks more of you than any person." The warrior added. "Yes, he may be your friend, but his heart has deep feelings for you."

Raising the skinning knife, Little Antelope pointed it at the Crow. "Red Hawk, I swear."

Red Hawk laughed. Raising his hands, he moved the spotted horse away from the dangerous weapon. The little Arapaho woman was back to her old self. Her tongue had become sharp again. "Your confidence in me seems to have faded."

"I am sorry, my friend." Little Antelope apologized. "I am just worried."

"Do you worry about Walking Horse or Crow Killer?"

"Watch your tongue, Crow." Little Antelope bristled again, then smiled. "I worry for both of my warriors."

Red Hawk felt they were being followed, but could not be certain. His powerful spotted horse could outdistance any horse that followed him. However, the bay horse, Little Antelope was riding, was not as strong or powerful, and the piebald could easily run down her horse.

"Can you travel further?"

"With that devil following me, I can ride forever." Little Antelope swore.

Red Hawk knew the Blackfoot had to be touched or had a strong belief in his medicine, but would he actually dare take on three warriors alone? Three against one were powerful odds, even against the great medicine of Bear Claw.

"Then we ride." Red Hawk turned the appaloosa. "Crow Killer would be mad if I lost you again."

Walking Horse reined in at the open area where Red Hawk had stopped to let Little Antelope and the horses rest. The signs were as plain as reading a book to the warrior. Red Hawk had been traveling fast, back to the east. He had no way of knowing how close the Blackfoot was behind him, or if he even followed. Walking Horse nodded with relief, the Crow was being smart by not taking chances with Little Antelope. They were at least two days from the river. At the pace Red Hawk was setting, Walking Horse doubted he would catch up to them before they reached the crossing. That was a good thing, at least he knew Little Antelope was out of the clutches of the Blackfoot, and safe in Crow lands.

The sorrel horse, Walking Horse rode, was tired. He could see the way the horse stood, he was done in and had become gaunt from the long trail. Crow Killer had pushed the horses hard from the river, and now, the sorrel would have to make the return trip to the east without rest. With Bear Claw, the Blackfoot, heading north and Crow Killer between them, Walking Horse knew he could spare the animal as best he could. He wanted to catch up to Red Hawk and Little Antelope, but the horse needed rest. In his condition, the animal would not go much further if pushed too hard. Walking Horse worried the animal would lie down on him and quit, leaving him afoot in hostile country.

Leading the sorrel, Walking Horse followed the tracks of Red Hawk and Little Antelope south. There was no rush now, knowing his beloved Little Antelope was safe with Red Hawk. The warrior shook his head. Who would have ever believed he would be grateful to the Crow for the second time. He studied his back trail several times as he walked south. He felt ashamed that he had left his friend alone, back in Blackfoot Country. He knew he should not have let Crow Killer send him back after Little Antelope.

For two whole days, Jed followed the trail of the Blackfoot. He had to be close, as the valley and mountains of the Blackfoot people appeared just as Tall Wind and Straight Arrow had described. They told him the trail, he followed, would widen as he neared the village, exactly as it was widening beneath him. After the long ride from Arapaho Country, following the Blackfoot, Jed flexed his powerful arms, surprised his strength had returned and the soreness had left his body.

Looking down at the tracks, he realized the Blackfoot village and the warrior Bear Claw would be waiting close ahead. Jed could tell from studying the warrior's tracks that on several occasions he had waited and observed him from a distance. The warrior was confident, he was riding the stronger horse and could get away from Jed any time he wanted. Jed knew the Blackfoot was not trying to escape, that was not what the warrior wanted. He wanted to lure the hated Crow Killer closer to his village. Jed knew Bear Claw was planning on challenging him in front of his people, to show off his medicine. Twisted Rope had given the Blackfoot the message of the bear people, and now, he thought he was invincible. Bear Claw had no fear in his heart, confident of the power of his name and his ability to defeat Crow Killer in single combat.

Winding through the beautiful tree covered trail, Jed had to catch his breath at the wonder of these mountains. They were as beautiful as his valley, only distinguished by higher mountains and larger trees. He could well understand why the Blackfoot resisted all trappers or immigrants trespassing into their country. As the spotted horse climbed carefully up the rocky trail, Jed noticed the Blackfoot had suddenly swung to the west. The village had to be somewhere in this range of mountains. Jed slowed the horse, studying closely every place of concealment the Blackfoot could hide himself behind.

He did not think the Blackfoot would ambush him, but this enemy was crazed, unpredictable. Jed was confident Bear Claw was driven by his desire for revenge. Worse, the warrior wanted everyone in these mountains to know he defeated the great Crow Killer in battle and took his bear medicine. He had to kill Crow Killer in front of many witnesses, so all would fear him. The old medicine man, Twisted Rope, had foretold of Bear Claw's victory over the Arapaho Lance Bearer, and now, the warrior wanted his triumph to be seen by all.

Bear Claw concealed the piebald behind a stand of maple trees and moved back up the trail to survey the pass. Fingering the Hawken rifle he carried, the warrior studied Jed as he slowly crossed a broad place on the trail. He grinned as the Arapaho closed the distance. Soon, he would be in rifle range. The dark, cruel eagle eye of the warrior took in the condition of the spotted horse and his rider. Bear Claw had to admire the Arapaho's courage, riding here alone, straight into dangerous Blackfoot Country. Crow Killer probably thought he would not be attacked here, as it would be a cowardly act and Bear Claw could not gain the bear's medicine power. Returning to the piebald, he kicked the horse into a hard lope. If the Arapaho was foolish enough to ride alone into the middle of the Blackfoot village, then he would die. Bear Claw grinned savagely. Tomorrow, he would have his revenge and the great power of the bear people would be his alone.

Jed followed the deep tracks of the piebald and knew why they were left so easy for him to follow. Trusting his instincts, he could sense the Blackfoot was watching his every move as he climbed higher into the mountains. The warrior was leading him straight to the Blackfoot's camp.

The high elevation had to be their summer camp location. It would be too cold and far too much snow during the winter months to keep the village in these high mountains. By the way his spotted horse was pricking his ears, he sensed other horses and the village could be close by. Maybe just around the next bend in the trail, he would come face-to-face with the one he sought.

Jed's mind thought of Little Antelope. He knew she was safe with Red Hawk, and Walking Horse should have caught up to them by now. Bear Claw had stolen his prize horse, but neither of these wrongs against him were the reason Jed rode alone, straight into his enemy's village. No, another reason lay heavy on his mind as he followed the warrior. He knew if he and Bright Moon were to have any peace and live safely in their valley home, the confrontation between him and the crazed one had to be finished and done with. One of them, the Blackfoot Bear Claw or the Arapaho Crow Killer had to die. Jed shook his head. The warrior was young, strong, and totally fearless. Jed knew when they meet, one would surely die, maybe both.

Red Hawk sat on the high ridge that stood high above the Yellowstone. Several Crow warriors joined him as he neared the river crossing. Long Leaper and two others had been watching the lower trail and reported Walking Horse was approaching.

"Are you sure it is the Arapaho, not a Blackfoot."

"Yes, my chief." Long Leaper frowned. "I know this Arapaho that follows your trail."

"Walking Horse has made good time."

Looking over at Little Antelope, the young warrior nodded. "She is the wife of this one following?"

"She is."

"I see why he follows. She is a handsome squaw." Long Leaper grinned.

"And she is my friend, Long Leaper." Red Hawk's eyes narrowed. "Say no more or I will let her husband have you."

"She is just an Arapaho." The young warrior looked at Little Antelope and smiled. "I would pay many horses for her."

Little Antelope heard the hard slap and watched the young warrior roll backwards from his horse. She knew something had been said about her, but she did not know what.

"Walking Horse will be here soon." Red Hawk stood before her.

"Thank you, Red Hawk." Little Antelope smiled. "You are truly my friend."

"No more of your sharp tongue?"

Little Antelope showed her pretty smile. "No, my friend, no more. I owe you my life."

"Here he is." Red Hawk raised his hand as Walking Horse rode in and slid from his horse.

Embracing Little Antelope, he then turned to where Red Hawk stood. "Again, I am in your debt, my friend."

"Where is Crow Killer?"

"He sent me after you and Little Antelope." Walking Horse dropped his eyes. "He was not sure where the Blackfoot was."

"And he followed after the Blackfoot?"

"Yes." Walking Horse looked around at the warriors. "He would not let me ride with him."

"He follows this warrior to get back the horse?" Red Hawk looked over at Little Antelope.

Walking Horse shook his head. "No, it is more than the horse or Little Antelope now. I think he wishes to have this fight over so he and Bright Moon can return to their valley in peace."

"I must ride after my brother." Red Hawk spoke sharply to Long Leaper to bring him fresh jerky for the long ride ahead.

"I will accompany you." Walking Horse spoke.

Red Hawk looked at the young Crow warriors. "No, my friend. I will go alone. You take the sharp tongue one home and look after her closely."

"You think the Blackfoot might return after her again?"

"The Blackfoot or some others, maybe." Red Hawk glared at Long Leaper.

Little Antelope spoke up. "Somehow the Blackfoot thinks I am Crow Killer's woman."

"You and your sister look alike."

"Watch over her closely." Red Hawk took the leather pouch of meat and swung up on the spotted horse. "She is truly one of a kind."

"Have a good trail, my friend." Little Antelope looked up at the Crow. "Bring my sister's husband home safely if it is possible."

Walking Horse grasped Red Hawk's heavy arm, then stepped back
as the warrior kicked the appaloosa back to the north. Watching him
ride out of sight, Walking Horse took her by the arm.

"Come, Little Antelope, we will cross the river." The tall warrior
lifted her effortlessly onto the bay horse, then turned to where Long
Leaper stood. "Tell Plenty Coups where his son has gone."

"Does the Arapaho give orders now?"

Walking Horse had been under a severe strain for several days with
no way of letting it out. A quick step toward the Crow and he grasped
the slender warrior by the throat, lifting him bodily from the ground.
Long Leaper's hands clasped the powerful wrist of the Arapaho, trying
to tear loose from his grip. Little Antelope's small hand touched
Walking Horse's arm, pulling it from the warrior's throat. Gasping and
coughing, the young Crow fell to his knees.

"Tell your chief, and do not turn your eyes at my woman ever again,
Crow." Walking Horse mounted his horse and headed toward the river
crossing.

The sun started to set when Jed rode down onto the sandy bank of
a small river crossing. He didn't know the river or its name, but it was a
beautiful flowing stream. The river, with its gravel bottom, was clear and
cold as its water flowed across small boulders. Both banks of the stream
were covered with wild flowers and lush green grass. The small valley, it
centered, stretched out flat, clear through the mountains.

Sliding from his tired horse, Jed let the animal drink a small amount
of cold water, then hobbled him on the ample grass. Dipping his cupped
hands, he pulled the water to his lips, drinking deeply. The water was
cold and crystal clear with every rock, gravel, and even the trout resting
on the bottom were visible. Jed still had a few pieces of dried jerky, but
he could taste the fish. A man could survive on the dried hard jerky, but
his mouth watered at the thought of fresh fish melting in his mouth.

Seeing movement from the corner of his eye, Jed turned to see five
Blackfoot warriors moving from the small cedars that had been hiding
them. None of the warriors showed any weapons. One of the warriors
held up his hand, the sign of peace used universally by all tribes. Jed
returned the signal and propped his Hawken against a dead log lying on

the bank. Riding to the water's edge, the warrior signaled again, asking Jed's permission to cross.

"I am Elk Man." The warrior tapped his chest. "Bear Claw has sent me here to protect you until he arrives."

"Protect me?" Jed almost laughed. "Does he not want to kill me?"

Elk Man nodded with a crooked grin. "Yes, Crow Killer, he wishes to kill you, but he wants no one else to harm you before he can do this."

Jed nodded. "I see, so you're here to protect me until this one has time to kill me."

The warriors all laughed. "The warriors, Tall Wind and Swift Arrow, say you are a good man."

"I have never unjustly killed one who did not try to kill me."

"But, Crow Killer has killed many enemies." Another warrior spoke up. "This is what we have heard."

Jed looked at the speaker. "Yes, I have killed many."

"They say you cannot be killed by man."

"Any warrior can bleed, and anyone can be killed."

"Our medicine man, Twisted Rope, says Chief Bear Claw cannot be killed."

The other warriors had built a small fire next to the dead log as Jed sat talking with Elk Man. Jed was curious as he felt no danger from these five warriors, and he felt their friendliness towards him. Watching curiously, as the warriors pulled fishing string and bone hooks from their pouches, they seemed to have read his mind about the fish. He smiled as they walked back to the stream and dropped their fishing hooks into the water. Jed watched as several trout were pulled from the stream and placed across the fire to cook.

"The Blackfoot knew what I was thinking." Jed smacked his lips. "This is the best fish I've ever tasted."

Elk Man grinned. "We saw how your mouth watered as you watched the little people under the water."

Jed felt stupid. The Blackfoot could have killed him anytime they wanted to, as he stood carelessly on the bank of the creek. Many times in the past, he had made mistakes, but today could have been the worst mistake of all.

"Do not worry, Crow Killer. We are here to protect you, nothing more." Elk Man leaned against the log. "We do not wish you any harm."

"At least not until Bear Claw is finished with me." Jed looked closely at the warrior.

Elk Man looked at the ground. "As I said, Tall Wind says good things about you."

"You have already told me that."

"Yes, but many of our people fear this one." The warrior nodded. "If Bear Claw kills you, he will be a spirit person to some. Tell me, who will he kill next or how many?"

Jed thought about the question and could hear the worry in the warrior's words. "For one, I figure he will kill Blue Darter for helping me in the battle that killed Lone Bull."

"Among others."

"You do not stand behind your hereditary chief in this matter?"

"I will say no more." Elk Man flattened his hands. "Only this; if you live, we will stand with you until you are safe."

"For this, I thank you." Jed nodded. "And you will forever be the friend of Crow Killer."

"This is good." The warrior studied Jed. "We have heard of your fight at Bridger and that you may still be weak."

"I am strong."

"Bear Claw knows we five stand against him. If he kills you, he will come after us next."

Jed was curious. "I understand if a chief kills one of his own people, he can no longer lead his tribe."

"This is true, but there are other ways to kill." Elk Man shook his head. "Since Lone Bull was killed, Bear Claw has gone crazy, mad for revenge. He will seek revenge against everyone he thinks was involved. He is filled with his own medicine thoughts. The seer has convinced him that he is invincible in battle and all-powerful."

Both warriors looked across the stream as another mounted warrior reined his horse in and splashed across the creek. Stopping a few feet from where they had risen to their feet, the warrior addressed Elk Man.

"Bear Claw says he will not come until the second sun shows in the sky."

"What has happened?" Elk Man looked up at the young warrior.

"Now, our chief has decided he wants the whole village here to watch him kill this one." The warrior pointed a skinny finger at Jed.

"Why don't I just go to the village?" Jed asked. "Be a whole lot simpler and quicker wouldn't it?"

"Are you in a hurry to die, Arapaho?" The warrior sneered down at Jed. "No, it will be as Bear Claw says."

Jed smiled back at the mounted man. "Perhaps, I'm in a hurry to kill the great Bear Claw."

"Bear Claw wants to kill you here." The warrior ignored Jed's words, looking down at him with disdain. "He says this place is where Twisted Rope foretold of your death in his smoke. The medicine seer says the fight must take place here."

"Why here?" Jed was curious why there had to be a certain place to fight and die.

"He will drain your blood into the stream and the water will be blessed by the spirit people." The warrior declared. "The mountains will be strengthened and stand for all time."

Jed looked up at the high mountains. "I figure these mountains will be here forever, long after the great Bear Claw is dead and gone."

"You are as dead, Arapaho."

"He's pretty sure of himself, ain't he?" Jed looked at the warrior. "I'm not dead yet."

"He is Bear Claw, the killer of the grizzly."

Jed laughed. "And, I've killed three grizzlies."

"Not with a knife." The young warrior sneered. "You are weak Arapaho. You can never stand against my chief."

"Go!" Elk Man glared at the warrior.

"Two suns when the sun is highest."

"I'll be here." Jed looked over at Elk Man. "He is right though, I never killed a grizzly with just a knife."

Glass Moon nodded. "Bear Claw is considered a bear now. Perhaps he will be the first bear you will kill with a knife."

Red Hawk had ridden the spotted horse as fast as he dared, but knew he would never be close enough to help his friend. He was just too far behind. Even the great spotted horse of the Nez Perce could not make up the long miles that stretched between him and the Blackfoot village. Slowing the horse down, he continued at a fast trot. At the worst, he would be in time to bring Crow Killer's body back home to his valley. Then, Red Hawk swore he would come back and kill this Blackfoot. In two days, maybe less, he would know, and he hoped he would be in time. He would pick up the tracks of Crow Killer where he had rescued Little Antelope.

CHAPTER 12

Walking Horse and Little Antelope splashed their tired horses across the small stream bordering the village and reined in by the lodges. They could see Bright Moon working over a small fire by her lodge.

Little Antelope looked over at Walking Horse. "What should I say to my sister about her husband?"

"The truth. She is Cheyenne and she knows warriors die in battle."

"But, she is so young and so happy."

Walking Horse nodded sadly. "If things should go bad, we will all be sad."

"What will you do, my husband?"

"Go to your sister, and tell her we know nothing." Walking Horse slipped from his horse and turned the tired animal loose. "I will speak with Slow Wolf."

"You will ride back to help Crow Killer?"

"If our chief gives his permission, I will ride back." Walking Horse assured her.

Little Antelope nodded, then dismounted and turned her horse loose. She walked to where her sister stood, waiting and watching her.

"My husband, is he dead?" Tears welled up in Bright Moon's eyes as she looked around for Jed.

"We do not know yet." Little Antelope wrapped her arms around her sister. "Red Hawk follows him, and Walking Horse is asking permission to go back after Crow Killer."

"A Lance Bearer does not have to ask permission to ride."

"My husband is asking our chief to take others with him." Little Antelope looked over to where Walking Horse was speaking with the frail Slow Wolf. "He needs permission to leave the village unprotected."

Bright Moon nodded. "Yes, of course."

Little Antelope watched as Walking Horse spoke to a village crier. The beating drums started their rhythm, sounding out across the village, calling for the warriors to assemble.

"He has our chief's permission."

"How many will ride with him?"

"This I do not know, but I think many will follow Walking Horse to help your husband." Little Antelope responded.

"The Arapaho think much of Crow Killer."

"Yes, everyone has much love for your husband." Little Antelope turned her face away.

Twenty warriors followed Walking Horse from the village with their horses in a high lope. Every warrior carried his war shield, weapons, and sleeping blankets, plus a good supply of dried meat. Walking Horse said his goodbyes to Little Antelope and Bright Moon, then rode away without looking back. He was leading his warriors into enemy territory where they would be badly outnumbered and up against some of the most savage enemies. Every warrior in the Arapaho village wanted to follow Walking Horse to help Crow Killer. These twenty were the best and strongest Lance Bearers in the Arapaho Nation. Slow Wolf would not let any more go, otherwise the village would be left defenseless.

Bright Moon teared up. "We will not see Crow Killer alive again."

"We may not see any of them alive again." Little Antelope watched the small caravan ride out of sight. "Many of the women here have husbands too."

"You are right. I am sorry."

"Do not be sorry, Bright Moon, be strong. Wait until we learn what the new sun brings."

Elk Man watched as the young warrior rode out of sight. "He is Small Bird, cousin of Bear Claw."

"I see. They are family blood huh?"

"Do you think you will defeat the crazy one when you meet?"

"I sure aim to try my best." Jed looked at the warrior. "Why?"

Elk Man laughed. "The Blackfoot are notorious gamblers. There will be many horses, weapons, wives, and furs lost on you maybe."

"Wives?" Jed was shocked.

"Providing they are young and pretty."

"You mean warriors would gamble away their wives?"

"In two suns, some will be totally naked if they lose." Elk Man explained. "It is the way of the Blackfoot."

Jed could only shake his head. "I guess your people are gamblers at that."

"Never have we had such a great thing as this, to gamble over." Glass Moon laughed. "Mostly horse races and wrestling matches, things like that."

"To answer your question, I do not know if I will defeat Bear Claw or not." Jed looked over at the warrior. "I guess it is in the hands of the people above."

"I think you will kill him."

"Why would you think this?"

"For one thing; you are more experienced. For another; the spirit people would not be so cruel as to let this one rule over us." Glass Moon added.

"Who will you wager on, what will you be betting?"

"I have already made my bets." Glass Moon chuckled. "You better win."

"Your wife?"

"Two of them and many horses!" The warrior exclaimed.

Jed did not know if the warrior was joking with him or telling the truth. He sure could not believe anyone would gamble away their wives. He had heard most Indian tribes were heavy gamblers and would gamble on most anything. The Cheyenne and the Arapaho were gamblers, but he had never heard of them wagering their wives. He didn't think Bright Moon or Little Antelope would think much on the idea.

"Crow Killer has one more day to rest."

"I'd as soon have it done with right now, and be finished with it." Jed complained.

"Do not rush your days, my friend." Elk Man handed Jed a large piece of fresh bark with two trout on it. "He will come in one day."

Glass Moon had been right. Jed watched as the whole Blackfoot village started filtering in along the little stream, lining up on the opposite bank to watch the spectacle of two great warriors do battle. Jed had seen two warriors challenge each other to deadly combat before, but he never knew of a whole village coming to watch such a fight. He could not understand why this warrior hadn't killed him while he was weak and unprotected, back in the Arapaho village. Maybe Bear Claw just wanted everyone to see him kill the great Crow Killer, the demon, and then his medicine would be feared throughout all the tribes. The whole village had taken on a festive mood as they arrived.

"Are you ready, Crow Killer?" Glass Moon stood beside the fire and looked down at Jed. "You do not put paint on your face?"

"For this, I don't need to paint my face." Jed replied. "Yes, I am ready."

"I have brought you the strongest horse I own." Glass Moon nodded at the big bay he held. "He is not the piebald Bear Claw stole from you, but he has plenty of heart and he has seen plenty of battles."

"Will this battle start on horseback?"

"Yes, and I advise you to unhorse Bear Claw quickly and fight him on the ground."

"Thank you for the advice."

"I have seen your piebald horse. He is a magnificent animal."

Jed agreed with him. "That he is."

"You will be at a great disadvantage on my lowly animal."

"I thank you for the use of him." Jed looked at the bay horse. "But, I will ride the spotted horse that brought me here."

"The spotted one is young and he has been ridden hard."

Jed nodded and looked to where Bright Moon's horse grazed on the abundant grass growing along the creek bank. "He is out of the greatest horse I have ever known. I will ride the spotted one."

"He is a powerful animal." Glass Moon looked over at the horse. "I think you should try to kill the piebald quickly and unhorse Bear Claw."

Shaking his head, Jed thought of his black and white paint horse. "I couldn't harm that animal."

"Not even to save yourself?" Elk Man questioned. "The piebald is just as strong as the one you ride, maybe stronger."

"No." Jed shook his head. "I will not kill the piebald."

The skinny warrior, Small Bird, rode to the small stream and sat his horse motionless for several seconds as Elk Man looked across the stream and nodded.

"He has come, Crow Killer."

Glass Moon brought the spotted horse to Jed and smiled. "He is only a man, Crow Killer, only a man."

"What weapons will we use?" Jed spoke across the water to the warrior. He had no idea how Bear Claw wanted to fight or with what weapons.

"You may carry your shield and war axe, and your skinning knife. Nothing more, Arapaho." Small Bird answered back.

"I will carry my lance, it is not a weapon."

"I guess the great Bear Claw will permit that." The warrior shrugged. "It does not matter, Arapaho. Your weapons are weak. You are weak. You are a dead man as we speak."

"We will see." Jed turned away from the warrior. "I sure don't feel dead yet."

"Prepare yourself, Arapaho, the great Bear Claw comes." Small Bird yelled out. "He will meet you in the water."

Jed removed his hunting shirt and prepared his weapons. The dark, heavily muscled body was covered with fresh scars from Leblew's blade. The long, pink scar across his stomach showed plainly where the knife had slashed him open. Sliding the bull-hide shield on his arm, he looked over where Glass Moon held a bay horse. The warrior was right as the bay horse he offered was a strong animal, but no match for the piebald in size or strength. He would use the spotted colt of Bright Moon.

Swinging up on the appaloosa, Jed looked across the water as the people let out a loud cry. In the middle of the villagers, sitting on the piebald with the morning sun shining across his features, Bear Claw seemed to shimmer in the morning light. The big warrior's body was painted all in black, except for a white streak down one side of his face and body. Jed had to admit, the warrior, with his size and muscle mass, looked to be a formidable adversary. Bear Claw passed before his people, exalting them, intensifying their chanting and screaming. Never had he heard such praise and worship given to a warrior, any warrior. Jed shook his head as he watched the Blackfoot people raise their hands to touch the warrior. Never had he seen such a spectacle as he was watching. The Arapaho or Cheyenne did not worship any chief as these people were doing. Jed watched as Bear Claw paraded the piebald back and forth before the people.

"He is a great warrior. Some have proclaimed him a spirit person." Glass Moon frowned as he watched the spectacle. "He is just a man, like any other warrior."

"I think he is much more, Glass Moon." Jed watched as the piebald pranced as he carried the warrior toward the creek. "I think this one really believes he is a spirit person."

Glass Moon was looking across the creek as the black and white horse moved toward the water. "Kill him quick, Crow Killer, we know you can do it. Then, these fools will no longer glorify him as they are doing."

Before Jed could turn the spotted one, Elk Man stepped up beside him. "Crow Killer, I will tell you this; the grizzly blinded Bear Claw in his right eye. That is why his face is always painted black. Keep to his right side and he cannot see you as well."

Jed nodded, and reined the spotted horse down river, away from the crossing. Maybe it was unfair that Elk Man had told him the warrior was blind in one eye, but Jed knew it was useful information for him to know. The water where he sat was almost knee deep on the horse. The heavy war axe was held in his right hand while the shield strapped to his left arm covered the left side of his body. He could feel the Arapaho Lance hanging across his back, touching against his bare skin. The Blackfoot moved upstream, away from Jed, all the while enticing the crowd to a fanatical frenzy as he waved his mighty war axe. Turning, he finally focused his full attention on Jed as he turned the big piebald horse to face his opponent. Jed noticed he had turned the horse sideways so his left eye only looked across at him.

Raising his axe, Bear Claw yelled out a challenge and whirled the piebald, throwing water up from under his powerful feet. Kicking the horse, he passed up and down the creek in front of the villagers several times. Then, with a loud scream, he charged straight toward Jed. Spray from the horse splashing up water as he ran through the knee-deep creek flew everywhere as he drew closer to the appaloosa. Kicking the young horse forward, both warriors screamed their bloodcurdling screams as they closed in on each other.

Jed didn't see him, but across the creek before the whole village, the old medicine man grinned as he held up his feathered lance, the token of his stature in the Blackfoot Nation. Pointing the long lance at Jed, Twisted Rope seemed to be saying something. Jed could feel the strength of the spotted horse beneath him. Over the last few months, the colt had matured into a powerfully built animal. Jed had trained him well for Bright Moon. The horse was a dream to handle, calm with no nervousness, and the least touch of his knees would turn the animal.

Jed knew to win the battle, he should try to kill the piebald on their first pass and unhorse Bear Claw. However, he knew he could never harm the great paint horse. Bear Claw was stalling, playing the fight out and wanting the battle to last as he reined the piebald away from Jed on the first pass. Prepared for the heavier horse to push into the young horse, Jed was surprised when Bear Claw pulled away. Laughing, the warrior raised his axe and screamed at the villagers, wanting their praise. Jed knew the warrior wanted the Blackfoot people to remember this battle and his great medicine.

Elk Man shook his head. "He shows off his medicine for the people."

"I think maybe, I will lose my woman this day." Glass Moon admitted sadly. "Perhaps, I should have bet on Bear Claw."

"If Crow Killer loses this battle, it will not matter. We are dead men, my friend." Elk Man was solemn. "Besides, your woman is ugly."

Again, both horses charged, this time smashing together almost unseating their riders. Jed knew Elk Man had spoken the truth. By staying on Bear Claw's blind side, the bigger warrior could not see him and missed with his war axe on the first pass. Jed's war axe had left a huge hole in the shield of the Blackfoot. On the next charge, the horses collided as the warriors leaned forward swinging their heavy axes. Almost face-to-face as the horses circled, pushing against each other, Jed could see the terrible claw marks that covered the warrior's face. Jed respected this fighter. Crazed or not, Bear Claw had been a brave man to track down a grizzly and fight it, armed only with a knife.

Again, the horses broke apart plowing through the water, and then whirling for another charge. This time, Jed faked going to his right, and with a slight touch of his leg, the spotted horse switched slightly and passed on Bear Claw's left side. Jed smiled as he had fooled the Blackfoot by staying on his left, delivering a powerful blow to the warrior's shielded arm. Reining his horse into the piebald's side, Jed rained blow after blow down on the bigger man as he dodged the other's war axe. Both horses were strong, powerfully built animals, and neither gave an inch as they pushed against each other.

"Maybe, I will not lose my wife after all." Glass Moon grinned. "I do not think our young chief is experienced enough to fight the Arapaho."

"Just a few minutes ago you were worried you would lose her." Elk Man watched the two combatants pull apart. "Tell me, Glass Moon, who was stupid enough to wager with you?"

"Tired Water."

"Tired Water?" Elk Man laughed. "Tired Water is blind, he cannot see."

"How else could I have made the wager?"

"They charge again." Elk Man was still grinning as this time Bear Claw did not seem so sure of himself or as eager about charging into Crow Killer again.

"I see doubt in our chief's face, Elk Man." Glass Moon pointed out. "He hesitates."

Elk Man had also noticed the look that Glass Moon had seen. "It is not doubt, my friend. He just stares in disbelief. He knows he will be defeated this day by a greater warrior."

The powerful horses slammed hard together again in midstream causing both warriors to be thrown into the water. Jed smiled as he watched the piebald and appaloosa being caught by Elk Man as they left the creek bed. It was a good sign because without the horse, Bear Claw had lost some of his great medicine. War axes clashed together as the two warriors slashed at each other, trying to land a killing blow. Water ran from their loin cloths and bodies as the two strong adversaries fought gallantly in the creek. Pushing and pulling, then wrestling each other as they rolled in the water, they once again broke apart and came to their feet.

Bear Claw was a powerful warrior, but he was young in years and not experienced as Jed was in hand-to-hand fighting. Now, fighting afoot, in at least a foot of water, their stamina would quickly tell the outcome of this fight. The villager's yelling and laughing ceased as they watched their warrior slowly giving ground as the Arapaho pushed him back. Bear Claw was bleeding from several deep cuts as he retreated, trying to avoid the war axe of the enraged Crow Killer.

"The great Bear Claw is finished!" Glass Moon exclaimed. "And we feared this one."

"Crow Killer has taken no deep wounds at all." Elk Man noted. "Just small amounts of blood show."

Bringing his war axe down hard on Bear Claw's broken shield, Jed felt the bloody handle slip from his grasp and splash into the water. The Blackfoot laughed as he saw his chance and lunged forward with his war axe raised, ready for the killing blow. Both men clashed together, each trying for the killing blow as they strained mightily with their strong arms. Both men, their hands wet and slick with blood, lost their grip on each other's arms. Suddenly, both warriors stood completely still as if they were frozen in time with their bodies clinging together not moving in the knee-deep water.

"What has happened?" Elk Man asked as the two fighters stood staring into each other's eyes. "Why do they not fight?"

"I do not know." Glass Moon watched searching for the answer, fearing for the Arapaho. "They do not move."

"Maybe both are dead."

The words hardly left Elk Man's mouth when Bear Claw slowly started to collapse before Jed, his huge body slipping lifeless into the clear stream. Both warriors watched as Jed pulled his long skinning knife from the Blackfoot's body where it had completely opened up the warrior's stomach. Picking up his fallen war axe from the bottom of the clear creek, Jed staggered from the water to where Elk Man and Glass Moon stood smiling. Walking tiredly to the piebald and appaloosa, he patted the horse's neck affectionately as he checked them over for wounds.

"That was not much of a fight, Crow Killer." Elk Man commented as he watched warriors massing across the creek. "Maybe, we will have another one now."

Jed looked across the creek where the warrior, Small Bird, was trying to convince the gathered warriors to avenge their chief and kill Crow Killer. The Blackfoot warriors were split in two sections as the young warrior pointed across the creek beseeching them to fight. Jed could see they were undecided whether to cross the water and fight, or ignore the warrior.

Mounting the bay horse, Elk Man rode across the creek and challenged Small Bird. The young warrior stared sullenly at the older warrior. Riding close to the warrior, Elk Man slapped the young warrior, knocking him from his horse. Slipping to the ground, Elk Man booted the cringing Small Bird several times before he slipped shamefully away through the crowd.

"My people, we have been lied to." Elk Man pointed to their medicine man, Twisted Rope. "He has brought us shame by his lies and false prophecies."

Walking to where Twisted Rope stood with his arms folded, Elk Man suddenly lashed out with his own war axe, killing the medicine man. "Now, do with me as you wish. I have killed this one who has brought shame upon the Blackfoot Nation."

Not a word could be heard as complete silence reigned through the villagers and warriors. Glass Moon and the other three warriors standing with Jed mounted their horses and rode to stand with Elk Man. Time stood still. Not a wisp of air or noise sounded as the entire Blackfoot village waited for the warriors of the people to decide the fate of Elk Man and Crow Killer.

Jed watched as all the warriors finally lowered their lances and war axes, then moved beside Elk Man. The body of Twisted Rope was trampled as a hundred mounted warriors crossed over it, showing their loyalty to Elk Man. Small Bird was dragged forward on the end of a rawhide rope by another warrior. Released, he was pointed downstream and told to run. Shaking in fear, his legs wobbling, the young cousin of Bear Claw barely moved as several arrows found his body.

Elk Man studied the other warriors closely. "Is there any others who wish to follow these?"

Not a head or arm moved as the warrior challenged them. Elk Man had killed the Blackfoot medicine man, but he had earned the respect of the tribe. Now, the warrior was a strong figure, and Jed figured he would become their new chief. In most tribes, if a warrior killed one of his own people, unless it was a challenge fight between two warriors, that warrior could never be chief of his tribe. However, Bear Claw and Twisted Rope had dishonored their people by bringing this shame down upon their village. If Bear Claw had won this day, then the future of the tribe would have been completely different. Jed knew if the warrior had been victorious, he would have killed many of his own people, including Blue Darter and some of Blue Darter's people in his crazed quest for revenge.

Suddenly, several of the Blackfoot pointed across the creek to where Jed stood. Turning, Jed's face broke into a smile as he glimpsed the proud spotted stallion standing with his neck arched and the equally proud looking Red Hawk gazing down from the higher swell above the creek. Kicking the appaloosa, the Crow made his way down the steep bank and dismounted beside Jed.

"It was a good fight, my brother." Red Hawk reached out his hand. "He was a worthy opponent, but..."

"But what?" Jed smiled over at the warrior.

"I think you should have killed the Blackfoot quicker." Red Hawk shrugged.

Jed looked down the stream to where Bear Claw's body stopped as it drug bottom in the shallows. "Maybe, I could have, if he hadn't been riding the piebald."

"You have fought tougher warriors." Red Hawk added. "The Nez Perce, Black Robe, and the Blackfoot, Standing Bull."

Jed nodded sadly. "He was like Small Mountain the Blackfoot, young and strong, but inexperienced in war."

Red Hawk recalled. "I remember you and Blue Darter speaking of Small Mountain."

Jed studied the body of Bear Claw. "He could have made a great chief, except for his lust for revenge. He should never have listened to the medicine of Twisted Rope."

Red Hawk nodded as he watched Elk Man and Glass Moon start across the stream. "The villagers are leaving."

"Tell me of Little Antelope and Walking Horse."

"She is safe and in her lodge by now." Red Hawk looked over at Jed. "She worries about her warrior."

Annoyed, Jed asked. "And Walking Horse?"

"I gave orders for my warriors to make sure they crossed the mighty river unharmed." Red Hawk assured Jed. "They will do as I say."

"I hope so."

"You know, my friend, Walking Horse is no fool." Red Hawk grinned. "He must know of her feelings for you."

"That is all there is, feelings, nothing more." Jed shook his head. "When I return, I will take Bright Moon and go home to our valley."

"Bright Moon will be waiting too, for her warrior." Red Hawk watched as the two Blackfoot warriors rode up, out of the creek.

Relieved to see the other Blackfoot warriors and the village people turning to leave, Jed smiled as he greeted the two men as they dismounted. "Thank you, my friends."

"We thank the great Crow Killer." Elk Man looked curiously over at Red Hawk. "This one is Crow. What does he do here in Blackfoot lands?"

"He is my friend, Red Hawk. He has come here to bring me back to our lands."

"You mean your body, if you had been killed by Bear Claw?" Elk Man laughed.

Glass Moon nodded. "I did not know the Crow and Arapaho could be friends."

"We have held each other's lives in our hands many times, Blackfoot." Red Hawk stared at the warrior. "Yes, we are friends."

Elk Man smiled and looked at the spotted stallion. "Even here in our faraway mountains, we have heard of Red Hawk and the spotted one he took from the Nez Perce."

"What now, my friends?" Jed looked over at a few mounted warriors who still sat their horse across the stream watching.

"We are friends now. Crow Killer may ride our land in peace." Elk Man looked at the watching warriors. "They are just curious."

"Do all Blackfoot say this?" Jed still didn't trust the waiting warriors.

Glass Moon agreed with Elk Man. "Yes, they will do as our new chief says."

"Then, me and Red Hawk will rest here tonight. Tomorrow, we will travel to the south with the new sun."

"We would like for you to be our guests as Elk Man becomes our new chief. Glass Moon smiled. "We will have a great fire, plenty of deer and buffalo meat, a great celebration."

"And pretty maidens to dance with?" Red Hawk asked.

"Perhaps, but I do not know if they would dance with a Crow." Elk Man shrugged innocently.

"And why not?" Red Hawk acted offended.

"Crow people are so ugly."

Both Elk Man and Glass Moon broke into a chorus of laughter. Red Hawk, knowing they were joking with him, joined in the laughter. He knew he had made friends, because enemies would never joke with one another.

"No, my friends, our people worry for us." Jed interrupted the laughter, declining the offer. "We must return quickly to our lands."

"I will bring fresh meat here and maybe catch us some more river people." Glass Moon smiled.

Jed and Red Hawk hobbled their horses on the lush grass of the creek bank, then settled back against the log as Glass Moon and his warriors fished and prepared their food.

"Why do their women not cook for us?" Red Hawk watched the men fishing.

Jed smiled. "Because, even here this far north, they have heard of Red Hawk, the woman stealer."

"I hope their women are prettier than their horses." Red Hawk looked over at the warriors, then turned his attention to the spotted horse. "You rode the colt here to do battle?"

"Yes." Jed looked to where Bright Moon's spotted horse grazed. "Today, he saved my life against Bear Claw and the piebald."

"See, I told you the appaloosa was a better breed of horse."

"Well, he was today."

Red Hawk studied all three horses. "The spotted ones are almost twins."

"Except in years they are."

"Your paint is a great animal too, my friend."

Jed looked to where his piebald horse grazed. "Yes, he is."

"Tell me, Crow Killer." Red Hawk shook his head. "How do you always get yourself in trouble when I am not with you?"

"My friend, this I hope is the last trouble I intend to be in."

The Crow laughed at the joke. "For a warrior who does not steal women or horses, you my friend stay in trouble."

Jed thought of Bright Moon and his valley. "No more, the only trouble I aim to get into is when I do something to upset Bright Moon."

Jed was still tired from his fight with Bear Claw, but found himself staying up late, listening to Red Hawk spin yarns of his escapades that no one but the Blackfoot could believe. Several times, he frowned over at the Crow as the stories became more and more unbelievable, but somehow, the warriors always asked for another story.

"You said you were there when Crow Killer stared the last bear to death." Glass Moon sat looking at Jed with awe.

"Yes, my friend." Red Hawk was very convincing as he answered the warrior with a straight face. "Crow Killer looked at the bear, then the bear looked back at him and just fell over dead."

"I would have liked to have seen that." One of the warriors whispered.

"I would have too." Jed whispered under his breath, then told the warriors he was going to his robes.

With the coming of the new sun, Jed and Red Hawk sat their horses, ready to head back south and home. Elk Man and Glass Moon, with several other warriors, accompanied them until they cleared Blackfoot

Country. They had said their goodbyes and were just turning their horses when Walking Horse and his warriors rode into sight, across a large meadow. Several of the Blackfoot warriors raised their bows and pointed at the oncoming riders.

Reining the piebald in front of them, Jed threw up his arm. "Wait, my friends. They are my people, coming to bring me home."

"They come for war." Glass Moon watched the riders. "They invade our hunting grounds."

Jed knew a fight could break out if Walking Horse rode up. "My friends, wait! I will send Red Hawk to turn them back."

"Go then, tell them to leave our lands."

"I am sorry for this." Jed reached out his hand and shook Elk Man and Glass Moon's hands as Red Hawk rode away. "Come to my valley. We will hunt and tell more of Red Hawk's stories."

"One day, we will come and see the Crow Killer." Elk Man laughed. "Have Red Hawk come. We enjoyed his wild stories."

Jed laughed. "You mean you didn't believe his stories?"

"Oh yes, we believed every one of them." Glass Moon replied, making all the warriors roar with laughter. "They were very good stories."

Glass Moon had given Jed his bay horse as a present to remember his friends, the Blackfoot. In turn, Jed presented Glass Moon his war axe to remember him by.

Looking at the axe, the warrior nodded. "It will hang in my lodge until I pass it on to my sons."

"His sons will probably be ugly." Elk Man laughed.

Jed looked at the warrior curiously. "Why is that?"

"Never mind, my chief." Glass Moon turned his horse back toward his village.

Elk Man leaned toward Jed and whispered. "His wife is ugly."

Waving good-bye, Jed kicked the piebald into a slow lope. Leading the spotted colt and bay horse, he hurried to catch up with Walking Horse and Red Hawk. Reining their horses to a stop, Walking Horse and his warriors surrounded Jed and pounded on his back.

"Our people will be glad to see you are still alive." Walking Horse laughed.

"I'm glad to see I am still alive too." Jed agreed. "I thought you would remain with Little Antelope at the village."

"Slow Wolf let these warriors follow me here."

"I am glad you are here."

"Red Hawk says the Blackfoot were not happy to see us."

Jed nodded. "I convinced them you were friends."

"You did?"

"Yes, but maybe we should leave this land quickly."

Raising his arm, Walking Horse kicked his animal into a short lope. "We go!"

Moving up beside Red Hawk, Jed looked over at the warrior. "How long were you watching from the knoll?"

"I was there when it started." Red Hawk admitted. "But, I did not think it wise to show myself. Besides, I knew you would win."

"And just how did you know that?"

"Easy, my friend, you were riding the better horse." Red Hawk pointed at the spotted young colt, and then pointed at the piebald. "Anybody mounted on that pile of bones you are riding now, just had to lose."

"One of these days, Crow." Jed laughed.

"You know, we could cross Nez Perce lands, it would be much shorter than taking the long way around the mountains." Red Hawk pointed off to his right. "Maybe, some spotted mares might follow us home."

Shaking his head, Jed frowned. "No, we will take the long way home and have no more trouble with anybody."

"Where is your sense of adventure?"

"I left it back there, about twenty miles or so."

Jed sat beside Walking Horse and Red Hawk, surrounded by Arapaho and Crow warriors, looking out across the mighty Yellowstone.

"Tell us, Crow Killer, did you kill the mighty Blackfoot Bear Claw?"

Nodding at Long Leaper, Jed pointed at Red Hawk. "I will let Red Hawk tell of the battle. He's a lot better storyteller than I am."

"We know this to be true." The warrior laughed. "Our young chief adds a little to each story he tells."

Shaking hands with Red Hawk, Jed rode the piebald into the river. "Come to my lodge and we will eat and get fat."

"I will come before the cold times arrive." Red Hawk waved before turning for his village. "Stay safe, my brother. Do not get yourself into any more trouble."

"Thanks to you, the mightiest warrior of all, we are all safe, my brother."

The pounding of the drums sounded before Jed was less than halfway into the village of the Arapaho. People streamed from their lodges to greet the mighty Lance Bearer, Crow Killer. Slipping from the piebald as Bright Moon sprang from her lodge, Jed picked her up and swung her in a circle.

"You are home, my husband." The dark eyes filled with tears as she laughed.

"I am home." Taking her by the arm, Jed walked her and the horses toward the horse herd by the creek. "The Blackfoot horse is a present for you from our friends, the Blackfoot."

"I have a great horse." Bright Moon took the lead rope of her spotted horse.

"Yes, you do."

Stroking the bay horse's neck, she nodded. "He is a beautiful animal. If my husband does not mind, I will give him to Little Antelope for all she has done."

"I believe she would be pleased with such a horse."

"Does this mean the hated one is dead?"

"He is dead. He will no longer be a threat to us." Jed turned the horses loose, then walked Bright Moon back to their lodge.

"I will fix food."

Walking Horse and Little Antelope had held back until Jed returned from his walk with Bright Moon. Shaking hands, the two warriors sat down in front of Jed's lodge. Little Antelope greeted Jed, then went to help Bright Moon with the food.

"We were worried for you, my friend." The warrior smiled. "Until we saw you and Red Hawk riding with the Blackfoot warriors."

"It has been a long and dangerous trail, for all of us."

"You are here, so that means the Blackfoot who took Little Antelope is dead?"

"He is dead." Jed looked to where the women were talking. "He will no longer bother any of our people."

"What will my brother do now?"

"Tomorrow, with the coming of the new sun, I will leave with Bright Moon for our valley."

"You cannot stay here to hunt the deer and elk for a few days?"

"Not now. I have been away too many days." Jed shook his head. "Rolling Thunder brings my white father to the valley when he returns from the west."

Walking Horse looked over at Jed and nodded. "Perhaps, I will come to hunt in the summer."

"Good, we will smoke the pipe and talk."

"And Crow Killer will tell me how he killed the mighty Bear Claw of the Blackfoot Nation?"

"That is a tale you will have to come to my valley for." Jed smiled. "I figured Red Hawk had already told you."

"He never spoke a word of the battle." Walking Horse replied.

"Did you ask him of the fight?"

"Yes, he said nothing." Walking Horse shook his head. "I think it will be worth the long ride to hear such a story."

"I warn you, I don't tell the story as well as Red Hawk does." Jed laughed. "Maybe you should have him tell it."

"It was strange, for once he was silent." Walking Horse laughed. "I guess I will have to wait for the story until we meet again."

"Send word to Red Hawk and ride with him to our valley." Jed suggested. "Then, he will tell you the story."

"I will do that." Walking Horse agreed.

"Come, let us go speak with Slow Wolf."

At daybreak, Jed had his horses and the little mule loaded down with his supplies from Bridger along with the sack of gold coins he had been paid for his furs. Bright Moon was already astride the spotted horse as Jed shook hands with Walking Horse and Big Owl.

"We will be waiting for you to come to our valley." Jed swung up on the piebald and looked down where Little Antelope waited. "Good-bye, little one. You take care of my brother while I am away."

"I will Jed." Her dark eyes stared up at him. "I thank you and Bright Moon for the beautiful horse."

Three days later, after leaving the Arapaho village, Jed looked out across his magnificent, beloved valley. Nodding slowly, he gave thanks as he was once again home and could tread the vast, beautiful land and smell the pure clean air.

Bright Moon reined in the spotted one beside Jed and stared out over the flower covered valley. She held her small hand up to shield her eyes from the western sun. "Perhaps now, the great Crow Killer can have peace."

"Peace, that is what I wish for too."

The long moaning cry of the great grey wolf recoiled and echoed from the mountainside as they sat smiling and enjoying their majestic view.

"Our protector greets us, my husband. We are finally home."

The End